"I don't believe we've met." Natalie kept her expression blank. *Not in this lifetime, anyway.*

"Natalie?" Lucien gave his head a little shake. "It can't be..."

"I *am* Professor Natalie Segova," she assured him politely. "Was there something you needed?" Natalie looked up at the hunky, gorgeous—ugh—*vampire* in front of her.

He tilted his head, his eyes narrowing as though trying to make sense of the insensible. "Uh, sorry, you—you remind me of someone."

"I must have one of those faces." She shrugged again and started to turn away.

"Wait—uh, Professor. Could I ask you some questions? About your studies," he clarified in that rich, deep timbre. God, it still had the ability to draw her attention, to suck her in and make her forget everything else around her. She remembered that voice murmuring softly to her in the darkness.

Yeah, she remembered a lot of damn things.

Shannon Curtis grew up picnicking in graveyards (long story) and reading by torchlight, and has worked in various roles, such as office admin manager, logistics supervisor and betting agent, to mention a few. Her first love—after reading, and her husband—is writing, and she writes romantic suspense, paranormal and contemporary romance. From faeries to cowboys, military men to business tycoons, she loves crafting stories of thrills, chills, kills and kisses. She divides her time between being an office administrator for the Romance Writers of Australia and creating spellbinding tales of mischief, mayhem and the occasional murder. She lives in Sydney, Australia, with her best-friend husband, three children, a woolly dog and a very disdainful cat. Shannon can be found lurking on Twitter, @2BShannonCurtis, and Facebook, or you can email her at contactme@shannoncurtis.com—she loves hearing from readers. Like...LOVES it. Disturbingly so.

Books by Shannon Curtis

Harlequin Nocturne

Lycan Unleashed
Warrior Untamed
Vampire Undone

VAMPIRE UNDONE

SHANNON CURTIS

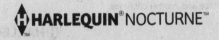

HARLEQUIN® NOCTURNE™

Recycling programs
for this product may
not exist in your area.

ISBN-13: 978-0-373-13999-6

Vampire Undone

Printed in U.S.A.

www.Harlequin.com

Dear Reader,

This book was such a challenge—and so much fun—to write. I created quite the problem for myself with the ever-fatal werewolf bite, an inescapable fate for a vampire. It created many an interesting conversation with gal pals and writerly friends in a variety of public places on how a werewolf bite could be cured—*if* it could be cured. The strange looks we got...

But then again, it was lovely getting this couple together, too.

There were also a couple of new characters here who kind of hijacked the story—you'll have to let me know who you want to see in a story! (I love getting those sorts of emails!)

I hope you enjoy reading *Vampire Undone*.

Take care, and until we meet again, happy reading!

With love,

Shannon Curtis

This story is dedicated to Allison Rogers—
Lucien is your hunk!

Thanks so much for the inspiration :-)

Chapter 1

"What about a nice, fresh Zinfandel?"

Natalie Segova ignored the suggestion and kept reading her book of poetry.

"Or perhaps a glass of Merlot? Something warm and full-bodied to ward off the chill evening?"

"You know you can't serve me anything, Terry," she whispered as she kept her eyes glued to the page.

"What about some nuts? Do you need some nuts? Advice? What's troubling you tonight, honey?"

Natalie adjusted her spectacles then rested her elbow on the bar and leaned her chin on her palm in a move that looked comfortable but also masked her mouth from others within the bistro. "Terry, we've been over this before. If people see me talking to you, they'll think I'm crazy. Shoo."

"Can I get you something, Natalie?"

Natalie looked up as Darren, the bartender, approached her with a smile. She smiled back. "I'd love a Chardonnay, please."

Darren winked. "Coming right up." He turned away

to ready the drink and Terry, the flamboyant ghost who refused to leave his job, folded his arms.

"Oh, so you'll give him your order, but not me, huh? What am I, chopped liver?"

Natalie rolled her eyes at the apparition's insulted expression and peered at him over her glasses. "Terry, for the last time, you're a ghost. Deal with it," she whispered as she again tucked her chin into her palm.

"Give me something, sweetheart," Terry whined, his hand moving in a flapping gesture as he leaned his hip against the bar. "I'm here all by myself and you're the only one who will give me the time of day." He eyed his fingernails. "Which is a crime, as far as I'm concerned, letting all this go to waste." He gestured to his form. Terry, fit and toned when he was alive, wore dark shoes, black trousers and a black bow tie, and that was it.

"I still can't believe that used to be the uniform here," Natalie said softly, eyeing his outfit—or lack of one.

Terry's smile was more of a grimace. "Well, this place used to have a very different clientele. Now they've snootied it all up." He sighed. "Friday nights used to be the best. The drag queens used to perform in that corner." He waved casually to a corner near the window. He arched an eyebrow as he returned his gaze to hers. "Now we get—what? Prissy chicks reading—" He tilted his head so he could see the cover of her book and winced in horror. "Oh, my lord. *Poetry*. This place is going to the dogs."

She smiled as the very corporeal Darren placed her glass on a coaster in front of her and then walked back to serve another patron.

"And you're still here," she murmured, sighing as

Terry's bottom lip protruded in a very good imitation of a sulk. She leaned back in her seat. "Fine. Give me some nuts," she whispered and waited patiently as Terry moved and unsuccessfully tried to lift the nut bowl further down the bar. Out of habit, she toyed with the silver chain lariat around her neck, her fingers sliding along the links as she watched her "friend" do his thing.

After a few more attempts, the ghostly bartender got impatient and swiped at the bowl. The bowl flipped off the bar and nuts spilled across the floor. The bartender and other patrons startled then froze, staring at the mess on the floor that seemed to have sprung from nowhere. Terry placed his hands on his hips as he walked toward her, frustration etching his forever-young features.

"You did that on purpose."

She shrugged, a tiny movement that was almost undetectable. Terry tried to serve her every time she came in to McKinley's Bistro, and refused to accept the limitations his phantom form put on him. But she did so enjoy watching him try. She dropped her chain and returned to reading her book.

"Did you see that?" an older woman sitting at the bar muttered. She gazed dubiously at the glass of amber-colored liquid in her hand before placing it gingerly back on the bar.

"Uh, must have been a breeze," Darren suggested quickly before ducking into the back room and returning with a broom and dustpan.

"I'm outta here," another man said, reaching for his laptop bag as he climbed hastily off his bar stool.

"Come on, Nat. So I can't serve you a drink. So what? I can still listen," Terry suggested as he placed his folded arms on the bar. "Tell Uncle Terry what's bothering you."

Natalie held the book of poems determinedly in front of her face. "Nothing's bothering me," she said, trying not to move her mouth.

"Oh, right. So you're here, all by yourself, every Friday night, and nothing's wrong?"

Natalie frowned. "I happen to like my own company."

"Honey, nobody likes their own company—not if they keep winding up in a bar," Terry said sagely. "Especially not wearing that." He gestured in a figure eight that both encompassed her outfit yet still managed to convey disdain.

Natalie's frown deepened as she glanced down at her collared shirt and jeans. Her outfit was presentable and comfortable. "What's wrong with what I'm wearing?"

"Uh, nothing..."

Darren looked over at her in surprise as he emptied the contents of the dustpan in the trash can under the bar, and color flooded her cheeks as she realized she'd spoken too loudly.

"Thanks, Darren," she said then focused intently on the works of John Keats she held in her hands.

"Do you mean that outfit is intentional?" Terry gasped, his hand rising dramatically to his chest. He shook his head. "And do you think that simple necklace is going to dress this up? It's worse than I— Oh, hello." Terry's attention whipped to the door of the bistro.

Natalie glanced over her shoulder and froze. Blinked. Whirled back around to bury her nose in her book. Her heart fluttered in her chest then took off in a thumping race.

Oh. My. God. *Him. Here.* It couldn't be. Her guardian angel.

No, not her guardian angel, she corrected herself. More like a devil in disguise. She knew exactly what he was and she wanted to run for the hills.

Natalie willed herself not to run, not to stare, not to flinch. Of all the bistros, in all the teeny, tiny college towns, in all of Argon, why did he have to walk into hers? His kind weren't common here. That was why she'd chosen to establish herself here. No shadow breeds, just humans.

The newcomer walked up to the bar and Natalie twisted away in her seat, trying to make it look like a nonchalant move as she closed the book she'd ceased to read. Maybe she could get out before he noticed her, recognized her. She slid the book into her bag, her fingers brushing, lightly grasping, then relinquishing the handle of the blade she always carried. It matched the one strapped to her ankle.

"Excuse me, I'm looking for Professor Segova. I was told I'd likely find her here…"

Good grief. That voice. Like smooth chocolate, all rich and dark and hinting of nights and mischief. He hadn't changed a bit.

Well, duh. He's a vampire. He's bloody immortal.

They didn't tend to age. Or change. Or die, damn it.

And he was looking for her. She didn't want to see him. She never wanted to see him. Never again. She sure as hell hadn't expected him to walk into her bistro, looking for her.

"Oh, wow, Mr. Hottie wants you," Terry whispered unnecessarily.

Mr. Hottie was an understatement. The man was undeniably handsome, in an intent, coolly detached way. He wore a black suit, a dark, collared shirt and no tie. With his dark hair and piercing blue eyes he looked every inch a potential dark angel. Shoulders broad, chin set at a challenging angle, he effortlessly commanded attention.

But not hers. Nope. Not anymore. She was too wise to his ways to let herself be entranced by a searing pair of stunning blue eyes and lips that suggested all sorts of steamy seduction. No, sirree.

She slid off the bar stool and turned away slightly, praying that Darren would get the message her body language was screaming, and send this particular patron on his way. She dug for her wallet and pulled out some notes to pay for her meal and drinks.

"Professor Segova? Yeah, she's right there."

Darren hadn't gotten the message. Well, there went his tip for the night. She put the money on the bar and busied herself with her coat. She lifted her bag to her shoulder.

"Ooooh, honey, he's on his way over to you," Terry sighed before biting his bottom lip.

Once again, Natalie did her best to ignore the ghost.

"Excuse me, Professor Segova?"

She forced a politely inquisitive look on her face as she turned to face him. Well, his chest. She'd forgotten how tall he was. Wow. Had he always been so…built? She forced herself to lift her gaze to his.

Er, wow. His eyes were still that stunning azure color. Nope. Not getting distracted. At all. She pulled her lips into a cool smile.

"Yes?"

He blinked. Gaped. "You! You— You're Professor

Natalie Segova?" Recognition battled with confusion. She hoped confusion won.

Showtime. "Yes?" she inquired innocently.

"Natalie?" he repeated.

She kept her expression bland as she nodded. "Yes, I'm Natalie Segova. How can I help you?"

"It's me—Lucien," he said. "Lucien Marchetta."

She continued to look at him blankly, then gave an apologetic shrug. "Sorry, I don't believe we've met." Not in this lifetime, anyway.

He gave his head a little shake. "It can't be…"

She raised her eyebrows, her expression turning expectant. "I *am* Professor Natalie Segova," she assured him politely. "Was there something you needed?"

"Oh, I'd be happy to help," Terry said suggestively.

Natalie shot him a grim look before turning back to the hunky, gorgeous *vampire* in front of her.

He tilted his head, his eyes narrowing as though trying to make sense of the insensible. "Uh, sorry, you—you remind me of someone."

She shrugged again. "I get that a lot. I must have one of those faces." She slid the strap of her tote up to her shoulder and started to turn away.

"Wait—uh, Professor. Please. I was wondering if I could ask you some questions? About your studies," he clarified in that rich, deep timbre.

God, it still had the ability to draw her attention, to suck her in and make her forget everything else around her. She remembered that voice murmuring softly to her in the darkness.

Yeah, she remembered a lot of damn things.

She started to back away from him, her expression still polite. "I'm sorry, I really have to go—but if you'd like to call my office, my assistant can make an appointment for you," she suggested. And she had absolutely no intention of keeping it. She'd be halfway across the Red Desert before he realized she'd fled town, fingers crossed.

This time his confused gaze turned serious, intent, and he met her gaze directly. "Wait," he said in a tone that took his voice to an even deeper timbre. "You want to talk with me. Now, as a matter of fact."

She could feel something fluttering along the edges of her mind and her smile tightened. He was trying to compel her, damn it.

Well, that put her in quite a position. If she resisted the compulsion, he'd realize something was up, that she wasn't the human she pretended to be, which would lead him to the next realization, that she could very well be the person he thought she was. She couldn't have that.

She tilted her head back, easily ignoring the shadowy effect trying to cloud her brain. "I'd love to talk with you," she lied. "Why don't you walk with me? My place is only a couple of blocks from here."

He smiled at her and she glanced away. He still had that sexy smile that was all mischief.

"After you," Lucien said, gesturing for her to lead the way.

She smiled through clenched teeth. Great. She just needed to play along with this farce long enough to get to her home, to safety. Okay, she could do this. She could act normal, even flirt if she had to, if it gave her enough time to get in her front door. She slid her hand inside her bag to clutch the handle of her blade as she walked out into the cool evening.

* * *

Lucien strolled along Main Street, surreptitiously glancing at the woman at his side as they went.

It was remarkable. She looked so much like Nina—but it couldn't be. Nina was dead. Years ago—it had made front-page news, everywhere. Besides, even if the papers had gotten it wrong, Nina would be in her sixties now. This woman looked to be in her twenties. Blond hair that fell in soft, barely-there waves to her shoulders, hazel-gray eyes behind black-rimmed glasses, and a pale complexion that was currently just the slightest bit flushed. She was pretty. Hell, she was more than pretty, but…well, it felt weird, thinking of her like that, particularly with the confusing mishmash in his mind with Nina. He frowned.

"Uh, I don't mean to be rude, but you don't really look old enough to be a professor," he remarked tentatively. He kept his tone light, perhaps there was even a hint of flirtation, but there was also some doubt. She looked like she should be a student, not the lecturer.

Her lips tightened briefly before curling into a smile. "I'm older than I look," she said. "Used to be a problem when I was younger and trying to get into bars."

Her response was light, but he got the impression his remark hadn't been received as a flattering compliment on her youthful looks.

"You wanted to ask me something?" she reminded him as she turned a corner down a tree-lined street.

"Uh, yeah. I hear you're an expert on all things mystical and mythological?" He still couldn't quite believe it. He'd thought, when Dave had mentioned this woman, that she'd be much older. He frowned. Hadn't Dave said she'd been here for some years? How did that work?

She nodded. "I've spent some time studying the old stories and legends," she conceded. "What did you want to know?"

He glanced around the street. He wasn't exactly eager to discuss his mission in public, but he'd detected a wariness in this woman and sensed this might be the easiest way to get her attention—and her assistance. He didn't have the time to leave it until some assistant managed to find an empty slot in the professor's schedule.

Fortunately the street was mostly clear of people. A woman walked her dog further along the block and a man carried two big bags of trash out to a bin on the curb.

"I'm wondering if you are aware of any myths or legends that discuss survivors of lycan attacks," he said casually.

Her eyebrows rose. "Well, yes. There are any number of ancient legends that include a lycan survival story. Particularly before the time of The Troubles, when humans still viewed werewolves as creative fiction. For a time, there was a belief that if one did manage to survive a werewolf's bite, one also turned into a werewolf." She smiled briefly. "We know that's not true now, though. We know that there has to be a bloodline, for example, for lycanism to develop."

"What did people do to survive the lycan's bite? In those legends, I mean," Lucien amended casually as she again led him around a corner. This street was quieter. Lights were on in some homes and the streetlamps gave a charming glow to the wide street. Shadows stretched between the lamps and colored leaves littered the sidewalk and gutters. He scuffed at a pile as he walked along, the movement almost instinctive. His lips curled briefly. Nina used to love the leaves. He glanced up and down the street. She'd love this neighborhood. He sighed. God, he hadn't thought of Nina in years. That familiar ache was still there, though, edged with regret.

"Oh, they didn't. Not really," the professor said. "Usually, the stories showed the victim dying a painful death, often shot with a silver bullet."

Lucien blanched. "At least they got that detail right," he muttered. Silver was toxic to both shifters and vampires, and the humans had used it to good effect during The Troubles.

She nodded. "It's surprising that some of the beliefs manifested in these legends were obviously born from some aspect rooted in reality."

She halted at the gate of a modest Colonial-style house with white columns on a wide porch. An old-fashioned coach light spread a warm glow in front of the red front door. "Well, this is me. Thank you for walking me home." She smiled, but the smile didn't quite reach her eyes. She turned away from him and suddenly he didn't want her to go, didn't want their time to come to an end.

"Let me walk you to your door," he said, following her through the gate.

Her eyebrows dipped. "Oh, no, you don't need—"

He met her gaze. "Please, let me walk you to your door," he said smoothly, using a light compulsion. He almost felt guilty, but he quashed the emotion before it caught a foothold. He reminded himself he was there to save his sister, and he didn't have time for polite pleasantries and stop-start conversations. But, deep down, he couldn't shake his fascination with this woman. Was it just that she looked so like someone he'd once known? Someone he'd once...felt something for?

Something flashed in her hazel-gray eyes—irritation?—then it was gone and a polite smile crossed her face.

"I would love it if you walked me to my door," she said in a low voice.

The husky sound curled deep inside him and he tried to think of any excuse to stretch out this meeting, this discussion, just a little longer. He took a deep breath as he walked down the garden path with her. He didn't need an excuse. His sister was lying in a coffin, slowly being consumed by a poison he desperately needed to find a cure for. This was not a first meeting. This was *the* meeting until he got what he needed.

She opened her bag, retrieved her keys, unlocked and opened her front door and then turned to face him. "If that's all, Mr. Marchetta—"

"Lucien," he prompted, and she dipped her head.

Her glasses had slid down her nose and she now pushed them back into position. He wondered if she realized she used her middle finger to do it—although the gesture looked natural.

"Lucien," she repeated. "I really have to go in and mark some papers—" She gestured with her thumb over her shoulder, but his gaze remained on the woman in front of him. She really was quite stunning. There was no reason why perhaps this meeting couldn't be an enjoyable one, for both of them.

"I'd love to talk some more," he said, his throat dry, his voice husky.

She tilted her head as she looked up at him, her eyes that fascinating blend of warm golds and cool grays. "Perhaps you'd like to call me some time," she said, her voice matching his in the husky stakes. She pulled a business card out of a pocket of her bag and offered it to him. He grasped the small rectangle of quality print stock and her fingers held it for just a little longer.

He lifted his gaze to hers. There was curiosity there, for sure, and an awareness of him that matched his unexpected appreciation of her. Something warmer flashed in those eyes, something he knew shone deep within his own. His gaze drifted down over her slender, straight nose to the sweetly curved lips.

"Perhaps we could continue this discussion inside?" he suggested softly. He placed his hand on the door-jamb and leaned closer. He could hear her soft intake of breath, the spark of surprise, the flare of heat that shifted her eye color to more golden than gray. Her lips parted.

He could feel the muscles in his groin stir, tighten, as her scent drifted to him, something soft and sweet, and yet…familiar. He leaned closer still, saw the pulse flutter at the base of her throat.

"I'm not in the habit of letting men I've just met inside my home," she replied, her gaze dipping to stare at his mouth.

His lips curled slowly and her teeth bit gently down on her bottom lip.

God, he wanted to kiss her. He was surprised by the flash of need that tore through him. She leaned against the doorjamb, shifting slightly so that she was half inside the house, half out. He heard a soft thud. She'd dropped her bag on the hall floor behind her.

"Invite me in," he suggested, his gaze flicking between her mouth and her eyes, and then he got distracted as her hand rose to the scarf around her neck.

"I can't," she whispered. She pulled the scarf away from her neck and he watched the fabric slowly drift over her skin. How the hell could removing a scarf look so damn sexy?

He caught a glimpse of silver around her neck. It was tied in what looked like an intricate lariat knot. He couldn't help but notice it would form a protective, painful barrier between her neck and a vampire's teeth—if one was so inclined...

The delicate chain dipped below her blouse and all he could think was how damn lucky it was. And sexy. Yep. Sexy.

"Invite me in," he whispered back. He grinned as she stepped inside the house, her palm sliding up the doorjamb so that she mimicked his stance. Her seductive smile was enough to melt any common sense he may have claimed as his own.

"I don't think so," she said as she parted the lapels of her coat. She wore a collared blouse that looked all-business but hinted at a body built for play, cutting in to reveal a slim waist. She shook her head, her blond hair sliding back over her shoulders as she gazed up at him with a flirty challenge in her eyes and a soft flush on her cheeks. She was magnificent.

"Invite me in," he coaxed, meeting her gaze and infusing his words with just the slightest hint of compulsion. He wanted in. In this house, in her arms. Inside her.

She arched her back, just a little, and his gaze dropped to her chest. That darned shirt draped over her breasts, hiding her curves. She leaned forward, just until she was in line with the door. She smiled sweetly, seductively, up at him, like an enchanting siren.

"No," she said slowly, drawing the word out in such a manner that he was briefly distracted by the O shape of her lips before he realized what she was saying. Her smile tightened and the warmth of her gaze took on a chill.

He blinked. "No?" What? But he'd—

"You should be ashamed of yourself," she told him, tsking as a frown marred her brow. "Fancy using compulsion to get into a woman's home—a woman you've only just met, too!"

He gaped at her. He'd used compulsion, true—but how the hell did she know? How the hell could she *resist*? She wasn't a vampire; he could still sense warmth and life within her. "What are you?" he asked in a low voice.

Her smile was brittle. "I'm the woman not inviting you in," she said sweetly as she reached for the door.

He held up a hand and encountered the impenetrable barrier to a home into which he wasn't invited. "Wait—I really do need to talk to you," he said as the door started to swing closed.

"Well, I really don't want to talk to you," she responded tartly. She shook her head, her disappointment stamped on her features. "Really, Lucien. When a woman says no, accept it."

The red door snapped closed in his face and the light on the porch winked out. He gaped at the door.

What the hell had just happened?

Chapter 2

Natalie groaned as she hid her head under her pillow. She wished she had a gun. If she couldn't shoot Lucien, she'd shoot herself to put her out of this misery. Maybe she should just use her chain? Lash him with silver. She needed to do *something*. He was outside her bedroom window, singing.

Badly. Which surprised her, because he had such a deep, sexy voice when he spoke… What happened in his larynx that he could sound like a brawling tomcat when he sang?

"Four hundred and sixteen bottles of beer on the wall…"

He'd started at one thousand bottles of beer on the wall.

She sat up in her bed and glared at the curtains shielding her window. She'd take one of those darn bottles and— Her hands fisted. She couldn't stand it. All evening, he'd tapped at the windows, the doors. He'd cajoled, he'd teased. Now he was trying torture.

She rolled out of bed, stomped over to the window

and whipped aside the curtain. He sat in the crook of the maple tree outside her window, looking way too comfortable for her liking. He stopped singing when she slid up the sash.

Lucien grinned. "Well, hello, minx."

The nickname stopped her cold. He used to call her that, all those years ago. It had been used in exasperation, affection, but never in that slightly flirty tone.

"Don't call me that," she snapped.

"What should I call you? Nina?"

She lifted her chin. Okay, so he knew. Didn't matter. It didn't change anything. "Don't call me that, either."

"Why not? It's your name."

"No. Nina died a long time ago. My name is Natalie."

He shrugged. "If that's what you'd prefer to call yourself—"

"It is. Now, please go *away*." How she didn't have the neighbors lining up to complain was a mystery. He must have compelled them, damn it.

He folded his arms, eyeing her figure.

She was wearing pajamas from her neck to her ankle. She hadn't felt comfortable wearing anything less, not with a vampire stalking her home.

"I need to talk with you."

"I'm not interested."

"I'm not leaving until you hear me out."

She glanced at her watch. "That's fine. Sunrise is in three hours. Nothing like smoked vampire with a side of bacon to go with my morning coffee." She raised her arms to close the window.

"Four hundred and fifteen bottles of beer on the wall," he began to warble.

She took a deep breath. She was tired, she was

cranky, and if this meant she'd snatch some much needed sleep, she'd let him say his piece and get it over with. "Fine, talk. You have five minutes—and then I'm going to sleep and you can sizzle, for all I care."

His eyebrows drew together and the downward turn of his mouth reminded her of Terry in one of his snits. "What happened to you? You used to be so nice…"

She snorted as she folded her arms and leaned her hip against the windowsill. "That was a lifetime ago, Lucien." Literally. She glanced pointedly at her watch. "Four minutes."

"I need your help."

She stared at him for a moment but his expression was enigmatic as he stared back at her. He, Lucien Marchetta, scion of the Marchetta vampire colony, needed her help. She burst out laughing.

He arched an eyebrow and her laughter trailed off. She blinked. "Good grief, you're serious."

His mouth quirked. "As a heart attack."

"How could I possibly assist the great Lucien Marchetta?" she asked, curious despite herself. The man moved in circles far removed from her own and, up until a few hours ago, he'd been completely unaware of her existence. From what she'd heard—and there were plenty of stories circulating about the man—he'd been living mainly on the west coast, establishing the family business…which was code for spreading the Marchetta influence to straddle the whole country.

And she…well, she was a professor of mythology and folklore studies, which was code for using teaching students as an opportunity to indulge her keen interest in stories set in bygone eras—and to find answers for her own problems. She couldn't help him with the Marchetta empire—the idea was so ludicrous, she almost giggled. Almost. She hadn't giggled in years.

"I was told you're the best in the field when it comes to everything arcane and mystical," he said quietly.

She arched her eyebrow. "Don't think you can flatter me," she said brusquely, ignoring the warm pride that bloomed in her chest that suggested he could, indeed, flatter her.

"I need to find something."

She kept her expression impassive but her mind started to race. What was he looking for? Something arcane and mystical, apparently. Something that drew him to a quiet little professor in a quiet little town. What mystical thing could a vampire want or need? A resistance to silver? No, there were any number of witches who could do some sort of protective spell for that.

An object that protected the wearer from sunlight? She knew of some stories that hinted at the existence of such artifacts. A book? Something that could reveal the clues to a lost pre-Troubles treasure? There were so many possibilities and her imagination was going wild.

"What?" She kept her tone cool, casual. She wasn't interested. Not really. Nope, not—

"Anything that would neutralize a toxin in a vampire's system."

Interested. She tilted her head and tried to look nonchalant. "What kind of toxin?"

"The lycanthrope kind."

She frowned as she digested the remark. Did he just say—? "A *werewolf* bite?"

He nodded. She lowered her arms as she straightened. "A werewolf bite," she repeated slowly to make sure he wasn't misunderstanding her and she wasn't mis-understanding him.

He said nothing, just met her gaze grimly.

"A *werewolf* bite," she said, this time rolling her finger in a circle. "You want to find a vampiric cure for a werewolf bite? You are hearing me, right? A were-wolf bite?"

His lips tightened. "Yes, I hear you. And, yes, you've got it right. I want to find something that will cure a vampire of a werewolf bite."

Oh, dear. Time had not been kind to Lucien. It was the only explanation she could think of, for him to have such a mental lapse. Strange, she hadn't heard of a human condition like dementia striking a vampire be-fore. Still, there was always a first time for everything...

Her arms rose to grasp the window, but he moved swiftly, his body a blur as he shifted to the end of the branch. "I'm serious, Nin—Natalie."

She shook her head. "No, you're bat-crap crazy, Luc-ien. Goodbye." She began to draw the window down to close, but he slammed his hand on the pane of glass, effectively halting her movement. She flinched at the anger in his blue eyes, the set of his jaw.

"Vivianne's been bitten and I don't have much time to find a cure. You're my last resort, Natalie. Help me."

His sister. She remembered how close they'd been, how he'd often spoken of her as his partner in all sorts of childish pranks, and how they'd supported each other when it came to his controlling, Reform-senator father. Family. It had always been so important to Lucien.

Yeah, well, family had been important to her, too, once upon a time. Anger warred with sympathy. Anger won. Her eyes narrowed at his words. "Me? Help you?

Where were you when *I* needed *you*, Lucien?" she snapped. "You don't get it, do you? You broke your promise to me and as a result I lost *everything*. Help you? I *hate* you."

She slammed the window closed, pulled the curtains across with a snap of fabric and stomped over to her en suite bathroom. She pulled cotton balls from the jar on her bathroom sink, stuffed them in her ears and stomped back to her bed.

Help him, indeed. She pounded her pillow into a comfortable pulp and lay down. She brushed away the tears trailing down her cheek as she glared at the wall.

No, damn it. She refused to care.

Lucien eased back along the branch toward the trunk of the tree.

I hate you.

He settled himself in the crook of the tree, staring at the darkened, covered window. He couldn't quite close his mouth, although his fingers clenched around the branches above and to the side of him. Shock. Annoyance. Frustration. Pain. Shock. The emotions tore through him.

He was still trying to process everything. Nina—no, *Natalie*—was alive. He could barely believe it. He'd suspected it was her when she'd slammed the door in his face. Not because she'd slammed the door, or because she'd resisted his compulsion—he still didn't know how *that* worked—but because of the way she'd said his name in such a familiar manner. It had sparked memories of a younger, happier woman.

Who currently hated him.

She was so angry, so bitter—nothing like the young

woman he'd once known, the woman whose memory he'd cherished. She also awakened a pain he'd buried deep.

He sagged against the tree. When he'd come looking for Professor Segova, he'd expected a quick, easy, polite discussion with a stranger. After all, he could simply compel the woman to tell him everything he needed to know. She was his last resort, though.

Vivianne had been languishing in her coffin for eight months. The witch, Dave Carter, had placed her under a suspension spell when she'd been bitten by a stray lycan, in an effort to give himself enough time to find something that everybody else didn't believe existed—a vampire's cure against the lycan toxin. Eight months, and he'd exhausted every option, had visited every elder, witch, monk, shaman—hell, he'd even tried the mundane human doctors. Nothing. Now, though, Dave had learned of a woman well-versed in ancient lore, who could possibly search through the dusty records for an oblique reference to the cure. Well, that was the plan. And he'd anticipated finding an older woman who would succumb to his compulsion and tell him everything he needed to know.

But, no. Instead he'd found a woman who could not only resist compulsion, but now showed no inclination whatsoever to help him save his sister.

She was right, though. He hadn't been there when she'd needed him. He'd promised and he'd let her down, and she'd paid the ultimate price. He shifted, guilt and shame weighing uncomfortably on his shoulders. He still couldn't quite believe it. Nin—no, Natalie. Natalie… He repeated the name over and over in his mind, trying to get it to stick, despite the shock. What the hell was he supposed to do now? His sister's body was slowly being eaten by the poison. His father would blame him for this death, too. He would lose the only family he knew.

He looked up at the sky. Already the dark was giving way to gray. He'd have to move soon, find someplace dark and protected from sunlight. He eyed the window. He didn't want to leave her.

She could be the key to saving his sister. She was also the only real friend he'd ever had. His eyes narrowed. He'd twisted himself inside out when he'd heard of her death. And here she was, looking remarkably healthy for a corpse. All those years—*decades*—he'd tortured himself with remorse for not being there for her, his regret for a treasured life lost had ripped him apart. He'd done dark deeds as a result of that pain, that desolation.

And it had all been for nothing. She lived. Anger tasted like ash in his mouth.

He hadn't been lying when he'd told her she was his last resort. Failure was not an option. Natalie Segova would help him save his sister.

He just needed the right leverage.

Natalie glanced around as she lifted her suitcase into the trunk of her compact car. She'd waited until the sun was truly overhead before stepping out of the house. There was no sign of Lucien. Not that she expected to see him. He was a blood-sucking vampire who sizzled to ash in the sunlight. She hoped he'd crawled back into whatever dark place he'd lived in for the past forty years.

Still, it was a relief he'd finally left. She wasn't sure

when, though. She'd stayed awake all night, listening. Hadn't slept a wink.

That was probably his evil plan, darn it. She'd had to wait for sunrise, though, before she could start packing. She hadn't wanted to clue him in to her plans for a speedy departure. It had taken her most of the day to get things sorted.

She lifted her sunglasses to rest on the top of her head as she strode through her kitchen and picked up a box from the table. She'd hastily packed her most prized possessions—whatever she could fit into her car. She'd lived as Natalie Segova for eight years, the longest she'd held on to an identity for decades, so she'd accrued quite a few things. Some old books that were dated pre-Troubles era—before humans realized the shadow breeds existed, and were quite telling of the time—some art, her tools, just in case she ever got close to a dig again. She eyed the contents, then gave a satisfied nod when she spied the small jewelry box tucked inside.

She peeled off her gloves and set them on the table, then reached for the velvet jewelry box. She lifted the lid and gently clasped the locket inside. She closed her eyes, trying to focus on the object in her hand, opening her senses. All she could sense, all she could feel, hear and see was a black void. Nothing. She closed up the velvet box and sighed softly in frustration. Still nothing.

She glanced around the room and made a face. She'd been here for so long. It was comfortable. Familiar. She liked it. She liked her work, she liked her students. Heck, she even liked Terry, and good old Rupert who haunted her office. She liked her name, too.

Damn it, she was two years too early. People started

to notice after ten years the lack of aging, so she generally made it a practice to move on before folks started to ask questions. But here—she liked here. Now she'd have to create a new name, a new identity. Where was she going to go? What was she going to do? It wasn't like job opportunities for historians came up regularly.

She tugged on her gloves and lifted the box. She had so much access to information here, information she needed to figure out what the hell was going on with her. Even now she struggled to think of a destination that would help her with her quest. She stomped to her car. She didn't like moving house. Had done more than her fair share of it. And why was her life in such a state of upheaval?

Lucien. It was all *his* fault. She dumped the box unceremoniously into the trunk and slammed the lid closed. She clapped her hands together, trying to dislodge as much dust as possible from her gloves. Why should she let another vampire ruin her life?

The thought brought her up short. Maybe she could just ignore him? She snorted. Like anyone could ignore Lucien Marchetta. The man was too good-looking, and too damn determined, to be ignored. She started to drift back toward the house. Send him on his way? Maybe she could get on with her life and to hell with Lucien Marchetta? Just go on living as Natalie Segova…? Her shoulders sagged. No. She couldn't risk it. If word got out about who—or what—she really was, she wouldn't have much of a life left, if any.

Being in this position, subject to the whims of a bloodsucker, was damn annoying.

She growled softly as she jogged back into the house to get her bag and keys. It was late afternoon and shadows were creeping across her yard. Dusk came early this close to the mountains. She had to get out of here before Lucien came back. And he would. If there was one thing she remembered about the man, it was how ruthless he could be when his family was threatened.

Her mouth turned down. What she would have given to have that fierce protection pointed in her direction. Well, obviously his regard for her hadn't cut as deep as hers had for him. She straightened her shoulders. If wishes were horses, there would be no shadow breeds, damn it.

She returned to her car, slid into the driver's seat and turned the key in the ignition.

Nothing.

She frowned, turned the key back to its original position and then tried again. Still nothing. She checked the fuel gauge. She still had a half tank of gas. Her eyes narrowed as she popped the hood and climbed out of the car. She lifted the hood, propping it open with the car rod, then rested her hands on the rim of the engine bay as she surveyed inside. It didn't take her long to notice the distributor cap was missing.

Son. Of. A. Bitch.

She heaved back off the car, her hands fisting as she took a few steps in one direction, then turned and stalked a few steps in another direction.

That weaselly, sneaky, clever bloodsucker. How had he known? She knocked the rod down and slammed the hood back into place. *Well played, Lucien. Well played.* She took a deep breath. Now what?

She whipped her phone out of the back pocket of her jeans and sent a text to her research assistant, Ned Henderson, asking to borrow his truck tomorrow. When the sun came up, Lucien would be forced to find cover, and she'd be able to flee. She nodded. That was the safest course of action. Sure, she hated delaying her escape, but it was better to be thorough and alive than impulsive and dead. She'd learned that lesson the hard way.

Great. Now she just needed to make it through the night. She grabbed her bag and keys, hesitated, then removed her suitcase from the trunk. She may as well be comfortable tonight. She hurried to her back door and had just opened it when she heard footfalls on the porch steps behind her. She whirled, surprised.

Lucien leaned against the porch railing, his eyes looking so startlingly blue with his dark hair. His black shirt was open at the collar and he was wearing a black coat that fell halfway to his knees. She frowned. She'd always thought he was handsome. Dreamy, even. Now, though, all these years later, she was aware of him in a way that was new and...unwelcome. She let go of her suitcase and subtly adjusted her grip on her tote, her hand sliding inside. She kept her gaze on him as she grasped the handle of her blade.

Despite the brisk breeze, his coat was open, revealing the dark shirt beneath. He folded his arms, the fabric pulling taut against his shoulders as he smiled. A slow, seductive curve of his lips. His gaze traveled from the top of her head to the tip of her sneakers, lingering on her curves. She swallowed. She wasn't used to him looking at her like that. Not for forty years. Not ever. It wasn't friendly, or exasperated, or even angry. No, it was provocative. She swallowed again and the corners of his mouth kicked up in a knowing smile.

She dropped her suitcase and bag and then whirled, stepping toward her doorway, to safety. She needed to get inside. He moved in a blur, slipping between her and escape. She gasped and jerked back, raising her hand. He caught her wrist and he slid his other hand up the doorjamb, skillfully using his body to crowd her back against the external wall of her home.

He eyed the silver blade in her hand with mild interest and squeezed just enough for her to wince at the pins and needles. Her grip relaxed. The dagger fell, its blade burying itself in the wooden slat of the decking. He let go of her wrist and brought his hand up to brace it against the clapboard at the side of her head.

He met her gaze intently as he leaned forward, effectively cornering her against her home. He tilted his head to glance at the suitcase at her feet and arched an eyebrow.

"Going somewhere?"

Chapter 3

Lucien inhaled. God, she smelled so sweet. So different to the way he remembered. She'd smelled of innocence and illness, a little sunshine mixed with poison. Sweet, but with a playful, daring sense of mischief. She'd definitely changed, though. He'd first met her when she was nine years old and had last seen her on her nineteenth birthday. Six years later, she was dead. Or supposed to be.

He shifted even closer. He could feel her warmth, her heat, could smell her, something floral with a spicy edge. Today she wore a denim jacket, a shirt revealing that enticing glint of silver at her neck and jeans that looked real damn good on her. He stared into her brown eyes, saw the startled fear morph into something darker, warmer. She definitely wasn't dead. Her gaze flickered briefly to his lips then back to his eyes.

He raised a hand to smooth her hair back behind her ear. "You weren't thinking of leaving, were you?" Annoyance edged with disappointment washed over him, confusing him amid a rising tide of attraction. Her intentions were obvious. He'd watched her briefly from the lengthening shadows. She'd crammed pretty much everything barring the kitchen sink into her car. Thank God, he'd thought to disable the car. If she'd left...

Well, she had. She'd been ready to turn her back on him and walk away without a backward glance, and that probably hurt more than last night's realization. He narrowed his eyes. Time for a different approach.

She lifted her chin. "I don't want to talk to you," she said. Her voice came out all soft and husky, and he could see the pulse fluttering in her neck, could hear the soft whisper of her breath and could almost feel the rise and fall of her breasts against his chest. If he leaned forward just a little more... He couldn't help the flare of curiosity—what would she feel like, her body pressed against his? Her eyes darkened, just a little, but he couldn't smell fear on her. No, there was something else, something innately familiar that his body recognized before his mind could.

Desire. It was like a shock, but a warm shock, as his body reacted before his brain could engage. This wasn't the little girl he'd once befriended.

He trailed his hand from her shoulder down her arm to slide in and rest on the indent of her waist. Soft curves. Warm heat. Blood pooled in his groin, his breathing quickened.

"Then let's not talk," he murmured and dipped his head. She gasped at the move and his lips took hers.

There was no slow familiarization, no tentative movements. Instant arousal, hard and sharp, gripped his body as his tongue slid against hers. Her hands rose to his chest and, for a moment, her palms flattened against his shirt and he thought she was going to push him away. He leaned his hips against hers, knew she could feel the effect she had on him. Her hands clutched at the fabric, pulling him closer, and she opened her mouth to him.

He crowded her back against the wall, sighing as his body pressed fully against hers, feeling the soft swell of her breasts against his chest, her pants as his hand slid from her waist to her butt, pulling her closer, tighter. And all the time, their lips and tongues played.

God, it was so hot, so fierce, this need to have her. She felt so damn good in his arms. His attraction to her last night paled in comparison to the rushing heat and desire swamping him now. He angled his head, deepening the kiss, feeling her breath mingle with his as she panted against him.

He wanted her. Now.

He shifted slightly, pulling her toward the door, and again encountered that impenetrable wall of resistance from the house.

He growled, bending low and clasping her around the thighs, lifting her up against his rock-hard arousal. God, she felt so warm there. His cock swelled and all he could think about was her, surrounding him. Her arms slid around his shoulders and she thrust her breasts against him as he wrapped her legs around his waist, his coat enveloping them both.

"Let me in," he whispered and rocked her against his hips.

She shuddered in his arms. Her nipples were tight little nubs against his chest. "Yes," she moaned before dipping her head to catch his lips.

He felt the invisible wall in her doorway disappear and he stumbled inside her home.

With one hand cupping her butt, he trailed the other one up her body, pulling her shirt along with it. Her skin—God, it felt so good, so smooth and warm. He could feel her stomach muscles shift under his touch, and they both moaned when his hand found her lace-covered breast.

He strode into the room, angling his head briefly to peer beyond her, although she kept distracting him with those soft little pants and those sexy little hip rolls that she did against him. He tried to find some place, anywhere— The kitchen table caught his eye and he carried her over to it.

The surface was clear—not that he cared—and he kicked a chair away, ignoring the clatter it made as it skidded across the floor. His senses were preoccupied by the smoking-hot, writhing woman in his arms. His own arousal was at fever pitch, clenching his body in a tight grip. He was so hard, so ready, stunned with the force of it, but willing to let it take control.

He kissed her hard and long, tongue lashing against hers as he rested her butt on the edge. He took hold of her ponytail and lowered her down on to the table, their lips and tongues tangling.

She moaned as he stepped into the juncture of her thighs and he could sense her heat, her dampness, right where he wanted to feel it most.

His lips left hers, trailing across her jaw and partway down to her neck. He stopped short of the chain. Her pulse was hammering away in her throat, matching his in a frenzied beat. He kissed her behind her ear, gently raking his teeth against the sensitive curve of her neck. She flinched. Tensed. Then shoved him with enough force that he flew across the room until he hit the kitchen island and fell to the floor.

She sat up on the table, her eyes glowing silver, as she clutched her neck.

"You bastard," she hissed.

How. Dare. He.

Natalie slid off the table, trying to calm her thumping heart, to wrestle her body under control. Her knees were like jelly and she had to lean back against the table for support. Tension gripped her; she couldn't identify whether it was fear or desire that made her feel weak. Probably both. She pushed the memories from her mind. That wasn't *now*. She wanted to run. She wanted to fight. She wanted to purr. She didn't know what she wanted.

"You bastard," she hissed again. She pulled her shirt down, trying to smooth it over her hips, wishing she could restore order to her pounding heart and desire-drenched body as easily as she did her clothing. Damn it, she hadn't even thought to use her lariat or the dagger in her boot. Hopeless. She eyed Lucien.

He shook his head, as though stunned, and eyed the distance between them. "What happened?" he said, his expression confused and maybe a little frustrated. He glanced at the kitchen island that had stopped his flight. A chip of caesarstone fell to the floor.

"Get out of my house," she said, her voice hoarse.

Lucien rose, rubbing the back of his head. He quickly composed himself as he leaned against the kitchen island. "No. You invited me in."

He wore that stubborn look that had always struck her as annoying but sweet. Now, though, she didn't think it was so sweet, just annoying. *I invited him in?*

She frowned and opened her mouth to argue, only a

faint memory of her panting "yes" stopped her. He had asked, and she'd invited him in. The fact he was inside her kitchen testified to it. Damn it. He'd used her. He'd kissed her, twisted her in knots, just to get his ass inside her home. Once in, you couldn't evict a vampire. At least, not easily.

"Nice place," he said, eyeing the interior of her home casually. He gestured to the frames that could be seen on the hall wall. "The photos are a nice touch."

"God, what is it with you vampires that you'll stoop so low?" she rasped, ignoring his offhand effort at conversation.

His gaze swept over her, pausing on her hips. "I was prepared to stoop much lower," he said in a voice that sounded deep, husky and just a little gravelly with tension.

It brought a tremble to her knees and a catch to her breath as images of what they could be doing right now, if she hadn't stopped him, flooded her mind as though on a rapidly spinning film reel...along with a good dose of mortification. Damn it. Seriously? This is *Lucien*. What was wrong with her?

"I can't believe you'd be willing to use your body to get what you want, that you would use *me*," she said, injecting scorn into her voice, and hoping she could inject her spine with a little bit of steel when it came to Locky-Lips Lucien. She shook her head. "I refuse to be some toy for you vampires to play with and then discard—or kill—whenever it suits you."

"I'm not toying with you," he snapped, bracing his hands on the counter behind him.

He had the audacity to look offended. She raised her eyebrows. "Oh, really? Suddenly, after all these years, you track me down because you actually want…me? You didn't even know I existed until yesterday. This," she said, gesturing between them, "isn't about us. It's about you, and how far you'll go to save your sister." She refused to give in to the hurt. He was playing a game. That's all *this* was.

His lips tightened. "I will do whatever I can to save my sister," he admitted. He tilted his head. "You would do the same, given the chance."

It was like a wave of frigid water sucked her down into a whirlpool—dizzying and frightening and oh, so cold, sucking the energy, the fight, out of her. "I can't believe you said that to me," she whispered. "You know better than that."

He stepped away from the counter, his frown harsh. "Do I?" He shook his head. "I *thought* I knew better. I thought you were dead—and you're clearly not." He ran his hands through his hair, his fingers tightening in the ebony strands. "My God, Ni—*Natalie*. I thought I'd lost you."

"You did lose me," she said through gritted teeth. "I know how much your family means to you, Lucien. Maybe this gives you some idea of what I went through."

He gaped at her for a moment then stepped closer, his hands at his sides. "Is that what this is about? Revenge? I didn't do this to you, Natalie."

Her smile was brittle as she stepped forward, closing the distance between them until she could look him straight in those gorgeous blue eyes. "I'll always be here for you," she whispered, satisfaction coursing through her when she saw him pale as she threw his words back in his face, the way she'd wanted to do for forty years.

"I watched my family die, and you were nowhere to be seen, Lucien. Now it's your turn to watch yours die, knowing someone could have helped but decided not to. Just like you did."

"I did not *decide* to abandon you, Natalie." His voice was low, like rocks spilling over gravel. "I didn't know. I was at one of my father's events."

Her lips tightened. His father... She thought Lucien had left Irondell because of her, because of that one stupid, innocent little kiss when she was just a little too drunk and a little less inhibited. Even now, her cheeks warmed at the memory. He'd been such a gentleman, too. Told her that she'd find a guy who was close to her age, and was ready to share with her all the adventures Lucien had already had. That he was too old, too cynical and world-weary for her, but that he loved her—as a friend. And then he'd left. Sure, they'd kept in touch via email—as friends. But every time he'd promised to visit, something always came up, and was always because of his father.

She'd followed all of his progress, reading anything she could find in the news articles, researching online. He'd been doing well, over there. Away from her. She folded her arms. "Yeah. I know. Looking after your family interests. Sorry, Marchetta. Your trip here was wasted. There is no cure for a werewolf bite, not for a vampire. You should go home and be with your sister." Her lips curved, but it wasn't a smile. "I know how much your family means to you."

His brow darkened and she watched the flicker of myriad emotions pass across his face until his expression was once again implacable. "Help me, Natalie. If not for what we once meant to each other, then for the sake of natural curiosity. I at least know that much about Professor Segova—her keen interest in the occult and cultural mythology."

So he'd done his research on her, huh? Well, it wasn't a secret that she loved her work and found it fascinating. She'd even managed to do a couple of field trips to track down arcane objects and sites of significant cultural importance. Then the rest of his words sank in. What they'd once meant to each other? Well, she knew that apparently she'd put more stock into their relationship than he had. She'd call him on it, too, if she could just put voice to those challenging words. What had she meant to him? But then she'd have to hear his response and she wasn't ready for that. Wasn't ready to have this whole damn conversation with Lucien, quite frankly. She'd drawn a line under that time in her life. All that had died when she had.

She shook her head, keeping her mouth shut. Just let sleeping dogs lie.

Lucien sighed and his breath whispered across her cheek. This close, she could feel his warmth, feel the life in his non-dead, too-gorgeous body. "What would it take for you to help me, Natalie?" His voice was soft, almost pleading—well, about as pleading as Lucien Marchetta could get. "Name it."

Her eyes narrowed as she leaned closer so that only a whisper separated her lips from his. She lifted her gaze to his eyes. "My family for yours."

She saw the instant that anger and pain flared in those eyes and rested back on her heels, triumphant for a brief moment at causing that reaction, quashing the shame that rode on triumph's tail.

She'd struck him in the heart. She knew from personal experience how important his family was to him, and how much he would sacrifice for them. It would eat him alive, this helplessness at not being able to help his sister. He'd crossed the desert based on a rumor of a cure to save his sister from a fate that was universally accepted as a natural, inevitable consequence. She just wished he'd fought against nature so thoroughly for her. Resisting him, not helping him—he would hate her for that.

And then he'd leave. And then maybe she could go back to her not-so-normal life.

She turned her back on him and walked toward her living room.

Lucien grasped her arm, turning her and forcing her up against the wall. His eyes were blazing red, his nostrils flared.

"Do you really hate me so much?" he yelled, the rage almost tangible. "Are you willing to let an innocent person die because of this petty, spiteful hate of yours?"

Her eyes widened as her anger coursed through her at his words that hit just a little too close to home. "Innocent? Your sister is a vampire, Lucien. She lost any dregs of innocence centuries ago. Petty? Spiteful? My family *died*. I *died*. Forgive me if that detail seems so trivial to you."

"Damn you, help me save my sister!"

She saw his muscles bunch, heard the thunk as his fist hit the wall, felt the wall shudder under the impact. She raised her chin. "Or what, Lucien? You'll beat me to a pulp? Maybe bite me a bit? That's what you vampires like to do, isn't it? Take little bites to torment and drain your victims? Or do you want to kill me?" She laughed as he blanched and stepped away from her. "Honestly, if you could figure out a way to do it, I'd be thankful. I've tried a few things and nothing has stuck."

He blinked as he backed up. "What do you mean?"

"I mean that you can't do anything to me I haven't already tried." She yanked off her gloves and held up her wrists, twisting them outward to show him the smooth skin. "See, I don't even scar now. Drowning? Well, that doesn't work, either. And electrocution stings, but the hangover when you come to isn't worth it."

His frown deepened. "You've…you've tried to kill yourself?"

His words were a little breathless, as though she'd punched him in the stomach. He was the first person she'd admitted that to, although why, she had no idea.

She shrugged. "Doesn't count if it doesn't work," she muttered. She eyed him as he turned away briefly from her, his hand rising to rub his chin.

"Why—" he cleared his throat "—why would you do that?" He turned to her, his expression pained.

She gave a sad sigh that sounded like a dying violin. "I have no one, Lucien. My mom, my dad… There is nobody left. Every night I come home to an empty house. There are no Christmases or birthdays. Anyone who once knew me, once cared about me, is long gone. I have no…" She swallowed. "I have no one." The last words came out in a whisper and she had to blink to fight back the burn in her eyes. God, she sounded pathetic, even to her own ears.

He reached for her but stopped midway and turned, his shoulders taut. He stood still for a moment and she desperately wanted to see his face, desperately wanted a clue as to what was going on inside his head— although she'd never had much luck reading the man.

He reached in and pulled an object out of his pocket. His face looked ravaged by emotion as he gently pressed the book against her chest, forcing her to clasp it.

"That's not true, Natalie," he murmured, his gaze meeting hers with an intensity that made her lower her stare. "You had me."

He walked through her living room to her front door and she glanced down at the book she held. She barely registered the sound of her front door opening and closing. Her breath caught as she recognized the dark red hardcover and embossed cursive font on the cover. Her old book of poetry from the Romantic era. Tears swam in her eyes, blurring her vision, but her hands clasped the tome tightly. He still had it, still carried it with him. She'd given it to him that last night, all dramatic and fanciful as only a nineteen-year-old girl with a massive crush could be. He'd just told her she was his greatest friend, and that he had to leave—for business. She should have just painted a bright red L on her forehead for loser. But no, she'd thought perhaps, just perhaps, there was a chance there could be more between them, and she'd pressed it into his hands.

Carry this with you and think of me when you read it, she'd told him. He'd smiled and hugged her close, and she'd hugged him back, cherishing the moment of being held in his arms just one more time.

And then he'd left and she hadn't seen him until yesterday. She hefted the book in her hands. She couldn't believe he still carried it with him. All these years…

Had he read it and thought of her? Had he actually missed her, maybe? She closed her eyes and held the book close to her chest and inhaled. The book carried faint traces of his scent, as well as the slight musk of years gone past.

"Puhleeze. Would you rather hug a book or that beautiful man?" A feminine voice sighed and Natalie jerked, her eyes popping open in surprise.

A young girl sat on the arm of a sofa, swinging her legs and popping gum. She wore a navy sweater, plaid skirt and long white socks. Her hair was pulled back in a curly ponytail. She frowned when she met Natalie's eyes. "Oh, my God. You can see me?"

Lucien halted at Natalie's front gate. A black BMW sedan was parked across the road, the windows tinted dark with tempered glass. Another vampire. The back passenger's window slid down and he sighed when recognized the vampire. He schooled his features as he crossed the road to greet his father. He didn't want Vincent Marchetta to see how devastated and shocked he was. Exposing that depth of vulnerability was a recipe for prolonged punishment from his sire. He should know; he'd modeled his own behavior on the man.

He braced his hand on the roof of the car. "What are you doing here?" he asked without preamble.

Vincent sat back in the seat, his face all dark and brooding in the moonlight.

"I would ask you the same question," his father responded, his expression closed.

"I need to track down a lead."

His father snorted. "I can't believe you bought into this fairy tale," he snapped.

Lucien ignored his father's contempt. He'd grown adept at doing it. He focused instead on the man's words. "I'm not sure if I've totally bought into it," he said, "but if there is a chance we can save Viv, then I'll do everything in my power to do so."

"So you go off gallivanting again while a member of your family lies dying," Vincent snarled.

Lucien's arm muscles tightened on the roof of the car for a moment. His father's words were full of anger, condemnation and something darker that Lucien didn't want to put a name to. They called up gruesome memories and pain—so much pain. And guilt. Shame. Anger. He shoved the tumultuous emotions behind a cold curtain of composure. He flexed his fingers on the smooth surface of the car and straightened.

"I didn't do this to her, Dad," he said quietly, gazing down the street. "I intend to save her."

"Well, we all know where your good intentions get people," his father muttered.

Lucien gritted his teeth, his muscles flexing in his cheek. It was dark now, although the sky still bore traces of burnt orange—the light of a sun reluctant to relinquish its grasp on the day.

"Your witch friend told me what you were up to," Vincent said calmly. Lucien's lips quirked. He wished he'd been there to see that. Dave Carter was renowned for not giving a damn about position or power, and wouldn't have given his father the respect the old man believed was his due.

Sometimes, he envied Dave Carter. Not a lot, but sometimes. Lucien said nothing, but turned to look at his father expectantly.

Vincent's brown eyes took on a serious glint. "Your sister's condition is getting worse. I understand a certain Professor Segova is proving resistant?"

Lucien glanced at Natalie's quaint little home. She still hadn't turned on any lights. "She'll come around."

"We don't have time for that. I'll leave Enzo here, to assist." His father indicated the driver's seat and Lucien leaned down to glance into the dark interior. His father's guardian nodded at him, his expression bland.

Lucien pinned Enzo with a lethal glare. "You won't go anywhere near her," he stated slowly and succinctly. "She is off-limits to you. And you," he told his father. "I'll take care of this." He was still upset with Natalie— furious, really—but he didn't want his father or the guardian prime to get involved.

Enzo arched an eyebrow and curiosity flared in his eyes as he briefly glanced toward the house. Lucien didn't care that his remark would draw more attention to Natalie. He knew what kind of "assistance" was being offered and he didn't want it anywhere near Natalie. Damn it, she'd already been through enough.

"I don't take orders from my son," Vincent pointed out mildly. "Whatever it takes, she has to tell us what she knows—and you know Enzo has certain skills to make people talk."

That was the problem. Lucien knew exactly what Enzo was capable of. Natalie thought she couldn't die—a fact that intrigued him. A woman who could resist compulsion, couldn't die, and possessed the strength of ten men—going by the way their kiss had ended so abruptly—yet she wasn't a vampire. She was all warmth and vitality in his arms, all soft heat and lush curves— Damn it, he wasn't going to think about that. But she thought death couldn't claim her. Well, she'd be screaming for death before Enzo was through with her.

A four-by-four pickup turned the corner and drove

slowly down the street. Lucien met his father's gaze briefly before the young man turned into Natalie's driveway. Lucien recognized the guy from several photos on Natalie's hallway wall.

He shook his head at Vincent. "I said, I'll take care of this." He stepped away from the BMW and crossed the street, back in the direction of Natalie's house.

Chapter 4

"**Y**ou *can* see me!"

Natalie's glance skidded away, but it was too late. The girl leaped off the arm of the sofa, clasping her hands. "Oh, my God. You can see me!" She jumped up and down, clapping her hands. "This is so cool. You don't know how long it's been since I've actually spoken to anyone. I'm Courtney."

Natalie glanced down at the book in her hands. She wasn't wearing gloves. Blast. She'd taken them off to show Lucien her scarless skin. "Look, I'm kind of in the middle of something right now—"

"Of course! You have to go after him. That was so romantic," Courtney gushed. "He has been moping over that book *forever*."

Natalie frowned. "Really?"

"For reals. Totally."

Natalie hesitated.

"And he's super-hot." Courtney waggled her eyebrows and popped her gum.

Natalie rolled her eyes, but still headed for the front

door. She'd deal with Courtney later. She pulled the door open. "Luc—"

Lucien was walking up her garden path to her door, hauling a resistant Ned Henderson with him.

"Ned," she gasped, then frowned. "What are you doing here?"

"I got your text," Ned said, trying to shrug Lucien off. He wasn't successful. "I was heading out to meet with some friends and thought I'd drop my truck off tonight instead of tomorrow." He tried to brush off Lucien's grip. "Let go of me, man." He winced as Lucien's grip tightened.

"That's very sweet of you," Lucien said, his gaze alternating between her and her research assistant. "You must be fairly close to be able to call in favors like that, Natalie."

Her frown deepened and sense of disquiet sparked at his words.

Lucien cocked his head as he smiled tightly up at her, his hold tight and unyielding on her research assistant's arm. "What was it you said?" he asked casually. "My family for yours?"

His eyes flashed red, his teeth lengthened. Natalie's eyes widened in horror as she guessed his intentions. She dropped the book and started running down her porch steps. "No!"

Lucien sank his teeth into Ned's neck and Ned cried out in pain. Her friend tried to struggle, but his eyelids flickered and he slumped to the ground.

Lucien watched as Natalie's expression paled.

"What have you done?" Natalie screeched as she skidded to her knees on the path. She pressed her hand to Ned's neck, trying to stop the flow of crimson blood that was now staining her path. She shrugged out of her jacket, wadding it up in her hand to press against the bite. He saw her hands tremble as she tended to Ned.

"Exactly as you said, Natalie," Lucien said calmly as he wiped a drop of blood from the corner of his lips. He watched as she tried desperately to save her friend. Much more effort than he'd expected, admittedly. He'd been right. For someone who had no one, she sure had a lot of photos of her students and coworkers. She might not admit it—she may not even be aware of it—but she had established connections with people in her life as Natalie Segova.

She glared up at him. "Fix him," she demanded.

He raised an eyebrow. "Oh, so you'd like my help to save someone close to you, huh?" He couldn't help the prod. He was so damn angry with her. He should have left, given himself time to calm down, to think rationally. But then, that would leave Natalie unprotected against his father's guardian prime. He tried to rein it in, but it was difficult. He was angry. Angry that he was forced to do this. Angry that she'd totally turned her back on him. She'd felt lost and lonely, and would rather kill herself then reach out to him. He'd— Damn it, he'd loved that young woman, in his own way. And she'd been prepared to bleed it all down a drain. Rage simmered within him, burying his shock and despair at her confession, and those softer, warmer feelings that had woken with that kiss. He smiled, his lips tight.

"Agree to help me save my sister and I'll save your... friend." He eyed the young man, his skin a pasty white against the dark flagstone of the path. He was just a friend, right? Not that he cared, or had any right to query her on that. Still, the curiosity jabbed at him.

"You bastard."

"So you've said. Clock's ticking. He's about to bleed out, Natalie. What's it going to be?"

She glared at him with narrowed eyes, the gray brightening against the hazel. Ned's breath started to rattle in his chest and she turned to her friend. She smoothed his brown hair off his forehead then nodded. "Fine. I'll help you look into a cure for your sister. I can't guarantee that we'll save her—there's never been a hint of a cure for the lycanthrope toxin," she said in warning, then dipped her head. "But I'll help you look. Save Ned."

He glanced at her for a moment. "No more running." It wasn't a request.

The muscles in her jaw clenched. "Fine."

Well, it would do for starters. "Deal." He held out his hand and waited for her response. She eyed his hand for a moment. Finally she clasped it briefly.

"Deal." She let go almost immediately. "I hope you're better at keeping your end of a bargain than you are a promise."

His lips tightened at the remark, then his incisors lengthened as he pushed his coat sleeve up and unbuttoned his shirt sleeve, rolling it back. He bit gently into his wrist. He leaned over and pressed the open wound to the research assistant's mouth, wincing as the young man tasted, then sucked at his offering. He pulled his wrist away.

The young man's eyes flickered open as the wounds on his neck closed up. He flinched when he saw Lucien.

"Take your car and go home—sleep it off. You were

too tired to visit Natalie," he murmured, his voice deep, his gaze intensifying as he compelled the young man. "You won't remember any of this. Oh, and Natalie doesn't need your car anymore." He helped the man to his feet and turned him in the direction of the four-by-four parked in the driveway.

"Will he be okay?" Natalie asked, rising. Lucien wondered briefly at her concern.

"He'll be fine." He turned to face her fully. "I appreciate your help, Natalie."

She gave him a harsh look as she rolled her blood-stained jacket into a tight ball. "Like I had any choice," she muttered.

"I just want to help my sister," he told her quietly. It pained him that he'd had to go about it this way, but for every minute Natalie refused to help him, his sister slid closer to death.

"We have a deal, Natalie. I've saved your friend, in exchange for your help. If you try to run again, I will kill him, and anyone else you call friend here in Westamoor. If you try to break our deal, I will kill everyone you've ever dealt with here." He kept his expression composed when she blanched, firmed his lips when the look in her eyes changed, dulled, and defeat crept onto her face. He stifled the regret that warred with self-disgust at forcing her to his will in this way.

Her lips curved, tinged with a sadness he wished he could remove. "Somehow, I didn't expect anything less," she murmured.

Pain speared him, and he straightened his shoulders in an effort to ward it off. "Where do we start?"

She pursed her lips and it was so obvious she hated the whole situation. "The institute. We might find something in the library." She held up the jacket in her hand and indicated the blood splatter on her shirt. "I have to change first."

He nodded. "I'll wait."

Natalie unlocked her office door and stepped inside, switching on the lights as she did so. Lucien followed close behind. She pushed her spectacles up on her nose into a more comfortable position. She'd almost forgotten to wear them. Shrugging out of her coat, she draped it over the coat hook next to the door, then crossed over to her bookshelves and started scanning the titles. She made sure to keep her gloves on.

Lucien frowned and jerked his chin in the direction of her hands. "Are you still cold?"

"Nope, just like wearing gloves, especially when I'm handling the books." She kept her tone clipped, trying to ward off any more questions about the gloves.

Lucien came to stand by her side, gazing up at the wall of books. "I see some things never change," he murmured, a slight curve to his lips. "You always loved to read."

She faltered at his warm tone, the indulgence of it, then continued to scan.

"Do you remember all those hours you used to make me read to you?" he asked, folding his arms and leaning a shoulder against the shelving to look at her. "One more," he said in a soft, singsong voice. "Always one more. One more page, one more chapter, one more story."

She steeled herself against the sweet memories he evoked. "Save it, Lucien. I agreed to help you. We don't have to pretend to be friends."

Lucien kept his gaze on her. "I always thought we were more than friends," he said quietly.

Her fingers paused on a volume of Celtic mythology. She'd thought so, too, but then he'd pulled that stunt on her front path. No friend would do that to another.

"What about wolfsbane? Did you think to try that to neutralize the toxin?" She changed the subject in an effort to distract both of them.

"Yes. It had no effect."

"Hmm. What about…silver nitrate? No, wait. That wouldn't work." Silver was toxic to werewolves, but it was also toxic to vampires. It might work on a human, but that particular remedy would probably kill a vampire.

She hesitated. "What about…null blood?"

"Too risky. It could possibly work on the lycan toxin, but it would also work on her vampiric biochemistry."

Meaning if it nullified the werewolf's toxin, it would also destroy anything vampiric in Vivianne. "She could wake up human…?" she suggested.

"Or maybe not wake up at all," Lucien pointed out. Natalie grimaced. He had a point.

"Oooh, I didn't realize we had a visitor," a male voice said from the doorway.

Natalie glanced over her shoulder, then glanced quickly back to the books. Rupert had arrived. He materialized through the door, his white hair a little scruffy, wearing his customary attire of cream-colored shirt, red bow tie and a brown cardigan. He used the hem of his shirt to rub his spectacles clean, then placed them back on his face and blinked at Lucien.

She'd been expecting him. The institute's resident ghost ambled further into her office and sat in one of the twin chairs opposite her desk. "To what do I owe this unexpected pleasure?"

"Look, if you want to find a vampire cure for a werewolf's bite, then let's just focus on that, shall we?" Her words were as much for Rupert's benefit as Lucien's. She pulled down a range of books on European history, pre-Troubles period, and turned toward her desk.

Rupert's eyebrows rose. "Did I hear you right? A werewolf cure?"

She eyed her friend briefly as she handed Lucien one of the volumes. "Let's go back to the very beginning." She went to sit at her desk and opened one of the books. "The first rumors of vampiric behavior date back to the Ottoman Empire," she said. "Let's look through these chronicles…"

Lucien flicked open a random page and read briefly. His eyebrow rose. "Transylvania? Isn't that a little kitsch? Besides, isn't that now Melania? That's been werewolf territory for nearly seven hundred years…"

"Hasn't he ever read *Dracula*?" Rupert asked in surprise.

Natalie's lips curved. "Yes," she said to her ghostly companion. She'd made Lucien read it to her when she was fourteen. She realized Lucien was looking at her in exasperation.

"Well, if it's just kitsch, why am I reading it?" he asked.

Natalie blinked, realizing her blunder, then turned as though she'd been speaking to him, after all. "As I mentioned the other day, folklore is largely based on fact. I believe Transylvania is the birthplace of vampirism."

Lucien shot her a skeptical look and she folded her arms and leaned forward to rest them on her desk.

"Think about it. Whenever you have a saturation of a certain breed, it's either a stronghold or—"

He finished her sentence. "They moved in and took it over."

She nodded. "Exactly. If Melania is a werewolf stronghold now, it's either always been that way or they overran the vampires. Look up any reference to Vlad—"

"Dracula?"

"Uh, he's not a total lost cause." Rupert sighed and pulled a pipe out of the breast pocket of his buttoned-up shirt. Natalie ignored him.

"Vlad Dracul was the father. We're looking at his son, Vlad the Third. Vlad the Impaler," she clarified.

Lucien frowned. "Why do you think Vlad the Impaler might be of help?" He moved to sit on the chair that Rupert was occupying.

"Wait!" She held up a hand and Lucien froze. "Uh, that one's more comfortable," she finished lamely, pointing to the empty seat. "The other one has a spring in it."

"Don't think I've ever been referred to as 'the one with the spring in it' before," Rupert muttered.

Natalie sighed, trying to keep track of the conversation she was having with Lucien. "I think we start with Vlad to search for a heretofore unknown cure for a werewolf bite, especially since he was the first person who understood how to kill the vampires."

"I thought he was rumored to be one?"

Natalie cupped her hand on her chin, her brows dipping. "I don't subscribe to that point of view. He may have been a human trying to rid his area of vampires."

Lucien shook her dry look. "By impaling them?"

"With wooden stakes," she pointed out.

Lucien's eyebrows rose. He nodded briefly, as though

acceding to her point, and started to read the book in his hands.

"You're not serious, are you?" Rupert asked as he removed a pouch of tobacco from his cardigan pocket. "A cure for lycanthropulism? My, you do find the most interesting projects. I thought the Cauldron of Daghdha was an ambitious undertaking, but you've outdone yourself with this one. Lycanthropulism…" Rupert started to chuckle as he packed the tobacco into his pipe.

"I'll find it," Natalie said in response, looking up at her colleague, and turned the page she'd been reading. The Cauldron of Daghdha was an ancient Celtic artifact rumored to leave nobody unsatisfied. At least that project had benefits for everyone. She'd found some maps of ancient Ireland and felt certain she was on the right trail for that.

Lucien looked up in surprise, then smiled. "We'll find it," he corrected. "We're partners now."

Her cheeks bloomed with embarrassment at being caught talking to the ghost, then realized how he'd interpreted her words.

"Oh, uh—"

Natalie placed her elbows on the table and covered her face with her hands. Ghosts. "That's not what was meant," she said, intending the words for Rupert, but glaring at Lucien. "We are not partners. You are blackmailing me to help you find this make-believe cure so that Ned and anyone else I know stays alive."

"Oooh," Rupert said, twisting in his seat to stare at Lucien.

"Which goes to prove my point that vampires can't be trusted," she said, glaring at the handsome man who sat across from her, staring at her warily.

"*I* can't be trusted?" Lucien leaned forward in his seat. "You're the one whose been playing dead all these years, Natalie," he argued.

"Because a vampire killed me," she shot back.

"Not just a vampire, though, right?" Lucien tilted his head and stared at her expectantly.

"Okay, fine. A vampire and a werewolf. Happy? For the record, I don't trust either breed," she muttered. She definitely didn't trust Lucien, either.

She eyed him now. "The sooner we prove or disprove this cure, the sooner you can be on your way."

Lucien leaned back in the seat and stared at her for a moment, then his nose twitched and he frowned. "Do you smell something?"

She glared at Rupert, who smiled back at her as he chuffed on his pipe. "Let's just read," she said tiredly and turned her attention back to her book.

Lucien glanced over at Natalie. Her chin was cupped in her hand, her eyes blinking ever so slowly, her face pale and drawn. They'd been at this for hours. Natalie had made several trips to the library, and there was still a book trolley with a large number of tomes to sift through. They'd spoken occasionally, when one or the other had found something of potential interest, but had mostly read in silence. It hadn't felt awkward, though. No, it had been eerily easy to slide back into that comfortable routine of reading alongside Natalie.

She'd changed a little, despite his attempt to cling to the past memories. Every now and then she'd shaken her head or nodded, as though having a silent conversation with herself. It was cute. Now, though, she'd been silent for the last half hour and looked to be fighting a losing battle against sleep. He wondered if she realized she'd been reading for the last two hours with her glasses perched on top of her head.

He closed the book with a snap and set it down on the pile that now reached the same height as the armrest of the chair he was sitting on.

"Come on, we need a break," he said.

Natalie jerked upright, as though startled awake. She frowned. "No, we can keep—" she paused to yawn "—going."

He glanced at the window behind her desk. The night sky was beginning to lighten. "I can't. I have to go before the sun rises, and you need sleep."

She yawned again then shrugged. "You're right. I guess I'm not used to pulling one of these study all-nighters, anymore. I'm beginning to skim a lot of this stuff, and I might miss something."

Or she might face-plant on her desk as she passed out from exhaustion. Lucien refrained from commenting.

"Okay, well…" She rose and walked around her desk as he stood from his chair. "I guess you go to whatever dark place you've found for yourself, and I'll meet you back here tomorrow night."

He remained where he stood and she had to halt in front of him to prevent herself from walking right into him. He surveyed her carefully. She looked weary. He realized this was her second straight night of little to no sleep, thanks to him. Guilt flared as she weaved a little on her feet, and he grasped her shoulders.

"Go home, get some sleep," he said in a low voice.

She frowned up at him. "You can't compel me, Lucien."

He sighed. "I'm not trying to compel you, Natalie. I just want you to get some rest."

She grimaced. "Right. So I can be back here, bright-eyed and bushy-tailed to help you search for something we don't even think exists."

"No, because I actually care about you, and you're exhausted." The words were out of his mouth before he could stop them and he frowned. Vulnerability never sat well with him. He hated it, but he couldn't stop his next words, either. "Will you be here tomorrow night?" She'd said she would, but he needed her to promise—she kept her promises. Or, she had, long ago.

Her eyelids flickered, as though she sensed his vulnerability and was as equally uncomfortable with it as he. "Yeah, I'll be here. We made a deal, remember? I'll keep my end of the bargain as long as you keep yours."

Thoughts of her packed car and that guy who'd offered his truck as a replacement haunted him.

Natalie sighed. She lifted her fist and extended her pinkie finger, encased in the soft leather glove.

"Pinkie swear, I'll be here," she murmured and then narrowed her eyes. "Pinkie swear my friends are safe."

He gaped at the gesture. She was the only one who'd ever pulled this with him. Good God, if any of his business opponents ever found out, he'd lose his dangerous edge in negotiations. All those years ago when they'd shared secrets by her bedside, she'd always held him to account. He knew how gravely she viewed a pinkie swear. He lifted his pinkie and curled it around hers.

"Pinkie swear," he said, his voice rough. "I'll keep you and your friends safe."

Her brow dipped at his words, but only for a moment before another yawn surprised her. She pulled her hand away from him to cover her mouth. "Oh, I'm so sorry.

Right, I'm off to crash for a couple of hours, and then I'll get back to this." She started to walk around him but he grabbed her arm gently to halt her.

She was so close, he could smell her, that sweet scent edged with spice. "Wait," he said. Her eyes met his in surprise, a flash of wariness tinged with curiosity and something a little warmer glinted as she returned his gaze before dropping briefly to look at his lips. He smiled and her stare returned to his. He raised both hands to the top of her head and removed her spectacles, folding them carefully before handing them back to her. "Don't forget your glasses," he whispered. He tilted his head forward.

A book flew off the shelf, hit him in the cheek, and he reeled back. "What the hell?" he growled in shocked surprise.

Natalie gasped, her hand covering her mouth.

"I'll defend your honor," Rupert said smugly, dusting off his hands.

"I'm so sorry," she whispered as Lucien rubbed his cheek and bent to pick up the book. Shakespeare's *Macbeth*. "It must have fallen off the shelf," she offered with a wince.

He eyed the bookshelf that stood three feet away. "Yeah, it fell," he said, not buying it one bit. He handed her the book, but held on to it briefly as she clasped it. She was still wearing her gloves, he noticed.

"I'm trusting you," he said softly.

She nodded solemnly. "That goes both ways, Lucien."

He dipped his head and strode out of the room.

He shut the door behind him then turned back to look at the plaque bearing the lettering Professor N.

Segova. His brows pulled together. She used to call him Luc, once upon a time. He sighed as he walked away. Well, at least now he had her cooperation.

Chapter 5

Natalie glared at Rupert. "*Macbeth*, Rupert? Seriously?" She shook her head as she placed the book back on the shelf. "That was rude." Rupert had been a ghost for nearly a century and had picked up some tricks through his research at the institute.

"You're welcome," Rupert responded before shuffling over to his chair. "Now, why don't you tell me exactly what's going on?"

Natalie took the seat next to him and told him everything. Well, nearly everything. She left out the part about the kiss. Rupert was like the grandfather she'd never known and there were some things she just didn't share with him.

"However did you meet Lucien Marchetta? Even I knew of him—and his family. You two don't look like you'd move in the same circles."

She laughed for a moment. "No, we did not. I met him when I was nine years old, in the hospital. I was going through a round of chemotherapy and dialysis, and he'd occasionally come and visit." She didn't go into the detail of their first meeting, or how she, a sickly nine-year-old, had negotiated unlimited visits from whom she'd later learned was a savvy business tycoon.

"Well, now I've heard everything. A philanthropic Marchetta," Rupert quipped.

Natalie smiled. "Well, we met there, but he continued to visit me, even after I left the hospital." She shook her head. "He'd wake me up in the middle of the night, and we'd chat for hours. Sometimes I'd read to him, sometimes he'd read to me…" She tapped a gloved finger on her jean-clad thigh. "He never treated me like some sick invalid. He'd take me on excursions and always had me back home before sunrise, and before my parents woke up."

Rupert tipped his head to the side. "I'm not sure if that's sweet or a tad creepy."

"Oh, sweet. Definitely sweet. He was always the perfect gentleman."

He'd never once acted as though there was anything more—not even when she'd gotten drunk on her sixteenth birthday and demanded a kiss as a gift. He'd given her a very chaste peck on her forehead. Then, when she was nineteen…well, that still belonged in the too-humiliating-to-remember file. Today? Well, today was a revelation, on so many levels. Natalie's cheeks warmed. Just remembering his lips on hers, his body against hers—phew. She pulled off her gloves. She always made sure she wore them at work—she never knew what she might encounter with some of these books and artifacts. Her hands were uncomfortably warm. She was uncomfortably warm. She swallowed, conscious that Rupert was watching her intently.

"In fact, he was like a big brother to me—you know,

like the program they used to run through hospitals and schools? I tried to apply for that, but got rejected on account of my terminal illness, but that didn't seem to bother him."

"He sounds like quite a friend."

"He was. My best friend—my *only* friend. At least, that's what I thought. He said he'd always be there for me, and I believed him. Until he wasn't."

"Natalie," Rupert chided. "What happened to you— that was unforeseeable. Surely you can't blame him—"

"I do," she interrupted. "He was in town, Rupert. I was out, because I wanted to see him. My parents were out with me, because I wanted to go see him. And then we were killed." She shrugged. "Never trust a vampire, Rupert. They'll say anything, do anything, to get what they want."

"But you told him you trusted him tonight," Rupert pointed out.

"No, I didn't. I told him trust works both ways." She did not, could not, trust that particular vampire. If the vampire and werewolf hadn't killed her, her broken heart would have.

"Relax, Rupert. I might be working with Lucien, but I don't trust him." She yawned noisily and Rupert grimaced.

"Well, he's right about something. You need some sleep. Off you go, and I'll keep going through the library."

Natalie smiled gratefully. "Thanks, Rupert."

"Yes, well, he's caught my interest. A cure for lycanthropulism." Rupert was still chuckling when Natalie left.

* * *

"I wasn't sure I'd see you back here," Lucien admitted as he stepped into Natalie's office. He made sure to keep his relief out of his expression. She glanced up at him in surprise, her glasses resting on the top of her head. Did she actually ever wear them?

Today she wore a pale pink tailored shirt. It suited her. With her blond hair tied back in a ponytail and minimal makeup, she could have passed as one of her students. He eyed the opening of her shirt. And again, he was reminded that she was old enough where it counted. Her top two shirt buttons were undone and the shirt was parted enough to show a hint of shadow between her breasts. He remembered how those breasts felt in his hands, all warm and soft, with just the right amount of shape and weight.

And then he noticed she was wearing gloves. Again. He frowned. It was chilly, admittedly, but not *that* chilly. Winter wasn't due for a few weeks yet.

"I'm not the one who has a problem with keeping promises," she pointed out tartly. She nodded at the pile of books by his chair. "You can start with those."

He shot her a dark look as he took his seat. He wondered if she'd ever get past that. He hoped she would. He wrinkled his nose at the scent of tobacco in the room. "Do you smoke? Like, cigars or something?"

"Nope." She didn't look up but kept reading.

"You can't smell that?"

"Nope."

He shrugged and pulled forward the first book on the pile. There was a faint scent of something in the air, but it didn't make sense. Natalie didn't strike him as the type to hide and smoke behind closed doors…

He opened the book and frowned. "Fairy tales?"

She shrugged. "Why not?"

Why not, indeed. He wasn't sure if the answer to his problem could be found in this book, or any other, but he'd keep searching, just in case. Natalie seemed to think the books held some answers.

They'd been reading for about an hour, and every now and then Natalie would look up something up on her computer, the sound of her fingers tapping on the keys so loud in the quiet of her office. She leaned back in her chair. "I need to go to the library." She rose, holding a book.

"Is it open?" It was Sunday night and he hadn't seen or heard anyone other than them at the institute all evening.

"It is for me," she murmured, swooping up her keys and walking toward her door, hugging the book to her chest. Pushing her breasts up… She passed him, and he eyed her denim-clad butt. She'd certainly filled out—

The book that rested on his lap snapped shut, trapping his fingers painfully between the pages.

"Ow!" he yelled and flung the book to the floor.

Natalie turned in surprise. "What happened?" she asked.

"Nothing," he muttered, glaring at the book. He stood. "I'll come with you." The books in here were being mean to him, damn it.

He followed her through the empty halls toward the library. It was on the other side of the administration block and Natalie's sneakers squeaked softly on the linoleum floors. Just him, and her, and squeak, squeak, squeak. Moonlight spilled through the glass that formed the wall to an atrium within the building, bathing everything in a silver glow.

"Do you really like working here?" he asked suddenly. He was innately curious about her. She'd been a bookish kid, with a keen interest in romantic literature and spectacles that had seemed too big for her face. Now he'd seen that her collection included journals from explorers—some he'd heard of and some he hadn't. He'd seen historical texts, government records and works of fiction in several different languages... He'd seen medical studies, religious references... There were all sorts of jars and vials of stuff that looked kind of gross, and old bowls and artefacts that looked like they belonged in a museum. Or a dump. Or a museum of a dump. He should have known little Nina would soak up knowledge like a starving sponge. No, not Nina. *Natalie*. She wasn't that little girl he'd first encountered in the renal ward at Irondell Memorial Hospital.

She glanced at him, surprised by his inquiry. "Yes, I do like working here. Very much, actually. I get to read the old stories, explore and test the beliefs, look into the science, and generally let my imagination go wild. And then I get to talk about it every other day with my students. What's not to like?"

His lips quirked. She'd found her ideal job. For a moment he envied her. He'd spent so many years working for his father, of trying to regain his trust, his forgiveness, he'd assumed similar aspirations to the extent that here, seeing Natalie doing what she loved, he had to wonder if his life was what he wanted it to be...or what he deserved.

Natalie unlocked the door and in moments had

switched on lights and a computer at one of the student consoles. He raised an eyebrow as she went to a set of drawers and started riffling through the catalog. It wasn't long before she strode down one of the aisles. He followed her. She wasn't looking at books, though, but a selection of long, round canisters.

"What are these?"

"Maps, mainly. I want to check them against some satellite imagery we have stored on file for a certain area."

He frowned. How did that have anything to do with a werewolf cure? "Why?"

She pulled out a container and walked to a long table at the end of the aisle, twisting open the lid as she went. "I just found an alpha prime's letter to one of his guardians from before The Troubles. From what I can tell, this is a pack that didn't survive the wars."

Lucien took a deep breath for patience. Getting information out of Natalie was proving a challenging process. "And?"

"He wanted his guardian to go look for his missing scion."

"And that's peculiar because…?" It didn't surprise him that a father was searching for his son or daughter. Of course, he couldn't really see *his* father searching for *him* if he went missing. But his family wasn't the normal bonded unit. Not since his mother's death.

"Because he mentions his son went missing in an area where there are no recorded shadow breeds."

"Null territory?" Some people called nulls the neutralizing agent of Mother Nature against everything non-natural. He preferred to call them freaks. A human breed that nullified anything supernatural or magical within their bounds, just by being. No effort required. Freaks.

"No, not to my knowledge. I've checked the old territorial outlines. There was no null activity anywhere near this place."

"There could be any number of reasons why a scion would leave a pack. Maybe he was taking a break? Maybe he was running away... Maybe he didn't like his father and was setting out on his own?" Lucien shrugged. He could relate to all options so far.

"In this letter, the father states that he wants his son found, to prevent WTH."

Lucien frowned. "What the hell?"

Natalie shook her head. "WTH is an old acronym that is no longer in use. Werewolf-to-human. In other words, the kid was trying to transition from shadow breed to human."

"What? Is that possible? Is that a thing? How did I know not about this?"

"It's not a thing. There are some people out there who strongly believe they should be something other than what they're born to be. I think this scion was looking for a way to transition, and I think maybe he found it. There are no further records of him anywhere, and teenage boys don't just disappear—not without press articles, missing persons reports, etc."

"Where are we talking?"

"The Aerion Mountains. Mount Solitude."

Okay, so now she had his attention. The Aerion Mountains were fabled for being shrouded in mystery, with a large number of indiscriminate disappearances—vampire, shifter, witch, human. It had once been the Great Trail Junction, where several picturesque mountain trails met in an axis. It was also close to the horrific incident that had triggered The Troubles.

Now, though, not many people ventured into the area. He remembered hearing about a similar place in the North Atlantic, the Bermuda Triangle, where ships and planes had disappeared. Vampires avoided the Triangle like lycan toxin. The very idea of being trapped, surrounded by salt water, was the stuff of even the toughest vampire's nightmares. The Great Trail Junction was no different. Vehicles, planes—anything that crashed seemed to be swallowed up by the surrounds. There was a rumor that the minerals in the earth messed with magnetic fields and that's why people got lost. Still, these were old myths, stories told by firelight by drunken teens or by grandparents to scare some sense into the young.

"This is just one lycan. A rebellious, flighty little lycan," he pointed out. He didn't understand how this could have anything to do with finding the cure for his sister. He sighed. "This is from before The Troubles, right? They wouldn't be recording shadow breeds as such. We were still thought of as humans back then."

"And the closest town to the base of the Mount Solitude kept meticulous records of everyone who 'disappeared.' They had to mount the search parties. This scion wasn't listed—as dead, missing, medical miracle, whatever. We know he was in the area. We know he was actively trying to transition from werewolf to human. Maybe he figured it out. Maybe there are others…"

"Or maybe daddy alpha got it wrong and the kid ran off in another direction."

"Maybe… But what else do we have to work on?"

"Good point."

His frown deepened. There was very little in that area. The terrain was rough and inhospitable, with some remote outposts that offered nothing more than an opportunity for a person to change their mind from venturing further. He leaned forward as Natalie flattened the map and placed his hands on two corners to keep it rolled out. Natalie glanced at the book in her hand, then down at the map, tracing along the legend of the map then peering down at areas. She shook her head. "I don't get it."

"Don't get what?"

"There is nothing in this area. It's so remote, yet the closest town reported more deaths and disappearances than the entire population."

Lucien frowned. "The town was wiped out?"

Natalie shook her head, frowning. "No, that's the problem. There was an attempt at coal mining in the mountains, but after constant cave-ins and loss of life, that was abandoned. There was also a tourism element, with the Grand Trail Junction, but this is more than just a bunch of tourists getting lost or falling into abandoned mine shafts. There was a high transient rate, I just can't figure out why."

Lucien peered at the map. "If it's such an inhospitable area, I can't see why people would flock there..." He leaned closer, as did Natalie, and her perfume tugged at him, distracted him. As she leaned forward her shirt gaped a little bit and he caught a glimpse of white lace.

"Here," she said, pointing to a spot on the map. He tried to shift his focus to her gloved finger. Visions of her hands on his body, without gloves, and what they could do to him, had his body tightening— *Wait.*

"What?" He shook his head then leaned closer to

the map. *Concentrate.* Vivianne's life was at stake, for crying out loud. His brow drew tighter. His sister was dying and he was behaving like a hormone-driven teenager. Sheesh. He peered at the map. All he could see was terrain. "There's nothing except forest and hills."

"Exactly." She strode back to the computer and tapped in some commands. "We have a bank of satellite imagery through the ages, some are just general, some are for sites of cultural significance, like potential Roman cities…"

"And you have the Aerion Mountains? What's so culturally significant about that area? Apart from the mystical 'lost souls' perspective?" Notorious, maybe. Culturally significant, not so much.

"Nothing, really, but it's dense forest. They used to monitor the area for bushfires back then. Here." She leaned to the side so that he could peer over her shoulder. So he did. And, yes, he was a juvenile for doing it, but it gave him a fantastic view down her shirt. So he looked.

Desire unfurled inside him and he breathed in her fragrance. He shook his head slightly. No, he didn't want it to fog his brain. He forced himself to concentrate on the screen she indicated.

"There doesn't seem to be much…" she murmured as she scrolled through the images.

Something caught his eye and he placed his hand on her shoulder. "Wait, go back."

She flicked back an image and then another at his nod. "There. Can you zoom into that?"

She nodded. "A little." She started to tighten the focus. The image started to pixelate.

"Wait. There, on top of that peak."

They both leaned forward, squinting at the blurry image. "Is that—?" Natalie blinked, then squinted again. "Is that—?"

"Solar panels." Lucien frowned, scanning the rest of the image. The top of the peak had been cleared of trees and the dark frames of the panels blended into the craggy bluffs. It was the highest peak in the range, and the panels were only visible from an aerial view.

"What is this place?"

She checked the map. "That is Mount Solitude. The highest peak in the Aerion Mountain range and one of the most rugged."

Natalie toggled the screen and opened up another database. She entered coordinates, then sat back in frustration when the search results yielded nothing.

"There are no wires, no services to this area," she said. "No amenities."

"Off-grid and completely self-sufficient." Lucien sighed. "There are some compounds like this in the deserts, where breeds go underground."

"You think there was a compound there?"

"It makes sense. It's remote. Whoever was there would be able to live in relative peace."

"But there is no record of any breed established in this area," she pointed out after doing a search in the RTDB—Reform Territory Database. The database, used by all breeds and authorities, was kept current and had been established so that those wanting to pass through certain areas could gain permission to transit—to avoid claims of trespass and resulting punishment. No breed was listed as owning the territory, or being in charge of the main town, Devil's Leap. It was a rare human stronghold. "No breeds. Ever." Her mouth pursed in frustration. "Not even a transitional. Darn. I thought for a moment…" she sighed.

A cleared area on one of the plateaus of the bluff caught Lucien's eye and his blood chilled. "Can you pan down to that?"

Natalie did as instructed and it took him a moment to process what he saw.

Natalie gasped. "Good grief. That's a crop," she said in disbelief. "But—there's no history of cultivation in this area. This isn't supposed to exist."

Lucien's lips tightened. "Verbena." He could easily recognize the toxic herb. All vampires were trained to identify all of its variations. Their lives depended on it.

"And wolfsbane," she said, indicating a separate area to the right. She turned her head to look at him just as he twisted his head to face her. They were so close he could feel her breath on him, dancing along his skin.

"When was this taken? Is it still there?" His voice came out a little rough.

It took Natalie a moment to turn back to the computer. She pulled up the latest collection of forestry satellite imagery. The peak looked to have been overrun with trees and shrubs, the forest reclaiming both the top of the peak and the plateaus.

"Those original images were taken before The Troubles. Whatever was there looks long gone," Natalie said.

"But, at one time, there was something there that was off-grid, off the record and with the supplies to kill vampires and werewolves."

"With a high transient-population mortality rate," she said quietly.

Lucien frowned. "What are we talking about here? What does this mean? That a potentially large number of vampires and werewolves traveling through the area were killed?"

Natalie shrugged. "Possibly. I can only assume that if some of the breeds died, more would come looking for answers, then more would die, more questions raised, and so on."

"But…you're talking about the systematic murder of hundreds of shadow breeds," Lucien said, shaking his head. "How could that go unnoticed and unreported?"

"Well, it's just a theory, for starters. We don't have any proof that's what happened," Natalie said, and her teeth worried her lip.

Lucien's gaze was drawn to her mouth, to that full bottom lip, and memories of that kiss once again flashed through his mind. He was a vampire, for Pete's sake. An immortal. So why, after hundreds of years of finding intimacy and release in any number of willing women, did that one kiss with Natalie plague him? Tempt him? Fascinate him?

"This may have nothing to do with your search for your sister's cure," Natalie pointed out, turning to him. Her gaze dropped to his mouth and he saw in her eyes the instant when she stopped focusing on the forest mystery and started focusing on him.

"It's better than nothing," he murmured, dipping his head. Her scent, her warmth—everything about her consumed his attention. His heart thudded in his chest and arousal flared. He was beginning to accept that was a natural state when he was around Natalie.

"It could be a…a wild-goose chase," Natalie said, her voice low and husky with a trace of uncertainty. And then she lifted her head up toward his. Her lips were so close, he could feel her breath whisper across his mouth.

Lucien smiled, his stare shifting between her beautiful hazel-gray eyes and that full bottom lip. "You should know by now, Natalie," he whispered, "I do love a good chase." He lowered his lips to hers.

Chapter 6

Natalie's breath hitched as she felt the pressure of his mouth against hers. Heat, intense and perfect, flashed through her as he kissed her slowly, as though giving her time to back away.

She should. She should run, frankly.

He was being so gentle—not tentative, though. There was confidence, there was tenderness, but there was no shyness. It was as though he was giving her time to adjust, to decide. No force, just seduction.

She reached for him, her gloved hand sliding through his jet-black hair, and it was as though she'd given him some form of permission. His hand rose to cup her face, his thumb pressing gently on her jaw, and she opened her mouth to him.

His tongue slid in to rub against hers and she sighed, instinctively licking him back. Her breasts swelled and heat curled between her legs. His arm slid around her waist, pulling her closer to him, and she slid off the chair and into his arms. He dragged her up against him, and she shuddered in his arms—her nipples tightening into firm peaks as he shifted, turning slightly to brace her against the table behind them.

She heard the rustle of paper as Lucien swept the map off the table, and her breath hitched as the muscles in his arms tightened. He lifted her effortlessly up onto the furniture. She sighed as she trailed her hands across his shoulders. He was so tall, so lean, with an innate strength that should have frightened her but instead had her panting as he leaned forward to kiss her again. He angled his head, deepening their kiss, and she moaned when his hands found her breasts, cupping them through the cotton fabric of her shirt. Her breasts swelled even further at the attention and the heat dampened between her thighs. He sighed as he fitted his groin to hers. She clutched at his collar, sliding her hands down to undo his buttons. Her pulse thudded in her ears.

Her gloves worked against her and he growled softly in frustration before lifting his head.

His pale blue eyes on hers, he took hold of one of her hands and lifted it to his lips. His teeth lengthened, his eyes heating with desire as he gently bit on the leather and drew it off her finger, just a little. He repeated the process on all her glove-tipped fingers, the move so damn seductive she would have melted on the table, if she could have.

He bit down on the leather and drew it completely off her hand. "I want to feel your skin on mine," he whispered before placing her now bare hand on his chest. She could feel the delineation of his pectoral muscle beneath her touch, and she luxuriated in the smooth glide of her hand across his shirt until she could fidget with that annoying little button. He tugged off her other glove, tossing it aside, then leaned forward, scooping her butt and pulling her even closer.

She tugged at another button and he dipped his head to kiss her thoroughly, languidly. Her heart was hammering in her chest now, and when she parted his shirt enough to slide her hands inside, just a little, she discovered Lucien's heart was also pounding. She smiled in satisfaction, heat spreading with the knowledge she had the same effect on him.

She heard a harsh thud and Lucien's head bumped into hers before he reared back, growling. He whirled around, and cool air twisted between them, bringing with it some rationality, some awareness. Natalie's cheeks bloomed with mortification at reality's intrusion. God, not again.

Lucien had managed to get past her defenses. Again.

A leather-bound book lay at his feet, and Lucien rubbed the back of his head, frowning as he glanced around the library that appeared empty save for him and the stunningly beautiful, smoking-hot woman he'd just been kissing. He glared at the empty aisles, listening intently, his senses on high alert, tension gripping him with an uncomfortable tightness.

Again, he smelled that faint trace of pungent smoke. He stepped away from the table, noting when Natalie jumped down to the floor, her breathy little pants slowly coming under control, just like his.

He scooped the book up from the floor and turned to face her. "What the hell?"

She shrugged, but there was something in her eyes, as her glance shifted to just behind him, that had him whirling again. "Who's there?"

"Nobody, Lucien. We're the only ones here."

Why the hell didn't he believe her? He glanced over his shoulder at her. Maybe because she was having a hard time meeting his eyes. "Then why did this book hit me?" He tossed it casually to her and she caught it, then stared at it in horror before lifting her gaze.

"It looks like a journal." She blanched, dropped the book and backed away. She shook her head as she focused on a spot to her right. "No," she said, her expression agonized.

"Natalie?"

She continued to shake her head. "No, no, please. No." She slid along the length of the table, closing her eyes and clapping her hands over her ears. "I'm not listening."

Lucien frowned, concerned by her abrupt change in behavior. "Natalie, what's wrong?"

"Nope. Not now." She stalked toward the door of the library, muttering to herself, until she removed one hand long enough to shake a finger at a shelf. "And you're a dick."

She slammed out of the library, leaving Lucien to stare after her in stunned confusion.

What the hell just happened? His gaze drifted down to the journal on the floor. And where the hell had that come from? It was as though the damn thing had just materialized to hit him on the back of the head. He glanced warily around the library. It was full of books and all of them were beginning to look like weapons. He picked up the journal and then scooped up Natalie's gloves and went in search of her.

He didn't understand what had happened. One minute they were kissing and the next...? She was running away from a book? He couldn't ignore the agonized expression on her face. He was beginning to suspect there was way more to Natalie than just an unnatural ability to dodge death.

What was she hiding?

Natalie hugged herself as she leaned against the atrium wall and glanced up at the night sky. Stars. *Just count the stars.* She began to silently count the twinkling beacons of light, until gradually her racing heart slowed to a more regular rate.

"I'm sorry," Rupert said quietly as he materialized by her side. "I was trying to help."

She looked down at the toes of her sneakers. "Do you mean the journal or...?" Or did he mean using a book as a cold water substitute to separate the horny folk? She couldn't quite formulate the words; she was so mortified.

"Both."

"Oh." Okay, that just pushed her embarrassment to a whole new level.

"He's more than just a friend, isn't he?"

"No," she denied instantly then frowned. Was he? How could he be? No, he wasn't a friend. A friend didn't abandon you in your hour of need. A friend looked out for you, had your back, and would...come find you.

But he did find you, a small voice whispered.

Shut up. Forty years later was forty years too late. He wasn't there when she'd really needed him. Because of that, her mom and dad were murdered. *She* was murdered.

"Well, you've never kissed me like that, and we're friends," Rupert pointed out mildly.

"He's not my friend." She didn't know what the hell he was, just that he wasn't *that*.

"No, I can certainly see he's something more."

She shook her head. No. She wouldn't allow that to happen. "He's a vampire. You know how I feel about vampires. And he's threatened to kill my friends here, my students, if I don't help him."

"Oh, I think you're both really enjoying your unique brand of help."

She frowned, ready to argue the point, but Rupert's arched eyebrow stopped her. Damn it, he was right. If she was being honest, she'd thoroughly enjoyed her time in Lucien's arms. What the hell was she doing, kissing Lucien Marchetta? Especially after everything he'd done to her?

"What was I thinking?" she sighed roughly, shaking her head.

Rupert pulled his pipe out of his pocket and lit it, puffing a couple of times, drawing on the tobacco. He finally met her gaze. "Then you have to do this," he told her quietly. "Just—be careful. Don't trust him. Don't trust anyone."

She nodded. "I won't."

The door to the library opened and Lucien made his way toward her, carrying that damned tatted book with him.

"Are you—are you okay?" he asked her. His expression showed concern, bafflement, and a keen wariness he had every right to feel. She'd just behaved like an idiot with him. A dark shadow moved behind him, and Natalie steeled herself once more. A woman, wearing green cargo pants, a shirt whose color she couldn't identify— somewhere between baby-poo brown and gastro-vomit green—and a badge on her breast stepped toward her, her expression angry.

"What is *he* doing with my journal?" she snapped, staring directly at Natalie.

"I'm fine," Natalie said in answer to Lucien. She eyed the woman. A law enforcer of some kind. But the uniform? That was old. Pre-Troubles, pre-Reform. She'd been viciously murdered. Natalie wanted to avert her eyes, but held firm. She wanted to apologize to her. When she'd first seen the woman, back in the library, she'd been shocked, and had reacted instinctively by trying to shut the ghost out.

The woman bore a neck wound, gaping and torn. Blood stained her shirt, her badge, and still glistened in the moonlight. Which meant her killer hadn't been brought to justice.

"Then do you mind telling me what the hell is going on?"

"I don't like him touching my journal," the woman said, stomping over to stand beside Lucien. "Take it off him. Now."

Natalie shrugged at Lucien. "Nothing's going on."

The look he shot her told her he wasn't buying it.

Rupert stepped toward the woman, a sympathetic smile on his face. "Hi. I don't believe we've met. I'm Rupert."

The injured woman looked at him briefly, curiosity flaring in her eyes before she frowned and turned back to Lucien.

"He's a damn vamp. I don't want him touching my stuff," the woman snapped again, glaring at Natalie.

Natalie held out her hand to Lucien. "Can I have my gloves, please?"

Lucien stepped closer to her and held out the journal. Natalie pulled her hand back sharply and Lucien's eyes narrowed. "Why are you afraid of a book, Natalie?"

"I'm not," she said through gritted teeth, tugging the gloves out of his hand. She could already see the ghost. That horse had bolted. She slid the gloves on, jamming her fingers into them.

"I know you can see me, hear me," the woman said, her hands clenching into fists as she turned to Natalie. "I don't want a vampire reading my journal. If you don't do something, I will."

Natalie sighed. Why did ghosts think they could actually *do* something? Rupert was the only one she knew who could marshal some control, but it was something he'd had to practice for decades. His aim was improving, though. She finally met the woman's gaze with a slight shake of her head.

The woman's eyes narrowed. Her lips tightened and her hand flashed out toward the journal in a vicious jab upward.

Lucien's hand jerked and the book hit him in the face. He swore as he clutched his nose.

Natalie gaped then turned to the woman. "How did you do that?" she gasped. She'd never seen a ghost manifest so much physical, corporeal power. She'd practically punched Lucien in the face. Rupert had only recently learned to move some objects, but he still had to concentrate on grasping the object and moving it, just as he had when he'd been living. This woman—ghost— had managed to do so without coming into contact with either the book or Lucien, almost as though she'd used power as an object.

"What the *hell* is going on?" Lucien bellowed, pulling his hand away from his face to stare at the blood on his palm. "Damn it." He glanced in disbelief at the book he still held in his hand.

The woman sagged a little, her face drawn, and she stared at the journal Lucien now gripped tightly as he tilted his head back in an effort to stop his nose bleed. Already, though, Natalie could see his self-healing abilities were coming into effect and the bleeding was slowing, if not stopping completely.

"I don't want a bloodsucker sticking his nose in my diary," she murmured, and she swayed a little on her feet.

Natalie eyed the ghost closely. Interesting. Using that much force seemed to have depleted her, just a little. Who was this woman? And how could she present with such force? She'd lost count of the ghosts she'd encountered, and only Rupert had displayed any ability to actually move things successfully. Others just fumbled around, causing 'accidents'—like Terry at the bistro. But this particular ghost had real strength and power. She had to read this journal, find out more about the ghost who guarded it.

"Let me see the book," Natalie said, holding her hand out for the tome.

"Not until you tell me what the hell is going on," Lucien said through gritted teeth. He pulled a handkerchief out of his suit jacket pocket and wiped the blood off his face.

Natalie arched an eyebrow. "You're the one holding the book, you tell me." She may know, she just couldn't say it. A ghost doesn't want you to read her diary, and is prepared to maim you in order to defend it. Yeah, it was highly unlikely he'd believe her if she did tell him, although why that should matter to her, she had no idea. Okay, so maybe she didn't want Lucien to think she was a complete nutter.

He shook his head, his eyes narrowed. "Uh-uh. How did who do what?"

Oh, so he'd heard her. The ghost's expression hardened and she took a shaky step toward Lucien again. Natalie sighed. "Just give me the damn book—otherwise I can't help you on this cockamamy quest and I'm walking out. Going home. Might treat myself to a nice hot bath, a glass of red and a good book." She shrugged. "Your choice."

Lucien's lips tightened and he stared at her for a long moment, then his gaze shifted to look around the otherwise empty atrium. He cocked his head, listening, before his gaze returned to hers. "I don't think I trust you."

After what he'd pulled with Ned, his words made her smile. "Right back at you, babe." He still hesitated. She sighed. "Fine. Bath it is. See ya." She turned away and took a step toward the door, only to bump into his chest. Damn, the man could move fast. She stepped back from the warm, solid contact. That broad, sexy chest...

He reluctantly handed over the book, holding on to it as she grasped it. "You will tell me. Eventually."

"Tell you what?" she asked, her eyes wide with pseudo-innocence.

"Your secrets."

She tugged the book out of his hand. "Dream on."

She gently opened the journal and squinted at the faded ink on the inside cover page. "'This diary belongs to...'" She leaned closer. "'Grace...'" She squinted. "'Pumkins'?"

"Perkins," the woman corrected.

"Perkins," Natalie repeated. "Grace Perkins."

"Who is Grace Pumpkins?" Lucien asked tiredly.

"Perkins," the ghost grumbled, glaring at him.

Natalie eyed the woman in uniform before gently turning some pages. "Looks like she was a police officer, maybe...?"

"Chief of Police, Devil's Leap Police Department," Grace proclaimed, folding her arms as she stared between Natalie and Lucien. "Not that it's any of his business."

"Why did Deputy Do-Little's diary hit me?" Lucien asked succinctly. "Twice. And what does it have to do with our search?"

Natalie surreptitiously eyed Rupert, who winced. "You need to read it," he said. "Particularly the entries about several, uh—" he cleared his throat "—disappearances." He smiled at the police chief. "Hope you don't mind."

Grace shrugged. "Not at all. Sometimes I think people should be reminded of what happened."

"Natalie?" Lucien prompted.

She blinked, bringing her attention back to him. "Oh, uh, well, it appears Grace Perkins was a cop at Devil's Leap."

"Police chief," Grace corrected.

"Police chief," Natalie stated then snapped the book close. She couldn't keep doing this, having multiple conversations at once. "I can't say why it just jumped out at you like that," she said. She wasn't lying, per se. "There may be a draft in the library. It may be be-spelled," she prevaricated. She shrugged. "I'm going back to my office to read this."

She started walking back down the hall and Rupert

trotted alongside her. Lucien followed. Natalie halted then turned. She grasped the book with both hands.

"I want to read this. Alone. It'll be quicker." Quieter. Easier. Whatever. "Please."

Rupert sighed. Lucien's eyes narrowed. "Does this really have anything to do with helping my sister?"

Natalie's shoulders dropped. "I don't know, Lucien," she replied honestly. "It's probably got as much bearing on finding a cure for lycanthropulism as any of those fairy tales back in my office. I just need a chance to sit down and—" she glanced briefly at Grace, who arched any eyebrow "—assess the information."

"Fine, I'll sit quietly while you 'assess the information,'" Lucien muttered.

Natalie winced. She couldn't very well talk with Grace if Lucien was sitting in the same room as her. "Maybe...not. If this book is be-spelled, obviously it's warded against you. It'll be much faster if I do this on my own. Take a break. Go have something to eat." She held up a hand and glared at him. "Some*thing* not some-*one*. Don't kill anyone. You promised."

"That promise extended only to your friends and colleagues," he reminded her.

Her lips firmed. "Then consider everyone in Westamoor my friend. This town hasn't seen any vampire activity for one hundred and nine years. They're a peaceful lot." A flash of inspiration hit her. "That may be why this book targeted you. You're a vampire, the first in over a century to come anywhere near it."

Lucien eyed the book warily and finally nodded. "Fine. I'll check in on you, later."

Natalie nodded. "Great. If everyone leaves me alone

for a while, I might get some results." She turned and headed toward her office, mentally preparing a list of questions she couldn't wait to ask Grace.

for … while. I might be … able to stop it. She turned and
looked … toward … he could … mentally registering effort at
each … this … expression, yet to … ask … once

Chapter 7

Lucien lifted his lips from the young woman's throat,
Natalie's words ringing in his ears. *Don't kill anyone.*

Well, don't kill anyone in Westamoor, he clarified. He'd driven to the next town, so, technically, he
could kill this victim. Despite what he'd threatened
with Natalie—and he was both satisfied and offended
she'd fallen for it—he didn't normally hunt to kill. Not
since his younger, wilder days. He'd learned the value
of life through the painful lesson of his mother's death,
and then Nina's. These days, he preferred to feed, not
kill. He let the woman lie back on the sofa. He'd found
her in a bar off the highway. He hadn't even needed to
compel her, she'd been eager to jump into his car and
invite him into her home.

He shook his head. Was it any wonder these humans
were viewed as easy pickings by his kind—by most
of the shadow breeds? He leaned back on the sofa and
gently touched his nose. It was healed, thankfully. Not
so much as a bruise. He still couldn't believe it. How
could books attack him? He couldn't help but notice it

had happened when he was close to Natalie. Was this the cosmos looking out for her? Or something more sinister? Was this Natalie's doing, defending herself against him? Was she somehow capable of teleporting objects across distances and with such force it could break bones?

He scoffed. Now he was losing it. Telepathy? No. Perhaps a witch's spell, like she'd hinted? Would she request that kind of protection from a witch? Could he blame her if she did? He still didn't know what had truly happened to her all those years ago, but if just a fraction of what he'd heard was true… Her comments about trying to end her life haunted him. All the news reports had told of a bizarre murdering duo, a vampire and a werewolf—something that was so damned unheard of, no wonder they'd gotten away with their crimes for as long as they had. It made sense if she'd bought some sort of ward against the vampires and lycans.

His mouth turned down at the corners. Did she need protection from *him*? She'd trusted him. Hell, she'd *fed* him. He would never hurt her.

He'd kissed her, though. Should he be ashamed? Proud? Hell. He'd met Natalie when she was nine years old and, despite the fact she'd pretty much grown up before his very eyes, he'd never thought of her as anything more than that sweet, precocious little kid.

He swallowed as images from the library flooded his mind. She'd been so hot and responsive, so willing in his arms. And now she couldn't even stand him being in the same room as her. She'd looked at him with such heat, such desire, in his arms and then she'd bolted. She'd kissed him. She'd pushed him away. She'd been so hot in his arms and so cold in her conversation. Now she'd asked him to leave—because she wanted to concentrate. So, was that because she found him unpleasant to be around or more of a…happy distraction? He rolled his eyes. God, he felt like some crush-fevered teen.

Stop obsessing over her. Think of something else.

He reached forward to pick up the book on the coffee table in an effort to distract himself and winced at the title. *Dating in the New Age—Navigating Inter-Breed Relationships.* He eyed the unconscious woman next to him on the sofa.

"Really? *Really?*" He frowned as he realized that as a perpetually single vampire, he couldn't really scoff. He didn't have problems dating, as such. It was more the committing part, the sustaining of those relationships. He wasn't ugly, he didn't have any disfigurements, and he kept himself in shape, so attracting women hadn't been a problem for him. Until now.

He glanced at his watch. Two hours. Surely that was enough time for her to flick through Officer Pumpkin's doodles…?

The woman on the sofa stirred next to him and he leaned over to watch her slowly regain consciousness. Her eyelids flickered open and he met her brown-eyed gaze intently.

"You're fine and you're safe," he said, lowering his voice as he mesmerized her before she could give in to the panic he saw in her eyes. "That sore spot on your neck is a hickey. We had a great time, but now it's time for me to go. You'll only remember me as a somewhat blurry, fun interlude."

She nodded, brushing her hair off her neck. "I had a great time," she repeated, smiling, a soft blush creeping over her cheeks. "But I think it's time for you to go."

He nodded, returning her smile. "I understand." He rose and let her walk him to her front door, but hesitated when she opened it, He tilted his head. She'd been a nice lady, if a little eager to please. He met her gaze intently, instilling a quiet confidence in his words. "Don't ever think you're not worth it. You're amazing, and you deserve the best kind of guy. Make him woo you and prove himself before you take him home."

She really needed to exercise more caution.

He turned to leave but halted when Enzo walked up the steps to the porch, his expression implacable. Lucien frowned. "Why are you here?"

"Following you," Enzo said simply.

"I told you, I don't need your help."

"Well, your father gives me my orders, not you, and he thinks otherwise." He lifted his chin toward the woman at the door—Lucien realized he didn't even know her name. "Who's she?"

"Nobody you need to worry yourself with."

Enzo stepped closer, his gaze steely as it flicked between Lucien and the woman. His lips curled. "A late-night snack, I see."

Lucien realized Enzo could probably smell her blood. He shrugged, not bothering to respond.

"Who is this guy?" the woman asked softly. Her chin lifted and she'd lost that eager-to-please look.

Enzo ignored her, focusing on Lucien. "Do you have any news? Anything for me to report back to your father?"

"Nope," Lucien said shortly. "If I did, I'd tell him myself."

"Well, I can't help but notice your learned friend is taking her sweet time with coming up with a solution."

Lucien frowned. "Up until now, my father has believed this to be a wild-goose chase, and now he's getting antsy for Nat—Professor Segova to deliver a fairy-tale ending. What gives?"

"He's concerned for his daughter, Lucien, and he's watching her slowly wither."

Lucien dropped his gaze. Maybe this fruitless search was the easy option, as opposed to sitting by his sister's glass-topped coffin and watching the lycan toxin spread like a black stain through her system, ravaging her as it went.

"Tell him I'm working on it," Lucien said in a low tone.

Enzo nodded. "He said you'd say that. He suggested I offer you an incentive."

The guardian prime moved like lightning, taking Lucien by surprise as he darted behind him. He heard the woman's neck snap, felt her slide down the side of his body and heard the dull thump her corpse made as it hit the floor.

Enzo stood over her body, adjusting the cuffs of his shirt. "Break's over. Find the cure." He stalked along the porch to the steps and skipped down them lightly. "Otherwise that professor of yours is next."

Lucien watched his father's guardian prime disappear into the darkness then glanced down at the body at his feet.

Well, damn.

"So, you covered up the disappearances?" Natalie said, shocked, as she turned the pages of the worn journal. Grace nodded as she lightly dragged her fingers across the spines of the books on the bookshelf.

"Yep."

"But there were so many of them…how did you manage it?"

"It's amazing what a town will do, given the right incentive."

"The whole town was in on it?"

Grace shrugged. "Eventually. Those we could trust, anyway."

Natalie shook her head, pausing on a page. "I can't believe a whole town conspired to kill so many people…"

Grace snorted as she turned to face her, leaning back against the bookshelf. "That's where you're wrong. These weren't people. These were animals. Monsters."

"Yeah, well, since Reformation they've been given equal rights."

"They're not equal," Grace snapped, and Natalie raised her eyes to meet the stormy gaze of the police chief. She'd hit a sore spot, apparently. "Have you ever been hunted in the dark by a werewolf? Do you think a human is equal against that kind of threat? What about the bloodsuckers, their speed and strength, the way they use those mystical powers to control the way you think, the way you act—is that fair and equal?" Natalie dropped her gaze. Yeah. She knew what that was like. And the police chief was right. It wasn't a fair contest.

"We were sitting ducks against them," Grace muttered. "There was no equality, no fair and just treatment. They were stronger and faster, and without a conscience when it came to killing good, honest people. It was them or it was us. We chose us."

Natalie tilted her head as she listened to a woman from another time. She was dealing with someone from before The Troubles, she had to remind herself. A time when the shadow breeds weren't recognized, where the general population didn't even know of their existence.

"What was it like?" she asked quietly. She'd always wanted to know what it was like to be completely oblivious to the threat around you.

Grace sighed as she walked over to one of the armchairs in front of Natalie's desk. "It was wonderful, before it wasn't." Her lips curled in a half smile. "I moved to Devil's Leap after working for several years in the city. Homicide," she clarified at Natalie's raised eyebrow. "After one too many deaths, I learned about this surprise vacancy and applied for the job." Her chuckle was derisive. "I was so pleased that I beat the other applicants on the force. I didn't find out until weeks after I'd made the move that I was the only person who'd applied for the job. That should have been my first clue, I guess."

Natalie rose, came around the side of the desk and leaned her hips against it. "What happened to the previous chief?"

"We had a lot of wild animal attacks in the area," Grace said, then leaned her elbow on the armrest and cupped her chin in her hand. "The former police chief fell victim to a bear attack. At least, that's what Doc Morton put on the autopsy report. Back then, if you claimed werewolf or vampire attack as a cause of death, you'd find the little men in white coats turning up to bundle you away in an ambulance."

Natalie folded her arms. "There doesn't seem to be any recorded settlement of shadow breeds in that area, though."

"There wouldn't be. Those monsters hid themselves

in plain sight, pretending to be humans—even the nightwalkers established themselves by working night shifts." She snorted. "If you can believe it, our county medical examiner was a bloodsucker. It was no wonder so many people were murdered in the area without anyone being the wiser. We beat the national average for 'accidental deaths.'" The police chief shook her head. "They were very clever, very sneaky." Grace leaned forward in her seat, her expression earnest. "You have to realize, back then there were no such things as monsters. It was all fairy tales and campfire giggles. If you insisted on their existence, you were considered crazy. If I'd reported a vampire in our midst, that town would have had another police chief by sunset."

"So—you were protecting your job?"

"I was protecting my family," Grace corrected, her tone stern. "And the town who placed their trust in me." She shook her head. "For years, we had this reputation for being the edge of civilization, with all the wild things in the forest." She smiled, but there was no humor in her expression. "So then we started to fight back. That's when we started to realize the numbers we were potentially dealing with."

"What did you do?" Natalie breathed, captivated by this firsthand account of a time for which many couldn't find any accurate historical information.

Grace shrugged. "We did what we could. We learned about our enemy. We fought against our enemy. When necessary, we called for reinforcements."

"There were more of you?"

"Right across the Pacific Northwest."

Natalie's eyes rounded in realization at Grace's

words. "Are you saying you and your town started the Resistance?"

Grace's eyebrows rose. "Is that what they called us?"

Natalie nodded. "Yes, but all the historical accounts we've been able to find suggest that a man, Jason Thorne, spearheaded that movement."

Grace's face softened and her lips curved into a sweet smile. "Did he just?"

"Did you know Jason Thorne?" Natalie exclaimed. He was only the father of the Resistance, and the reason humans weren't completely annihilated during The Troubles. There was a statue of him in Reform Square, within view of Government House.

Grace's smile broadened. "Well, that's a whole other story."

"There is no mention of Devil's Leap in any of the historical accounts," Natalie murmured. "No one has ever considered that area as a place of interest."

Grace's smile broadened with satisfaction. "Then we did our job right."

"How so?"

"Those 'breeds,' as you call them, started to notice others of their kind going missing from the area. They started to come in greater numbers. We knew that if they kept disappearing, then we'd get more of their kind coming through, and that meant more of our townspeople being killed. So we had to make it look like an accident. We created natural disasters, mining accidents—it was very risky, living in Devil's Leap."

"But—so many, Grace," Natalie breathed, still shocked by the numbers. "How did you hide the bodies?"

Grace looked down at her shoes. "They didn't all die…straightaway."

Natalie's eyes widened. For once there was a shadow of guilt that crossed Grace's features.

"What did you do?" Natalie asked in a low voice, almost afraid of the answer.

"We didn't know how to kill them. Not at first. Especially the nightwalkers. You'd think you'd killed them, and then the next night they'd be back trying to kill you. It was exhausting. We lost a lot of good people."

"What did you do, Grace?"

"Doc Morton lost his wife to these things. We needed to learn more about them," Grace explained.

Natalie cringed. "What did you do?" she whispered as horror brought out her goose bumps.

"We…held them," Grace whispered back.

"Held them? What do you mean, you held them?"

"We had a place, this old bunker from the Cold War," Grace said, then cleared her throat. "We used it to hold them and…find out about them."

Natalie blinked as she processed the words. The Cold War? God, that was going back in time. A lot of countries had been renamed as part of Reformation and territories had been split or merged, depending on which breed was awarded them. If memory served her correctly, the Cold War was a political war between east and west, with an impressive arms race and a world poised on the brink of atomic war. Bunkers had been built everywhere—she'd even seen one in what was formerly known as Russia—to provide an escape haven from potential nuclear disaster.

"Ah, the mountain," she said in comprehension. "You used a bunker in the mountain to—what? Keep them captive? Observe?"

"We did more than observe," Grace admitted and a shadow of shame crossed her face.

"More...?" Natalie frowned. If you needed to learn about the enemy, what else would you do than observe? Suspicions edged with dismay rose within. "Experiments?"

Grace grimaced. "It wasn't something that I was in favor of, but I can't deny some of those 'experiments' gave us the weapons we needed to fight the monsters."

Natalie's eyes narrowed. "Did you know that a werewolf's bite could kill a vampire?"

Grace nodded. "Yes, but we didn't need to experiment to learn that. We saw that evidence with our own eyes. I know that breeds now have territories, but back then it was open season between those creatures. We learned from some of their tactics."

"Were there any experiments on a cure for that toxin?"

Grace's expression shuttered and both of them started when the door to Natalie's office was thrust open.

Lucien walked in briskly, his midlength coat billowing out behind him like the wings of a dark angel.

"What have you got for me?" he asked abruptly.

Natalie frowned at his cool demeanor.

"Nothing," she lied immediately. Gone was the hot, sensual man who'd kissed her breathless in the library. This man was determined, focused...cold.

"You can't tell him. That bunker is a secret," Grace warned. Natalie gave a small shake of her head as she kept her gaze on the vampire stalking toward her.

"You forget, Natalie. I know you. I know when you're lying." There was no missing the impatience in his tone.

Her frown deepened. Was he still pissed about earlier? His whole disposition had changed. "What's gotten into you?"

"My patience is running out. This process is taking too long," he said, his blue eyes bright. "We can't afford to waste any more time reading fairy tales. If you can't find something, you're in breach of our deal."

She held up a finger in warning. "No. Our deal was for me to help you look—it had nothing to do with actually finding something that nobody believes exists. This is what I'm doing. I'm helping you look." And in return, he wouldn't hurt or kill her students, friends or the residents of Westamoor. She eyed him as he stopped in front of her, so close the toes of their shoes were almost touching.

"Well, you might be content to hide behind these books while life passes you by, but my sister doesn't have that luxury." He reached around her, pulling her against him.

She opened her mouth to protest the contact but stopped when he slid the phone out of her back jeans' pocket and held it up.

"Tell me what you've learned or I'm calling that little friend of yours. When he gets here we'll have a late dinner. And by 'we,' I mean me."

Natalie shoved at him. For a moment she didn't think he'd budge, but he eventually stepped away from her. He held up the phone. "What was his name? Nigel? Nerdster?" He snapped his fingers. "Oh, that's right. Ned. Shall I call him, Natalie, or do you have something?"

She stared at him stonily.

"Don't," Grace warned.

"This is a wild-goose chase, Lucien. I can't find any reference to a cure for the lycan poison." She was tell-

ing the truth. Kind of. What Grace had mentioned—
that bunker—wasn't cited in the diary, and it may have
absolutely nothing to do with Lucien's quest. "Besides,
you can't call Ned. You need the pass code to get into
my phone."

Lucien glanced at the phone. He made a face. "You're
right. Well, I'll just go do a door-knock for him, shall
I? Work my way through this quaint little town until I
find Nerdy Ned…?"

He turned and was halfway to the door before she
could take in his words. He was going to—?

"Wait," she cried out when she realized that, in this
mood, Lucien was prepared to kill more than her research assistant. Visions of other people, people she
cared about, all maimed and killed, swirled in her mind.
Westamoor townsfolk wouldn't know what hit them.

"Don't," Grace warned again.

"Devil's Leap," Natalie blurted, ignoring the ghost.

Lucien halted. Turned. Frowned. "What?"

"You might find something at Devil's Leap."

Lucien's eyes narrowed and he was still for a moment. "What?" he asked finally.

Natalie shrugged. "I don't know," she said honestly.
"It could be another wild-goose chase or it could be
something. There's a bunker there…"

He nodded slowly in realization. "The mountain."

"Yeah, the mountain. There might be a reason why
no shadow breeds settled there," she finished lamely.

Grace made a noise of disgust and disappeared. Natalie grimaced. The police chief probably thought she'd
betrayed her trust. And, to an extent, she had. But if she
didn't give Lucien something, the people in Westamoor
were in danger.

Lucien looked at the window then grimaced. "Fine. We have just enough time for you to pack."

"Me? Pack?" Her eyes widened and she shook her head. No. *He* was supposed to leave. Not her. Besides, that was what he was good at.

He smiled as he advanced toward her slowly, his eyes brightening a little as he stepped into the light cast by the lamp on her desk.

"You didn't think you could get rid of me that easily, did you, Natalie?" He tsked as he shook his head. "Oh, no. Until something happens one way or another with my sister, you and I are like green on grass." He grasped her arm lightly, but in a grip that she knew would be difficult, if impossible, to break. He smiled. "Think of it like…two friends becoming reacquainted."

Chapter 8

Lucien squinted behind his sunglasses. The road they were on was slowly rising from the desert floor and he couldn't wait to put the rolling sand dunes and rocky outcroppings behind them. There was nothing quite like a desert to make a vampire nervous. Deserts didn't offer much shelter from the sun. He eyed the landscape. Everything just looked so damn scorched under the midmorning sun. So damn desolate and dreary.

A movement caught his eye and his lips tightened. A dunerunner from the looks of things. The coyote shifters dwelled along the fringe of the desert. He hadn't seen any sandstalkers crossing the valley floor, but that didn't surprise him. The werecats could take camouflage to a whole new level. As long as he and Natalie kept to the Reform highways, paid their tolls and didn't stray onto the secondary roads, he wasn't worried.

He adjusted the air-conditioning. It was warm, and he chose to ignore the temperature reading outside his car. Not for the first time, he thanked the ingenuity of vampires before him who had created the night-tint tempered glass and light-armored vehicles. It meant he could travel during the day in his car, if necessary, but he was stuck in it until he found a place to park in the dark.

He eyed the silent woman in the passenger seat next to him. Stuck with Natalie Segova. He could think of worse things.

"Are we seriously going to drive in silence all the way to Devil's Leap?" he asked her.

She turned to give him a glacial stare that was only mildly muted by her sunglasses, then returned her gaze to the desert slowly giving way to stunted shrubbery as the road rose toward the foothills of the mountain range.

Apparently so. Lucien sighed. So much for getting reacquainted. Natalie was pissed and making no effort to hide it. He checked the rearview mirror. The winding road along the floor of the desert valley had low-volume traffic, but he knew that Enzo was in one of the tempered vehicles. His father's personal guardian had an uncanny ability to track him. It made him lethal. Dangerous. Bloody annoying.

He glanced again at Natalie. He couldn't blame her for being angry with him, but he didn't have the luxury of waiting for Natalie to reveal her findings.

That professor of yours is next. Enzo's words haunted him.

While his sister was in her current state, Lucien was the Nightwing Vampire Prime, but their colony's hierarchy was…unusual. When his father had become a Reform senator, Vincent had been forced to secede from his position as Vampire Prime of the Nightwing Colony to avoid conflicts of interest. Enzo had gone with Vincent, so, while Lucien was now in charge of

Nightwing, he had no authority over his father's personal guardian.

He may not be able to control that guardian, but he would do whatever he could to keep Natalie safe from him. Even if she hated him. He sighed.

He'd known as soon as he'd opened the door that Natalie had learned something. She'd looked disturbed, startled and just a little guilty at his appearance. He knew her tells. *And* he could hear her elevated heartbeat when she'd lied to him.

Natalie shifted in her seat, her denim-clad legs brushing against her oversize tote bag. Along with her laptop, he could see two books in the unzipped opening, and he had to force his gaze back to the road. Officer Pumpkin's journal, and their book. There wasn't any other way he could think of it. It had been their book, the one she'd loved to read so often as a kid. He could recite the poems by heart, he'd read it to her so many times.

She'd been such the romantic, and he'd loved it. Not that he'd admit it, but the way she'd looked at the world, with the innocence and optimism of an ingenue was... Refreshing. Charming. It had made him look at things differently—until she'd died, that was.

Warmth flooded him at the memories of "before." He remembered lying next to her on her bed and gazing up at the phosphorous stars she'd stuck to her ceiling. How many hours had they spent counting stars? Or playing cards? But she'd loved that damn book and he'd had to read from it each visit.

Now, she'd brought the book with her. Surely that had to count for something, right? He eyed her hands and his brows dipped. She'd also brought her gloves. They'd just spent the last four hours passing across the top corner of the Red Desert and she was wearing gloves. His lips tightened. Eventually she'd tell him. Still, this silence was eating at him.

"So what did you find, exactly, in that journal?" For a moment he thought she was going to continue to ignore him, but he heard her sigh eventually.

"They didn't appreciate shadow breeds in Devil's Leap."

"Why do I get the impression that's an understatement?"

Natalie glanced briefly over her shoulder toward the backseat.

He glanced in the rearview mirror. What was she looking at? "We put your gear in the trunk," he reminded her.

She blinked. "Uh, yeah. Of course."

She'd packed mainly hiking gear, with some implements she'd used on archeological digs, she'd told him. Tools. Tools that she never left home without, she'd said. And then she'd said pretty much nothing ever since. Until now.

"Uh, the missing people were mainly…shadow breeds."

He frowned. "What happened to them?"

She shifted in her seat. "I'm not exactly sure, but I suspect it wasn't pretty."

"Why do you think that has something to do with Vivianne's situation?" He'd called his father just before he'd left. The toxin was now visibly creeping through his sister's system, the dark poison noticeable in her veins. Dave Carter was trying to slow it down, but it didn't sound good. Lucien couldn't afford to be off on a fruitless search. Still, going somewhere, doing *something*, had to be better than sitting around a dusty library reading stories from cultures long dead and pretty much forgotten.

Natalie sighed. "I don't know," she said, and he heard the honesty in her voice. "I don't even know if what we're looking for actually exists…but with what we saw on the satellite imagery, and some of the cases noted in Grace Perkins's diary, people in this area were figuring out how to deal with the shadow breeds before the world knew they even existed. In doing that, who knows, they may have come across something for lycanthropulism. It's as good a place to start as any, I guess." She shrugged. "I can't think of any other avenue to follow."

He stared at the road in front of them. "Well, it's more than any of the other experts turned up in the last eight months," he admitted. And she'd found it in less than forty-eight hours.

He heard the leather creak as she shifted in her seat, turning to face him more fully. "You must love your sister very much," she murmured.

He flicked her a glance, his brows pulling together. "Of course. She's my sister. I'd give up my own life to save her, if I could."

"Why?" There was open curiosity in her tone.

"What do you mean, *why*? She's family." He knew there weren't too many family-based vampire colonies, but they weren't that unusual. Of course he'd do what he could to save his sister. They may not always see eye-to-eye, but she was blood kin.

Natalie yawned and he realized she'd gone three nights without much sleep at all. He didn't know if she'd managed to catch some sleep during the daytime when he wasn't around, but he had the impression she'd worked through, trying to find a solution for his sister's problem. He appreciated her effort, but there was still a little spot inside him that cared for the fragile human he'd gotten to know. He told himself that having a well-rested Natalie was better than an exhausted Natalie, for the purpose of their mission, and that was why he worried about her lack of sleep. It would probably do them both good if they took a break. Soon.

"And family is everything, huh?"

He glanced at her again. Wasn't that obvious? "Well, yes."

She tilted her head and he felt like her shielded eyes were boring holes into the side of his head. "You were always alone when we met," she said. She yawned again.

He didn't respond. He may have told Natalie stories about his sister, perhaps even some about his parents, but he'd never mentioned the sickly girl to his family. She would have been seen as a weakness, a waste of time...a distraction. Distractions needed to be dealt with.

She remained silent and he knew she was waiting him out. The fact that she was finally having a semi-normal conversation with him made him want to keep her talking. Damn it, though, when he said they could get reacquainted, this wasn't quite what he'd intended. He'd wanted to know about what had happened that night and every night since. Still, maybe if he shared a little, she'd share a little.

"I love my family but they're not without...flaws," he said finally.

"I was sorry to hear about your mother," she said.

His fingers tightened on the steering wheel at the unexpected turn in conversation. Okay, he was happy with silence now.

"Crap happens."

"You started to travel to the west coast, 'round about that time, didn't you?"

The same time she'd kissed him as a nineteen year old, and he'd tried to be the good man she'd made him want to be. The same time he'd tried to be noble, and honorable, and ignore the way she'd tempted him. The same time he'd tried to convince her there was a better man out there for her. The same time his mother died.

"Yes."

"But your father and sister stayed on the east coast?"

"Yes."

"You all must be really tight."

He pulled a little on the wheel and had to correct. What the hell? "What makes you say that?" He didn't know whether to be amused or offended. He and his father were not tight. And Vivianne? Well, they'd been in the middle of an argument when she'd been attacked.

"Well, take a look," Natalie said, casually gesturing to the receding view of the desert as the road continued to climb. "You've driven across a desert—in daylight. You've threatened to kill I don't know how many people. You kissed me to get me to help you…" Her voice trailed off and his sideways glance took in the blush on her cheeks. "You are doing things you'd normally hate, to save your sister. It's just…weird to see you like this." She paused for a moment. "Okay, maybe you like the killing people part. You know, being a vamp and all that."

He blinked. "That's the part you think I like?" He hated to break it to her, but kissing her wasn't a chore. Did she really think that was the only reason he'd do that? He thought about it. What was the reason he'd do that? Yes, he'd told himself he'd use whatever tool was at his disposal. But, if he was honest with himself, he'd have to admit he thoroughly enjoyed that particular method of persuasion.

"I don't remember you being so…ruthless."

Of course not. She probably remembered him as some indulgent pseudo-uncle type who'd read her bed-time stories and kept her company through her illness. He flicked a glance at her. She'd changed into a blue cotton blouse with a light scarf draped across her shoulders. He could see the silver lariat chain around her neck, dipping low between her pert breasts.

"I don't remember you being so…grown up." Now would be a good time to remember that pseudo-uncle vibe.

"That's because you never saw it."

He sighed. She had a point. His trips west had grown longer; he'd last seen her when she was nineteen. "I'm sorry I didn't visit more often."

She moved in the seat. If she could have morphed through the door, he thought she would have. "Don't lose any sleep over it," she muttered.

"I did, you know." He'd lost a lot of sleep when he'd heard the news.

"Don't."

"No, you started this. I realize I was away for a while—"

She made a noise that sounded suspiciously like a snort.

"But I was coming back to see you."

She remained silent for a moment then her chin dipped. "I know."

His fingers tightened on the steering wheel. She knew? "How?"

She laughed, the sound harsh and derisive. "You're famous, Lucien. Every time you made one of your massive deals, every time your family's holdings increased to the capacity it could wipe out world debt, every time you dated a new woman—we heard about it. The most eligible vampire's activities always made front-page news. I knew you were in town."

He frowned. "Oh." He'd been in town the same night she'd died. He'd fully intended to step out of the fundraiser ball his father had dragged him to and go visit her, but his father had insisted on his presence. Unfortunately his days of skipping out of balls had ended the night his mother died. He'd fully intended to visit Natalie, though. He'd heard the news the following night.

He hesitated then took a deep breath. "When I heard about what happened to you…" He shook his head. It was hard for him to put into words what that news had done to him, the dark devastation that had swamped him. The guilt. He glanced over at her. Her face was so still, as though she'd been carved from rock.

"How did you survive?" he asked her, his voice rough with emotion.

The muscle in her jaw flexed. "I didn't."

"And yet here you are." He was still trying to adjust to that. What was it she'd called it? Weird? Yeah. Weird. He'd mourned her and now he was like a pendulum, caught between the joy of discovering she was still alive and the grief of the realization that she was now so different to the person he'd once known. It was like losing her all over again.

He saw the road sign he'd been looking for and took the next turn off the highway.

"Did the papers get it wrong?" he prompted her.

She shook her head. "No, they got it right. I died."

"But you're not a vampire," he said, confusion twisting his face as he tried to make sense of the inexplicable.

"No, I'm sure as hell not."

His eyes narrowed. "You make it sound like a bad thing."

"Because it is." Her tone was clipped. Cold.

"You used to like vampires," he reminded her. "You used to like me. You used to believe every breed had a place at Mother Nature's table."

She snorted. "I used to believe in fairies, unicorns and a pot of gold at the end of every damned rainbow. I was an idiot."

"We used to be friends," he reminded her. "You could—and would—tell me everything." Even when he'd wished he could cover his ears and sing la-la-la when she talked about the kid at the back of her history class or the latest teen celebrity crush.

He turned down a long, tree-lined drive that hid the valley from view and could sense the temperature drop outside. The area was cultivated, with the rocky outcroppings of the desert giving way to rolling green hills and fields bordered by planted trees. It was quite tranquil after the harsh desert.

"We were friends," he repeated softly. She'd never seen him as the son of Vincent Marchetta and scion to the Nightwing Vampire Prime. She'd never treated him like a rich and powerful businessman. She'd made him play at tea parties with her teddy bears and make cotton-thread bracelets. She'd reminded him so much of his sister, Vivianne, when she was younger, and when he and his sister were still human. She'd tugged at the heart he didn't realize he still had.

"Yeah, well, nothing lasts forever."

Natalie pursed her lips. She refused to fall into the lull of sweet memories, to remember Lucien from back then, to forget what had happened, or to forgive what he was now. The man sitting next to her was so different. So…intense.

"If I have to listen to any more of this, I'm going to throw up," Grace Perkins said from the backseat.

"No, this is *so* romantic," Courtney exclaimed softly. Then she frowned. "Wait, when he says 'friends,' does that mean, like, just friends-friends or like boyfriend and girlfriend?"

Natalie ignored them, as she'd tried to do for the full journey, and glanced out the window, finally realizing they'd left the highway. They were on a private road that twisted and curved into the hillside. She glanced around with a little more curiosity. She knew they'd been passing through coyote and bobcat territory, but what was this area?

Outside her window was a wall of trees that gave way to a rising embankment of grass. On Lucien's side was the vista into the desert valley, all rich shades of red and gold in the midday sun that was occasionally masked by trees as they drove along the curving road. It was so weird being with him out in the daylight and watching the play of dimmed light and shadow across his handsome face. He had a strong jawline, a straight nose and lips that looked like they were made for kissing, darn it. She shouldn't have been surprised that he wouldn't let a little annoyance like the sun prevent him from going about his business. She slid her fingers across the polished timber inserts on the passenger-door panel. His car definitely beat her little sedan in the comfort stakes.

"Where are we?" she asked.

"We need a break. We'll catch some shut-eye here and continue on at sunset."

Her fingers clenched on the armrest. "What?" Together? Where? What was this *we* business?

"I can dr—" she was interrupted by a yawn "—drive," she finished.

He shot her an exasperated look. "Forgive me, but I'd rather get to where we're going, and not become a roadside statistic. We're taking a break."

She reached for the journal and withdrew her spectacles from their case. He put his hand out to stop her from putting them on, clasping her wrist gently.

"Seriously? You don't need them, do you?" He raised her wrist, and just briefly managed to peer through the discs. Just as he thought. Glass. She needed glasses about as much as he did.

She pursed her lips as she tugged her wrist out of his grasp.

"Force of habit," she muttered.

"Or a disguise?" he asked. "Although, it's a lousy one, seeing as you wore glasses as a kid… Did your eyesight improve around about the same time as your death?"

"That's none of your business."

He pursed his lips. He wanted to make it his business. His curiosity about the woman seated next to him was growing to uncomfortable proportions. He didn't respond, and Natalie sighed, then placed the spectacles inside the case and dropped the case back in her bag.

"I guess there's no point wearing them if it's just you," she muttered.

He tried not to smile.

He drove around the final bend and a large steel gate set into the hill opened to reveal a dark void. Natalie's eyes widened as she took in the gaping maw and the gargoyles perched on the top of the entrance. Goose bumps rose on her arms.

"Uh, Lucien," she began, leaning forward. Her knuckles whitened as she clutched the armrest. "What is this place?" Her heart started to hammer in her chest.

He drove through the opening, the underground drive darkening as the gate started to slowly close behind them. "It's a hotel."

She yanked off her sunglasses. "What kind of hotel?" She twisted in her seat to peer through the rear window. She didn't like this, not at all. Too dark, too closed in. No. this wasn't good at all.

He shot her a puzzled frown. "It's a roadside rest spot." As though it was normal for someone like her to be in someplace like this. She felt like her world had dropped out the back end of her stomach.

He braked gently as they pulled up to an expansive portico tastefully lit with subdued lighting.

"A vampire roost?" she asked in a low voice.

He nodded. "Well, yeah. I'm a vampire. It makes sense to stay at roost."

Almost always underground, roosts allowed limited sunlight under controlled conditions. A vampire couldn't utilize a human lodge unless they were happy to be bound by night, as simply walking from the front door to the parking lot was suicide. Roosts provided vampires with all the shelter they needed during their travels.

The problem with being in a vampire roost was that it was full of vampires.

"Get me out of here," Natalie said as she glanced wildly around.

He frowned. "I can't drive for much longer, Natalie. I need a break and so do you."

"Not here." She shook her head, her eyes wide as she stared at the steps leading into the architecturally designed subterranean hotel. "I won't stay here." *No way, no how.*

"Well, I can't stay anywhere else," he responded as he shut off the ignition. She watched as the concierge descended the steps toward the car. A vampire concierge. His fangs flashed as he smiled in greeting. Cold sweat broke out on her forehead and she had to fight off other images of fangs.

She whipped around to face Lucien and he paused when he met her gaze. She tried to control the rage, the fear—but her heart was beating a staccato and every instinct screamed at her to flee. How could he? After what had happened, how *could* he?

"You brought me to a roost?" Her voice was low and his puzzlement gave way to wariness. "Screw you, Lucien," she said hoarsely.

Comprehension finally dawned in his eyes. "You'll be safe, Natalie. You're here under my protection. You'll be safe." His voice was gentle and just a little husky.

Her eyes narrowed as his words awakened other memories. *I'll always be here for you.* Fangs. Growls.

Pain. Nothing. "Forgive me," she rasped, "but I know your protection is worth diddly-squat."

She launched out of the car, muscles bunching as she bolted toward the door built into the side of the gate.

"Natalie," Lucien called as he climbed out of the car.

She could hear a couple of guests coming out of the hotel and she glanced briefly over her shoulder. More vampires. Her heart felt like it was clawing its way out of her chest in an effort to race her to safety. The concierge called out to her in protest. She ignored him. If she opened that door, that sunlight would stream in and turn any vampire out under the portico to ash. Including Lucien.

"Natalie!" Lucien started to bolt after her.

She could hear his feet slapping against the concrete of the drive. "Go to hell, Lucien," she yelled over her shoulder as her hand reached for the latch.

She heard a small pop, then felt something tearing into her shoulder, the impact shoving her against the steel gate with force. She fell to the ground, her shoulder burning, her breaths coming in hoarse pants as heat rolled over her. Her vision started to turn gray at the edges.

Lucien dropped to his knees, his face harsh with concern as he reached for her.

She tried to fend him off, her movements sluggish. Pain in her shoulder. Like before. Dizzy.

"No, please," she wailed, although her voice failed her, coming out as whispery moan. Pain. Heat. Fangs. She needed to get away. Find Mom and Dad. Before they killed her.

"Natalie," Lucien whispered, his hand cupping her cheek.

His features blurred and tears welled in her eyes as she could feel her control slipping away from her. "Help me, Luc. Save Mom and Dad." Darkness swept over her and there was no more Luc.

Chapter 9

Lucien's brows dipped with concern. Damn it. Natalie was unconscious but still alive. He could hear her heart slowing to a more reasonable rate, see the soft rise and fall of her chest. Her features were slowly relaxing from stark fear to slumber. He'd never seen such fear in her eyes as when she'd pleaded with him to help her. She'd called him *Luc*. God, that had twisted that decrepit muscle in his chest, tugging at it, forcing it to *feel*. She'd begged him. He raised her shoulders gently. A dart protruded from her shoulder, a small stain darkening her coat.

He heard the soft pad of feet running toward him and glanced over his shoulder. The concierge and two other vamps jogged toward him and he recognized one of the others. His lips pursed but already he felt calmer.

"What did you use, Heath?" he asked the tall, brown-haired vamp as he approached.

Heath Rafferty grinned. "Relax. It's a tranquilizer laced with verbena," he said loudly. He hefted the pistol in his hand to reveal the extra cartridges in the custom-made chamber.

The concierge and the other vamp hesitated, disappointment and annoyance twisting their features as they stopped and turned to walk back to the hotel. For them, the light snack in Lucien's arms had just turned into poison.

"Why did you tranq her?"

"It was either that or let the other two feed on your reluctant little plaything, here," Heath said, gesturing to the unconscious Natalie on the ground. "They weren't going to let her open that gate. Neither was I."

Lucien slid one arm under Natalie's knees, one arm behind her back, and scooped her up. He started walking toward the hotel entrance. She'd been ready to pull open that door and let the sunlight stream in. She could have killed all of them in her frantic need to escape. The concierge wouldn't have allowed it. And her darting off from Lucien like that? Well, she must have looked like fair game to them. Lucien hefted her in his arms, holding her firmly.

He got it. He'd been slow, admittedly, but he'd finally realized what was going on. It was hard to miss her terror. She'd been killed by a vampire. Well, a vampire and a werewolf in some sick and twisted killing spree love duo. And he'd brought her to a place where she would be surrounded by more of the same. She'd gotten spooked. His lips tightened at his carelessness. She'd panicked. She'd tried to run, just like she'd tried to run after his first visit. Damn it. What the hell happened to her all those years ago? It was as though she'd segued into that time, pleading with him to save her, save her parents. His muscles tightened. Is that what had happened? Had she cried out for him all those years ago? So frightened, so vulnerable, had she called his name during the attack?

God. No wonder she hated him. He felt like a douche. A mean-spirited, manipulative douche, forcing her to help him by threatening to kill her friends—just like she'd been killed—forcing her to face her very real, genuine fears.

"Mind telling me why you're bringing your unconscious friend into my fine establishment?" Heath inquired as he sauntered alongside him.

Heath made a casual gesture to the concierge and the vampire immediately crossed over to Lucien's car and started hauling out the bags. Another vampire jogged out to help. Lucien shook his head when the man offered to carry Natalie. No. He wasn't letting her go. The man turned to assist the concierge with the bags.

"She's...helping me."

Heath's eyebrow rose. "Oh, so that's what help looks like."

Lucien shot him an exasperated look as they entered the hotel lobby. The decor was the Rafferty's signature black, white and chrome. Ultra modern, with gray marble on the floors, white, polished wall tiles that caught the light from the stunningly elaborate chandelier, and black-and-silver accents in the furniture, light fixtures, art sculptures and wall trims. It could have looked tacky but somehow it looked elegant and stylish instead.

"I like what you've done with the place," Lucien commented. Heath was one of the first friends he'd made on the west coast, and they'd worked together on a number of lucrative projects. His friend had just taken over the family's hotel chain. Heath shrugged as he crossed the lobby to the reception desk. "It's a work in progress."

"I see you've left the skylights," Lucien commented, eyeing the tempered strip of glass that ran the width of the building's roof. The rest of the ceiling ran beneath the hill. The glazing on the window allowed a muted light to shine through, but not enough to cause the vampires inside any pain.

Heath grimaced. "I hate it, but Mom likes it and wants it to stay. I'm going to wear her down, though." He winked at the hotel receptionist, who blushed and smiled back. He tapped away on her computer keyboard and, within moments, had programmed a keycard. "Mr. Marchetta is a personal friend of mine," Heath told the receptionist. "I'll take him and his…guest…to his room."

Heath indicated the far wall and stepped out to escort Lucien to the elevator. As soon as the doors were closed, Heath pressed a button, folded his arms and leaned against the mirrored wall. He eyed the unconscious Natalie in Lucien's arms as the elevator descended into the side out of the mountain. "She's pretty. Haven't seen you have to run down a date before, though."

Even though the comment was casually uttered, Lucien could hear the curiosity in his friend's voice.

"She's not a date," Lucien said. "She's helping me with Vivianne."

Heath sighed. "I'm sorry, man. How is your sister doing?" Heath was one of the first people to offer him help when his sister had been attacked by chasing down a voodoo witch in Old Orleans. He was one of the few who didn't waste his time trying to tell Lucien what a hopeless quest he was on. For that, Lucien would call him friend for the ages.

"Not so good. Time's running out."

"And how does this little one fit into the picture?" Heath reached to touch the tangled blond ponytail and Lucien shifted as the elevator came to a smooth halt. Heath's lips twisted in a dry smile at the protective move. "Ah. I see."

"No, you don't." Lucien didn't "see," didn't really understand what was going on between him and Natalie, so Heath couldn't "see" a damn thing. She made him feel angry. She made him feel confused. She occasionally made him feel like a right royal schmuck and sometimes she made him feel like he was going to combust from desire. Now, though, she made him feel tender, and caring. Damn it, enough with the feelings.

"She's not one of us," his friend said as they stepped out of the elevator. Thick, plush, charcoal-colored carpet stretched along the hallway, with strategically placed wall sconces that shed a muted, cool light. Lucien hoisted her a little higher in his arms, trying to ignore the warm curves pressed against his body—because if he allowed himself to get aroused carrying an unconscious woman, he deserved every criticism Natalie could level at him.

"No, she's not."

"You might want to keep to your room," Heath suggested, looking at him briefly over his shoulder before walking on down the hall. "She looks tasty enough, and we have enough guests here who might confuse her for a feeder."

Feeders were humans who willingly offered their blood to vampires. Heath's hotel chain always had a sumptuous feast on offer, and Lucien knew Heath made it a point to protect his stock. One of the infamous Rafferty's Rules—you couldn't completely consume any of his feeders. He offered enough variety and quantity that it never seemed to be an issue.

Still, Lucien did not want Natalie exposed to that kind of risk, especially if the mere sight of a vampire sent her running for the hills—literally. "Point taken."

Heath stopped in front of a door, swiped the card and swept into a room. Lucien followed. Well, more of a suite than a room. Split level, the living area two steps down into the room, with a thick black rug on the floor, large armchairs and a sumptuous sofa upholstered in black leather. Two bedrooms opened off the far landing. He could see through the open doors two expansive beds covered in white linen and black throw cushions. Two beds. Lucien tried to ignore the small spark of disappointment.

Heath indicated the suite. "So, this is yours for as long as you need it. Room service can get you everything you need."

Lucien strode past his friend and gently laid Natalie on the sofa. He picked up a light gray wool throw off the armrest and draped it over her sleeping form, making sure her neck was supported by a cushion before he stepped back. He turned to find his friend gazing at him intently.

Lucien cleared his throat and tried to distract his friend. "I, uh, wasn't expecting to see you here," he said. "I thought you were refurbishing your properties in the north."

Heath grimaced. "That's where I'm supposed to be,

but I need to sort a few things out here, so this roost gets refurbished first."

Lucien's eyebrows rose. "Anything to do with why you're walking around one of your properties with a tranq gun?"

"Maybe."

"Anything I can help with?"

Heath shrugged. "Not sure, yet. Will let you know. So, where are you headed? I would have expected you to be a little further south, if you were heading home to the west coast."

Lucien shook his head. "No, we're headed to a small town up in the Aerions—Devil's Leap."

Heath's eyes narrowed. "Devil's Leap? What's up there for you?"

Lucien shrugged. "Maybe nothing, but Natalie thinks there might be something there to help Vivianne."

Heath's gaze slid to Natalie on the sofa. "Can you trust this woman?"

Lucien turned to look at her. Her features were so sweet, so relaxed, in her drug-induced slumber. But there was something going on with her—and her books—that he just didn't understand. Something she was trying to hide from him. She'd tried to lie to him. And today she'd been prepared to turn him and Heath to ash in her effort to escape a vampire roost.

Somehow, though, he believed in her. Believed in her ability to help Vivianne. Believed in her sincerity and integrity. From their very first meeting, she'd helped him, at great sacrifice to herself.

"Yeah, I trust her," Lucien said quietly.

Heath shook his head. "You are such a sucker. She

nearly nuked us, and now she's taking you to Devil's Leap. There are stories about that place, Luc."

Lucien arched an eyebrow. "I never thought you were the one to believe in campfire stories and fairy tales, Heath."

Heath snorted. "I'm not. But that place is not friendly to the shadow breeds."

"What do you know?"

"Nothing much—like you said, campfire stories and fairy tales. I do know that Eventide got a foothold in this area because the ridgewalkers disappeared."

Eventide was Heath's colony. "Ridgewalkers?"

"Werewolf pack that held this territory before The Troubles. They were wiped out."

Lucien rubbed his chin. "Interesting. Ridgewalkers, huh? What happened to them?"

Heath shrugged. "Don't know, don't care. The day a wolf pack disappears is a good day for me. I'm not going to lose any sleep over it, especially as Eventide benefited from it. Anyway, can't stand here yapping. You know that saying…have tranqs, must shoot."

"Must have missed that one." Lucien frowned. The tranqs worked well on humans, obviously. But protect them from vampires…? He wasn't sure if that made any sense. "The verbena means you won't be able to feed."

Heath waved a dismissive hand. "Oh, that. It's only a mild dose. Humans metabolize it within a couple of hours. Vamps wake up with a hell of a hangover. Werewolves— well, there's a nice little measure of wolfsbane in there, too, so they don't wake up at all. One shot can neutralize pretty much most shadow breeds."

Lucien whistled. "One tranq that can knockout everything? Where did you get that?"

"It's my own concoction." Heath said, a touch of pride in his tone.

"Is this a new sideline for Rafferty Inc.?"

Heath had expanded the family business of high-end luxury accommodation and leisure activities to encompass pharmaceuticals and technology. And now it looked like he was venturing into munitions.

"Just something I'm dabbling in at the moment. Your father's shown an interest in investing."

That didn't surprise Lucien. If there was a way his father could develop weapons to be used against lycans, he was interested.

There was a knock at the door and Heath leaned forward to open it. Staff stood outside, carrying Lucien's and Natalie's bags. Heath stepped aside to let them in.

"Right, well, much as I'd like to catch up with you, I've got work to do. Call me if you need me."

"Thanks, Heath."

Lucien tipped the staff and closed the door. He turned. It was just him and Natalie now. An unconscious Natalie. Lucien frowned as he stepped toward the sofa. He crouched until he was level with her face and brushed a strand of blond hair off her face.

"I will keep you safe," he whispered to her, leaning forward to brush a soft kiss against her forehead. He adjusted the blanket to cover her more fully and then turned to their bags. May as well make himself useful.

Natalie stirred. Winced. *Ow.* Her head throbbed as though she'd drunk her body weight in bourbon. Her eyelids flickered and she squinted at the light that lanced through her lashes.

"Finally," a woman's voice muttered. "Your boy-friend's been snooping through my stuff."

Boyfriend? Whaaat? Natalie frowned, raising her hand to her head to try to make sure everything was where it should be. Namely, her brains on the inside. Thump. Thump. It took her a little longer to realise she no longer wore her gloves. She could feel her pulse in her ears, in her temple and at a painful spot at the back of her neck. What the hell?

Fleeting memories of a dark tunnel and vampires in weird uniforms swam in a blurred mess in her mind's eye. Running. Running for a gate. A burn in her shoul-der. Then nothing. She jolted when those fuzzy memo-ries coalesced into something with clarity. A vampire roost.

"Hey, sleeping beauty," a deep voice said to her left. Her head whipped around and she regretted the swift movement as her vision swam and her stomach heaved. Lucien closed a familiar-looking tattered book and placed it on the small end table next to him—right next to her gloves.

His gaze deepened with concern as she clapped a hand over her mouth.

"I think I'm going to be sick," she said. Her stomach roiled and her mouth felt like she'd chewed on sand-paper.

"Here, have some of this." Lucien was by her side immediately, holding a glass of water to her mouth.

She drank, gulping the cool liquid to ease the rough-ness in her throat.

"Easy, minx, easy," he cautioned gently.

She lifted her head to look at him and he smiled as he wiped the last drop of water off her bottom lip. That simple caress heightened her senses even further. She could feel his breath stir her tangled hair, smell that seductive scent of patchouli and sandalwood, feel the warmth emanating from his body. She could feel herself softening, relaxing.

"Better?"

She blinked at the tenderness in his gaze, his touch. Heat bloomed inside her. A heat she firmly swamped with cool rage as she took in the room around them. Black furniture, gray carpet, white walls with—framed art, and tasteful lighting. All opulent and luxurious, all screaming cold, bloodless comfort. Right down to the bottle of red wine and two crystal glasses placed oh, so stylishly on a silver platter on the dark coffee table in front of the sofa. God, she hoped that was wine.

"Where are we?" The words burned along her throat.

His expression became shuttered. "We're at the roost." He placed his hand on her shoulder when she tried to launch toward the door. "It's okay, Natalie. You're safe. I know the owner. We won't be disturbed."

"Is that supposed to make this okay? You say some empty words and poof—" she snapped her fingers "—everything is going to be all right?" She tried to rise again and winced as her muscles screamed in protest. Her shoulder ached. She subsided against the sofa. "What the hell happened to me?"

"You were shot with a tranquilizer. It was either that or be taken down by some very concerned vamps." He frowned as he surveyed her. "I was told it would have worked its way out of your system by now."

She brushed his hand off her shoulder. "Well, you were told wrong. You should have let me leave."

He shook his head. "This is a roost, Natalie. You

were going to open the tunnel gate. Any vampire within the sun's reach would have turned to ash. We're going to have to wait until sunset."

She glanced at her watch. Four hours. She'd have to survive four hours inside this hell hole. Her eyes widened as she noted her skin. It was pale—like, really pale—and her veins looked light gray in color. "What was in that shot?"

Lucien shrugged. "A bit of a cocktail, I'm afraid. Sedatives, verbena, wolfsbane—Heath was covering his bases."

Damn. No wonder she felt like crap. She flexed her hands and took a small comfort as the color of her skin started to revert to a more normal tone; the veins starting to lose that gray look.

"I promise, Natalie. You'll be safe here."

"A human? Safe? Here?" She shook her head. "Only a vamp would say that. A human walking into a roost is pretty much committing suicide."

"Not here. You're not a feeder, you're a guest. *My* guest."

She rubbed her forehead. "That sounds so wrong. I don't want to stay here."

"I know, and I'm sorry," he murmured as he moved to sit beside her on the sofa. "I didn't think. I use this particular chain for all of my travel, and I didn't think of how it would affect you, after what happened... I'm sorry. We'll check out as soon as the sun sets."

She glanced at him, surprised by his apology. His voice was warm with sincerity and she could see regret etched into the grooves of his face. When he was all genuine and caring like this, it was easy to remember him as an oh, so patient, yet slightly naughty benevolent figure who'd once kept her company. When pain had racked her body during the night, when she'd lain awake, terrified of her nightmares and feeling so lonely and low, he'd been there. Playing games, taking her on secret excursions her parents claimed she was too ill to indulge in... Everyone had treated her like she was dying, but Lucien had showed her that even the undead knew a thing or two about living.

She looked away from him. She didn't want to remember him like that. He was a vampire. She'd been hurt so much by vampires, had lost so much because of vampires. It had been so easy to blame them all for what had happened to her. After all, it was their very nature to prey on humans. They all did it. Lucien did it. It had been so easy just to avoid them all, wherever possible. She'd managed to avoid shadow breeds for nearly forty years.

And now she was sharing a room with one, in a hotel full of them. The old panic started to flare deep within her again.

Lucien cleared his throat. "Uh, back there in the tunnel, you asked me to save your parents." He met her gaze and she could see the agonizing guilt there, something she'd never expected from him—from any vampire. "What...what happened, Natalie? I have been sitting here, trying to imagine what it must have been like for you... If I'd known..." He growled softly and rose from the sofa to walk a couple of steps. "Why didn't you tell me? Why didn't you come to me afterward? I would have helped you." He paused, then his expression gentled. "Please, help me understand."

Natalie's eyes narrowed. "It was in the papers."

Lucien's eyes widened in frustration. He gestured to

her. "Obviously the reporters left a few important details out of the story." He sat back down, his lips tight.

He kept asking for this and, damn it, maybe if he knew, he wouldn't drag her in to any more vamp roosts or other deplorable situations.

"You want details, Lucien? Fine. I heard you were back in town. So I thought I'd surprise you. I wanted to go into town, and with the crappy weather Mom and Dad offered to drive in with me. We'd just opened the garage door when they came."

She swallowed. She didn't know whether it was the tranquilizer or the emotional toll of revisiting the most horrific night of her life—and death—but her stomach felt like it was a frog caught in a blender. Gross.

"It was snowing," she said unexpectedly. That detail had always stuck with her. That strange quiet as the snowflakes fell and muffled sound. The pristine-white cover that got sprayed with blood. So much blood.

"The wolf attacked Dad but didn't kill him. He made Dad watch his vampire friend kill Mom first."

Even now, just talking about it, goose bumps rose on her arms. "They did this little creeped-out sicko signature thing, where they'd feed their victims their blood, then kill them." Tears fell down her cheeks and she clenched her fingers tighter. She could still hear that gagging noise Mom had made as she'd tried not to swallow, the pleas her father had uttered, all bloody and torn from the werewolf's claws. Mom had screamed when the vampire bit down on her, but that scream was silenced. Natalie knew she'd screamed. She knew she'd called out for help...

"They took a perverse delight in my father's frustration, in my fear. I think killing Mom in front of us was the most devastating thing they could have done. She was always so sweet, so gentle. It was cruel, how they hurt her." She didn't mention what else they'd done, how they'd used their teeth to puncture her.

"Dad was so helpless. He went nuts trying to get to her." She glanced down at her tightly clenched hands. "I couldn't stop them." That confession was so hard to face. She'd tried, and the vampire had shaken her off easily. She'd broken her arm when she'd landed across the road from his casual fling. "I screamed your name," she admitted. "I don't know why. I mean, there was no way you would have heard me, but you were the first person I thought of for help." She lifted her gaze to Lucien's.

His face was haggard, but he didn't interrupt her.

"Dad told me to run." He'd screamed it at her and those monsters had laughed as they'd tackled him to the ground, biting and tearing at him. Her father's screams had rung in her ears as he'd been torn to shreds.

"I tried to run, but I was hurt and—" It was hard for her to put the rest into words.

"And?" Lucien prodded hoarsely.

She grimaced through her tears as she met his gaze. "The cancer had come back," she whispered.

His eyes shut, hiding the pain that glimmered there oh, so briefly.

"I'd just done my first round of chemo. I was so weak—I didn't get very far."

Lucien left his chair and crossed to her, kneeling to cover her twisted hands with his.

It was as though his touch gave her a quiet strength to go on. She hadn't spoken openly about that night in years, but she carried the memories with her and, every now and then, when she least expected it, she relived it, slipping back into the nightmare of her mind. Just as she had out in the tunnel where, for a brief moment, she'd thought she and her parents were being killed all over again.

"They forced me to drink their blood." Her stomach heaved at the memory. "Everything they'd done up to then started to heal. My broken arm—"

"They broke your arm?" Lucien repeated.

She watched his pain give way to anger. Surprisingly, she took a little comfort from that.

"They weren't very nice," she whispered in what had to be the understatement of the century. "By that time, though, the neighbors had called the cops. They arrived just as the monsters drained me." She shuddered at the horrific memory. She'd once thought that death wiped all senses out, but she now knew better. She'd felt every claw as it mangled her flesh, had felt every fang as it punctured her skin and tore through muscle. And then she'd felt her own heart slow then stop.

Lucien rubbed her wrists. "Did the vampire try to turn you after you died?"

She shrugged. "I don't know. I think the lycan blood would have inhibited it, but then I was revived in the ambulance." She laughed bitterly. "A simple blood transfusion and good old CPR, and suddenly I was back in the land of the living."

She chewed her lip for a moment. "It's ironic, really. A mix-up at the blood bank—a blood bag from a half-null—and, hey, presto, I'm back."

Only she'd come back changed. Different. Her own variation of monster.

Lucien frowned. "Then why were you reported dead?"

"Because I was dead. For a couple of minutes. The vamp and the wolf managed to escape. I was accompanied in the ambulance by a police officer, and he and the paramedics thought that if word got out I'd survived, the killers would come back for me to finish the job. So that night, Nina Stewart died."

And that's when her hell truly began.

She wiped at her tears then took a deep, cleansing breath. Wow. She felt wrung out, exhausted, and yet, somehow stronger. She'd been through hell. He still didn't know the half of it, but at least he knew the half that affected him.

She twisted her hands out of his grip. "So you see, Lucien, I don't like vampires. Or werewolves, for that matter. Your type killed my mother, my father—and me. You, who I'd considered my best friend, who had promised to visit, to keep in touch—to have my back..." she said, quietly emphasizing the last words. "You weren't there when I desperately needed you, when I called your name. I knew you were in town, but you weren't coming to me. After all your promises, you weren't there when I needed you the most. That's what killed me, Lucien. Those psycho dudes just finished the job you started."

Lucien flinched and Natalie rose to avoid seeing the stark pain she knew her words had caused him. She picked up the bottle of wine on the end table and started to weave her way toward one of the bedrooms, her muscles feeling like hot lead as she forced her body to move.

"I'll go with you to Devil's Leap, but then that's it. If we do or don't find something to help Vivianne, that's not on me. Either way, once we've checked out Devil's

Leap, you and I are done. After that, I don't want to see you ever again." She held up the bottle of wine. "Oh, and I'm taking this and I'm going to get drunk. Don't interrupt me."

Chapter 10

Lucien turned and waited for Natalie to catch up to him. The moon was just beginning to rise, bathing the forest in a light silver glow. She climbed up over the boulder then jumped down. He could see the puffs of her breath in the cool night air. She was surprisingly fit, he'd noticed. Even if she was incredibly hungover. He watched as she took another long swig from her water bottle. She was still wearing the gloves.

He'd also noticed a change in her since their conversation earlier in the day. Before she'd seemed... reactive. No, that wasn't quite the right word. She'd been resistant, but she'd still been fairly obedient. Now she was...strong. Gutsy. She'd walked through the hotel foyer with her shoulders back and her head high, almost daring any vamp to try to sink his teeth in her. He'd lost count of the number of vamps he'd had to stare down—including Enzo.

She hadn't encouraged conversation, either. She'd said her piece and that was it. He turned to look up at the mountain. They were almost at the summit of

Mount Solitude, and she'd climbed, with a pack on her back, steadily through the evening. No complaints. No requests for rest. She was...determined.

His brow dipped. She was on a mission. When they found this damn bunker, wherever the hell it was, she'd help him look and then this, whatever the hell this was, was over. She'd be on her way home. After what she'd shared with him, he wouldn't stop her. He wanted to—hell, he so wanted to—but he wouldn't. Couldn't.

God. He'd had no idea. She'd told him her story, but he knew she'd glossed over some of those details. Like her absolute terror, her grief, the torture she'd endured at the hands and teeth of those monsters. His hands clenched into tight fists. Logically he'd accepted she'd been murdered, and violently so. He'd imagined what that had entailed, had experienced anger, grief and sorrow at someone so gentle and sweet dying in such a harsh manner. Now, though, he realized that what she'd experienced didn't compare to the dark scenes he'd imagined.

Now he understood why she'd felt abandoned by him. Christ. He'd felt as big and manly as a slug when she'd told him that little detail. She was on her way to see *him*. He blinked. The reason they were outside the house, and prey for that vampire, was because she was coming to see *him*. He'd fully intended to come visit her, had been hoping to sneak out of a charity event his father had roped him into, but his father had proved difficult to shake. So he'd stayed.

And Natalie had died.

He knew without a doubt that had he been there, things would have ended differently. Had he been there, she would have survived, and her parents, too—because she loved them and he would have seen to it.

If only he'd left the party… If only he'd told his father no in the first place… If only he'd treated her like the priority she was… If only…

What pained him the most, though, was that she now classed him in the same category as the monsters who'd killed her. She'd endured such pain, such horror, at the hands of his kind—God, no wonder she hadn't invited him into her home that first night. No wonder she was reluctant to help him. No wonder she didn't want to have anything to do with him. She didn't trust him. She'd told him some of her story, but he would bet his ancestral home that that wasn't all of it.

He'd called Heath while she'd slept in her room. He could tell she'd awoken from that tranquilizer in pain. He'd seen it in her movements, he'd seen it in her veins, the drug turning her circulatory system a light gray that had reverted to a warmer tone as she'd sat up and moved a little. Heath couldn't explain it. No human had had that reaction in the testing phase, he'd said.

Natalie had flung him easily across the room. She had conversations with herself. Oh, she didn't think he'd noticed, but he had. And he didn't mean the cute tea-party-talking-teddy-bear sort of conversations he'd seen her do as a kid. No, he was talking a full-on chat fest with someone who wasn't there. Was that a remnant from her traumatic experience? Hallucinations?

She shrugged off her pack and moved her shoulders under the light jacket she was wearing. He could see the sheen of perspiration on her forehead, despite the chill in the air. Yet she wasn't out of breath. They'd covered far more terrain than he'd estimated and she'd been able to keep up with him.

She glanced over her shoulder, nodded and then turned back to him. "It's not too far from here. Just a little further up the trail. I guess," she ended hurriedly at his inquiring glance.

He nodded at the journal she held. "Is there a map in there?" He knew the answer, but he was hoping she'd explain some more things to him. She hadn't referred to it once since they'd driven through Devil's Leap. She hadn't let him stop in the small town for directions, had just told him to keep driving. A small number of people had been in the streets, and all of them had stopped to watch his vehicle roll by. Nobody had smiled.

Damn creepy place.

And now he was climbing a mountain in the dark on the say-so of a woman who spoke with imaginary people.

She glanced at the journal, blinked as though surprised to see she still held it. "Uh, not a map, exactly. More like directions."

Should he break it to her now that he knew she was lying? He'd gone through that book while she'd slept. Sure, there were journal entries about people going missing but there'd been no mention of a bunker. No mention of something that could be used on a vampire to neutralize the lycanthrope toxin, either.

Heath's words came back to haunt him. *Can you trust her?*

He thought about that first time he'd seen her, sitting in that massive, reclining, single-lounge chair, her body so small and withered beneath the voluminous hospital gown she'd worn. Those big hazel-gray eyes staring up at him in greeting, only mildly startled by his appearance in the renal ward. What she'd done after that...

He sighed. Yes. He trusted her.

"Okay, then. Let's go." He reached for her pack but she shook her head, lifting it up to shrug into the shoulder straps. She started off, halted, then changed direction slightly.

"This way," she said, and he let her lead. He was staring at her denim-clad butt and long legs, but at this rate, this might be the last time he had the opportunity to do so.

Twenty minutes later Natalie halted.

Lucien frowned. "What's up?"

"We're here." She let the backpack drop from her shoulders and opened the top to shove the journal deep inside.

He glanced around. "Here?" He could see the trail kind of end in a wall of foliage and rock. He retreated a couple of steps, looking carefully about. It was just forest. Trees, bushes, creepy things rustling in the leaves and a light show between the dark and silver as clouds trailed across the moon.

"Here," Natalie repeated. She pulled a sheath from within her backpack and removed the blade, and his eyes rounded as he stepped back. She had a damn machete.

"Whoa, minx." He trusted her. He trusted her. He kept repeating the phrase over and over in his head as the moonlight caught the edge of the blade, causing it to gleam briefly. That knife could almost fell a damn tree.

Natalie shot him an exasperated look. "Don't worry, Lucien. I know how to use this."

"That's what I'm afraid of."

She shook her head but didn't quite manage to hide her smile from him as she turned to the foliage.

Minx.

He strode up to the branches of nettles and other bushes and started pulling at them. It was rough work and, after a few moments, he dropped his pack, shrugged out of his jacket and attacked the greenery with renewed vigor. It didn't take long for Natalie to also slip out of her jacket.

Slowly, though, he could see what she was getting at. Behind the foliage, behind the branches with the nettles, what he'd originally thought was the rock face of the mountain proved to be a massive concrete door.

He stepped back to survey it. "How do we op—?"

"Here." Natalie yanked back on a branch, the snap loud in the night forest. She revealed what appeared to be a large wheel lock.

He grimaced. It looked rusted.

Natalie started to pull on it. After a moment there was a low squeak. He crossed over to help her and the wheel creaked as it slowly started to shift. He grunted, gripping at the wheel tightly, sweat beading his brow as he pulled down. The wheel shifted some more, protesting as it did.

Natalie growled softly as she put her shoulder against it, her face twisting with the effort, and the wheel creaked some more.

Lucien could feel his biceps bulging with the effort as he tore at the wheel until it gave way. He spun it gradually, until he heard a thunderous click inside.

Natalie halted, panting, and looked at him, excitement, anticipation and curiosity in her expression. She was looking at him in exactly the same way she had when he'd showed her the grotto on his family's property. Just like then, he grinned back at her and winked, then hauled back on the door. The hinges groaned as decades of dirt and grime slid free and the gigantic door swung inward, just a little.

A cool breeze crept out to tease his hair; a blessed relief despite the cold night air. Clearing the door had been hot work. He stood next to Natalie and glanced at her briefly. Her blond hair was gilded platinum in the moonlight, her face bore dirty streaks where she'd absently brushed at perspiration, and her jeans and shirt were filthy.

She looked so damn gorgeous.

"We're here."

"Wherever 'here' is," Lucien conceded. He felt like he was standing on a precipice, about to take that one step into the great unknown. Was Vivianne's cure inside? Or would they find another clue? Or would it be a complete bust? He couldn't remember the last time his blood thrilled at the uncertainty, at the newness of a situation.

She crossed to her pack and shrugged into it again, then strapped the sheath to her thigh and slid the machete inside. "Let's go. We need to be back down the mountain by sun up."

He sighed. Okay. No time for high-emotion moments.

She pulled the flashlight from the clip on the side of her pack as he shrugged on his gear. She walked through the doorway and he jogged to catch up with her.

"Wait a minute, Nat—" He ran into an impenetrable wall, then a painful jolt threw him back three feet onto his butt.

Natalie whirled around, frowning as he swore. He rose and advanced slowly toward the gaping maw of a doorway, hands outstretched. He flinched at the small spark that bit at his fingertips. He curled his hands into fists and tried to beat at the invisible barrier, only to be repelled across the trail again, the sides of his hands burning. This time he swore long and loud.

Natalie grimaced and tentatively reached out, waving her arm through the opening. Nothing happened. "There's an ownership claim...?"

He folded his arms as he approached the doorway, halting just short of getting fried again. He frowned. "Yes, but it's boosted. Damn thing is frying me every time I try to breach it."

Natalie aimed her flashlight at the lock mechanism on the inside wall. She shrugged. "It looks pretty standard to me. No wires. An old-style pulley system. My guess is circa World War Two. Still, who owns this place now? There are no records in the system for it."

"Well, just because it's not in the Reform database doesn't mean a title doesn't exist," Lucien stated.

"But the barrier's got a kick to it. I've never seen that before."

"Damn witches," Lucien muttered as he glanced up at the frame of the opening. This wasn't chemical, and it only worked on him, a vampire. A witch had to be responsible. Blast it.

"Oh, I have to meet this witch," Natalie commented in admiration. "This spelled barrier reacts to force. The more you apply, the greater the kickback. Very clever."

He pursed his lips. "Well, I'm so happy this has intrigued you." He jerked his thumb. "Okay, let's go. We'll go find who owns the title and seek permission."

Natalie frowned. "Hey, it's only you that has a problem getting in there, not me." She backed up a little into the darkened corridor, her light flicking from side to side. "No, I'm *allowed* access."

His eyes narrowed and a shady trail of disquiet rose at her words. "You can't go in there," he told her, surprised she'd even consider it.

Natalie gave him a look over her shoulder that he roughly interpreted as "whatever." She walked a little further inside and his disquiet gave way to concern.

"Natalie, come back."

She turned to face him, an eyebrow arched in challenge. "Are you saying you're prepared to walk away? We're talking about your sister, Lucien. If this place is spelled against vampires, do you seriously believe that if we can track down the owner—and I do mean *if*— that they'd actually consider allowing you access to something that is specifically protected against you?" She shook her head. "It could take weeks, maybe even months, trying to obtain the proper permissions. Or," she said, raising both arms to indicate the dark cavity around her, "I could take a peek here and now."

He shook his head. "No, it's not safe."

She laughed. "What makes you think that? You saw the lock. This place hasn't been opened in decades. Apart from the average creepy crawly, what could possibly be down here that could hurt me?"

"Come back, Natalie," he ordered. "I mean it. I don't have a good feeling about this."

"Why, Lucien, you're beginning to sound like one of those witches you so love. All moods and portents. Don't worry. Think of this like an expedition. I'm an old hand at those."

"Get back here."

"No. We have the opportunity to find out more about what happened all those years ago and if they have something here that can help your sister, I'm going in."

"I can't keep you safe," he protested.

She halted then sighed. "You never could, Lucien."

That frank statement hit him with more of a jolt than any witch's barrier spell could deliver. He wanted to keep her safe. He wanted to protect her, damn it. She turned and proceeded into the dark corridor that was wide enough to fit a pickup, her flashlight sweeping from side to side.

"I forbid it, Natalie," he yelled after her, his hands on his hips.

"Well, it's a good thing you're not the boss of me," she sang back over her shoulder. She halted, grimacing. "Wow, that sounded so juvenile—yet so right." She smiled broadly, gave him a cute little wave and turned a corner in the corridor, humming to herself as she went.

"Natalie!" he roared. He watched as the beam from the flashlight slowly dimmed, hearing what sounded suspiciously like the work chant of the seven dwarfs' movie she'd once demanded he sit through.

"Damn it!" he kicked at one of the fallen branches, watching as it sailed off into the distance. How the hell could he keep her safe if she refused his protection? He'd never felt so damn helpless.

Chapter 11

"This place is amazing," Natalie said softly as she swung the flashlight beam across the corridor. "And creepy," she admitted. The corridor stretched on in a gentle decline. The air was cool, but not as chilly as the night air outside. Her shoes made slight scuffing noises along the concrete. Concrete floor, walls and ceiling. She felt like she was walking through a tomb. And quiet... Her fingers rose to play with the silver lariat around her neck. Too quiet. Not even the scurry of little legs disturbed the silence.

Grace Perkins grimaced. "I haven't been here for a while. It's all so different now. Dark."

"You'll need to show me where to go," Natalie told the ghost, ducking under a fluorescent light that hung in the corridor, one of its cords frayed and worn through. She'd already tried a light switch, but whatever power had been hooked up to this facility had long since been disconnected.

"This is the main corridor. The trail we came up is overgrown, but it used to be a track you could drive up."

Natalie's eyebrows rose. Wow. It had been difficult to follow it in the moonlight, so wild and overgrown as it was. If Grace hadn't been beside her, guiding her, she and Lucien would never have found it. She glanced behind her. After all of his threats, the danger he presented, the risks he'd forced her to take, she should be happy he was stuck outside. Oddly, though, she found she missed his presence.

They turned another bend and Natalie gave a low whistle as she stepped into a huge, dark cavern. She aimed the beam around the area, but found it shed only a dim light on the walls, so far away were they. "This place is massive," she gasped.

"It was built during the Second World War, just before the first atomic bomb was dropped. It was intended to be a military base of operations, in case things escalated." Grace explained.

Natalie frowned. "But if it was military, then the former government would own title. Those vamp barriers only work on private title."

"The land was purchased a few decades after the war ended," Grace supplied. "One of the wealthier families in the district. I don't know who owns it now, though."

The flashlight beam illuminated a dark shape and Natalie stepped closer. "Good grief, it's an old Jeep." She'd never seen one outside of a museum.

"There are a lot of antiques in here," Grace murmured. "Come on, the medical center is this way."

Natalie followed her toward one of the corridors branching off from the main chamber. It was so damn silent. They stepped through a gate that hung askew on its hinges. It was the first of many.

Natalie frowned. "What happened here?"

Grace shook her head as she stepped through another damaged gate. "I don't know. This isn't how I remember it."

Natalie swept her light over a wall and froze, her eyes widening. She slowly moved the light back, trying to find what had caught her eye. A chill crept over her arms as the beam highlighted claw marks in the concrete, deep and bloodied. "Oh, my God."

Grace looked around, her face anxious. "I don't feel so good, Natalie. Something isn't right."

Natalie pursed her lips. "As a ghost, it goes against the rules for you to get spooked." She turned back, but something moved out of the corner of her eye and she whirled around, the flashlight beam flickering with her unsteady movement.

"What was that?"

"What was what?" Grace whirled, peering into the darkness.

"I thought I saw something." Natalie hesitated, but the light only illuminated more corridor, more doorways with damaged doors. They stepped through one and into what looked like an antechamber of sorts, with a desk and some screens. Three doors hung open, revealing three corridors. The doors were thick, constructed of steel and in varying states of disrepair. Claw marks were visible in the steel. Natalie grimaced at the dark shadows on the floor. "Is that—?"

"Blood. Yes."

Natalie gulped then nodded. "Good to know."

"Security checkpoint," Grace informed her. "From here you have the clinicians' offices," she said, gesturing to one hallway, "the patients' cells—"

"Cells? Like, prisoners?"

Grace gave her a dry look. "This place wasn't a vacation for those monsters, Natalie."

Natalie nodded. Of course. God, it sounded so wrong, so...harsh.

"And the operating rooms are down that one."

Natalie stared at that doorway and shuddered. This place really was beginning to creep her out. She couldn't begin to imagine what it must have felt like for those imprisoned here. Her grip tightened on the flashlight when she realized she could have easily qualified as one of those "freaks of nature" to be observed and experimented on.

"This is all levels of wrong," she muttered.

She was trying to gauge which hall to enter when another dark shadow moved. She turned, squinting in the darkness. She shone her light in that direction. Nothing save more marks on the wall—God, was that a bullet hole? What the *hell* had happened here? Otherwise, nothing moved.

"What is it?" Grace asked.

"I thought I saw something again." She shook her head. "My imagination is running away with me. Let's go take a look at the med staff offices. There might still be some information in there." Her heart started to beat just a little faster as she chose the hall that lead to the clinicians' offices.

"Dr. Morton's rooms are down here," Grace stated.

Natalie nodded. Great. The man was fast becoming quite the sicko in her mind.

Lucien strode along the barrier, halted at the end, turned, and strode along the barrier. Damn it. He glanced at his watch. Forty minutes. She'd been in there for forty minutes. Alone. What if something happened to her? What if the roof caved in? God knows, the place was decrepit. What if she fell down a hole? What if she was bitten by a snake? Okay, so maybe it wasn't the right time of year for snakes, but still—anything could befall her, and he was stuck outside, cooling his damn heels.

He surveyed the dark cavity. "Damn witches." He strode along the invisible perimeter. What was he thinking? He should have left her at the car. He stopped. No. He should have left her back at the roost. *No.* He shook his head. He should have left her back at Westamoor, where she was safe and secure among friends.

Well, except for Enzo. He paused by a birch tree and gazed out over the valley. The town of Devil's Leap was about three-quarters of the way up the mountain. They'd passed some natural waterfalls on the way up. It had been quite pretty, and now, in the late evening, the town sat in a sleepy golden glow. It was quite picturesque, for a freaky, murderous little town. His hand fisted on the trunk of the tree.

There was something off about this whole place. And Natalie was by herself, unprotected and alone. He didn't like it. He wanted to make sure she was safe. God, he'd never felt so damn helpless.

A twig napped in the wilderness and Lucien froze. That wasn't a bird. Probably wasn't a deer, either. He peered into the darkness, his eyes narrowing as he discerned shape from shadow. His lips tightened. Great. Three figures were slowly climbing the mountain toward him. From this distance he couldn't tell whether they were human, vampire or shifter. All he knew was that from the way they were trying to creep up on him, they weren't friendly.

Natalie stepped inside the dark office, not for the first time wishing she could switch on a light.

"I think I'll go," Grace said, glancing around. She seemed quite skittish.

"I don't know where," Natalie commented dryly. "I'm carrying your journal in my pack." She strode over to the desk and trained the light over the surface. Papers had been left in disarray, but they were mainly supply orders, prescriptions and medical journals. She moved to a filing cabinet and tried to open a drawer. The darn thing was locked.

She slid the machete out of the sheath and slid it into the gap between drawer and case, using it as leverage. She tapped it forcefully with her fist and the drawer shuddered open under protest. She grinned as she slipped the blade back into its sheath. Such a versatile tool.

She drew the drawer open further and eyed the documents inside. Old-fashioned manila folders, with papers. "So many papers. Didn't you guys know how to use a computer?"

"Yes, but a computer could be hacked. This way you actually have to physically get your hands on the documents, and this place was well-protected." Grace rubbed her arms. "This place is really cold."

Natalie glanced at her briefly. "Since when do ghosts feel the temperature?" If they did, then Terry would have worn a shirt years ago. She smiled at the thought.

Grace shrugged, but said nothing.

Natalie withdrew a folder and propped it on top of the drawer, raising her flashlight beam to read the contents. Her smile slowly died. Good Lord. She took out more folders and dropped them on the desk, flicking them open. It was difficult to turn the pages with her gloves, so she quickly removed them and shoved them in her jeans' pockets.

"He's called them test subjects. No names. Holy crap," she breathed as she read the medical report on Test Subject #139. Did that mean the one hundred and thirty-ninth prisoner? Holy friggin' hell. This guy—he'd been put through hell. He was listed as a male lycan, seventeen years old. *Seventeen.*

"'This one appears to have a high pain threshold,'" she read aloud. "'It is unclear whether that is due to his limited age or the purity of his bloodline, whether his father's alpha status offers greater strength, and therefore a better grade of protection against pain.'" Her eyes widened. "You captured a scion?" A prime's children were scions and held an elevated status in the new Reform society. There was an unspoken level of protection on scions. Mess with a scion and you were basically declaring war with that pack, colony or coven.

Grace nodded. "More than one. Lycan. Vampire. We even managed to catch a cougar, once." She grimaced. "That one was particularly vicious. The primes were harder to capture."

Natalie turned back to the report. "'The subject displays advanced healing qualities. Cuts and grazes close up quite quickly, but bones take a little longer to…knit.'" She swallowed. "You broke their bones?"

Grace sighed. "I told you, I didn't necessarily agree with everything they did here."

Natalie turned the page. She sagged against the desk when she read the next entry. "'It appears that although these creatures display miraculous healing powers, they cannot regrow limbs. Open wounds will close, but fatality is confirmed with decapitation.'" Tears filled her eyes. "You tortured him. He was a kid."

Grace frowned. "Let me see that." Natalie slid the folder toward the police chief, who read it silently, shaking her head. "I knew about some of the experiments, but this…" She lifted her gaze. "Number one-thirty-nine. A scion…" She closed her eyes. "Matt Anderson. Damn it."

"What?"

"The Anderson family came looking for Matt. I didn't know he was a werewolf. I thought he was human. I asked Doc about him."

"Let me guess, the good doctor lied to you?" She didn't hide the contempt in her voice.

"I swear, Natalie, I had no idea. There is no way I would allow this kind of treatment to a teen. God, I have—had—a teenage son and daughter. Doc knew the children were out of bounds."

"Well, he conveniently ignored that restriction." She turned back to the pile of folders, angry at the police chief, at this damned Dr. Jekyll, at this town for what they'd done to those who weren't like them.

"Natal—"

"Save it," she interrupted Grace. "Let's just see if there is anything they used here that can save a vampire against the lycan toxin." She quickly skimmed through the notes, her lips tightening as she read the horror stories. They'd placed shifters in the same cells as vampires, just to see what would happen. They'd placed shifters that knowingly had a natural aversion to each other—like a bobcat and a werewolf or a bear and a cougar—together in cells. Damn. This was just plain sick.

She opened another drawer, quickly flicking through folders. She shook her head. More of the same. She crossed to another filing cabinet, forced the lock and started going through its contents. She shivered a little. Grace was right—it was getting quite chilly in here.

She sighed as she reached the doctor's "defense" reports. Dr. Morton had kept copious notes on his victims— she refused to call them patients—and he'd prepared some documentation for what he'd referred to as "The Executive."

"This is more like it," she breathed. The effects of verbena on vampires, of wolfsbane on the lycans, oleander on the cat shifters…her eyebrows rose. Black nightshade was poisonous to all shifters, but silverleaf nightshade was poisonous to all breeds, including humans. She flipped through the reports, dating back several years. Good God, he'd done this for so long. She kept flicking through the pages.

They'd discovered so many weapons, she realized. Some of them were well-known now, two hundred years past Reformation, but some were quite surprising. She paused and had to flip back a few pages. There was a side note to wolfsbane… She trailed her finger down the page, looking for the reference. Wolfsbane, wolfsbane…she nodded her head. Yes, incredibly toxic to lycans, acts as a corrosive to the skin. Yes, yes. Can be neutralized—Natalie halted, her eyes widening.

Wow. Okay. Um. Well, that was surprising, and yet, holy crap, it made so much sense. She shivered.

"Natalie," Grace said quietly.

"Not now," Natalie murmured. "I think I have something."

"So do I."

Natalie lifted the report, turned and halted. Her heart seemed to shudder to a stop, then start again at a thunderous rate.

A young man stood in the doorway, blood seeping through the white bandage that encased the stump that was once his left hand.

Test Subject #139, she presumed. God, he looked so young, so haunted, with dark shadows under his eyes and skin stretched across gaunt features, as though he was half starved. His eyes narrowed when he met her gaze. Natalie gulped as his mouth tightened over fangs and a thunderous growl erupted from his throat. He hunched forward and Natalie flinched at the sound of his bones breaking, reforming, as hair sprang up all over his body. Fabric tore as his body morphed and, in seconds, a growling werewolf, one paw missing, glared up at her.

She swallowed, holding out a shaking hand. It was just a ghost. Just a ghost. "Nice doggy," she said hoarsely, closing her eyes as the wolf launched at her. Just a gho— Her eyes flicked open in horror as she felt claws sink into her shoulder.

Chapter 12

Lucien turned toward the bunker entrance. Was that…? He heard the scream again, terrified and pain-filled, and his throat closed up. He raced toward the dark opening, stopping just short of being fried and flung off the side of the mountain. His heart hammered in his chest. No, no, no. He raised his hands to his head. Damn it. Just like when Mom died. The inability to act, to rescue, to *save*, ate at him like acid on an open wound. He couldn't let this end badly, not like Mom. He had to get in there. He had to help Natalie. He glanced back down the mountain. The figures halted, as though they, too, had heard the screams, then he saw them pick up their pace.

He turned back to eye the bunker. He couldn't get in there. Natalie was inside, being hurt, being frightened, and yet again he couldn't do anything to help her, to save her.

He picked up a branch and hurled it at the cavity, growling as it sailed through the opening. The barrier didn't stop *that* from entering.

A branch snapped behind him and he whirled. The first had arrived.

"You're not welcome here," the man said. He was brawny, broad-shouldered and muscular beneath his plaid shirt and grass- and mud-stained jeans. With a thick beard, a baseball cap and a brutal expression, he looked like a lumberjack spoiling for a fight. He raised a handgun and aimed it at Lucien. Human then. A shifter would just shift and a vampire would just come at him. Only humans kept their distance.

Lucien lengthened his fangs, growling at the threat the man presented. Natalie was inside and this *fool* was wasting his time. His eyes glowed with bloodlust. "Leave. Now."

The man shook his head. "Nope. This is *our* mountain." He cocked the gun and fired, and Lucien dodged the shot. The bullet lodged in the trunk of the tree behind him and he caught a brief glimpse of the carved base. A wooden bullet. He sneered as he turned to face the enemy who was already cocking the gun for another shot.

Lucien launched himself, changing angle at the last minute as the man withdrew a wooden stake and held it in a defensive stance. The man lashed out. Lucien ducked, punched him in the gut and then danced back. "Give it up," he told the man. "I'm faster than you. Stronger. Give up and go back."

The man shook his head, baring his teeth as he changed his grip and threw the stake at Lucien's chest. Lucien twisted to the side, avoiding the weapon, then struck out with his feet, catching his opponent behind the knees and sending him crashing to the ground.

Lightning fast, Lucien raced behind him and caught

him, one arm snaking around the man's shoulders as he grasped his chin. "You made the wrong decision," he whispered to the man. He dipped his fangs toward the man's neck and smelled the verbena on him just in time. The man chuckled when he sensed Lucien's hesitation. Annoyed, Lucien snapped the man's neck. He dropped the body to the ground, staring grimly down at the man. "I refuse to be killed by a lumberjack."

His blood chilled as he heard yet another sound, although this one sounded more like a yell than a scream.

"Natalie," he roared through the opening.

Natalie screamed as she fell back under the weight of the lycan, the pack on her back breaking her fall. Her shock wore off almost immediately as he snapped at her. She dodged his jaws, grabbed the bloodied stump of a paw and dug her nails into the wound.

The werewolf howled, reeling back off her. She rolled to her feet and burst out into the hall. She started running down the corridor, gasping in fear as she rounded the corner into the security zone, and saw more shadows materializing down the other halls. She could see eyes glowing red in the dark as the vampires caught the scent of her blood. Could hear the growls and grunts as the shifters morphed into their predatory forms. More alarmingly, she saw humans stumbling along, leaving trails of blood on the walls as they yelled at her. Oh, God. There were so many of them, so many ghosts, and all of them were, fundamentally, royally pissed off.

She tore down the corridor that led to the main chamber, bumping against walls as the ghosts of the guards tried to haul her back. What the hell? She struggled against them. This wasn't supposed to happen. Damn it, ghosts shouldn't be able to hurt the living. She tripped, fell. She kicked off the hand of one of the guards, saw him weave a little. She stumbled to her feet, ran.

She could hear a low growl right behind her then felt a force hit her square on the back, and she went down. Whatever was attacking her was trying to rip and bite its way through her backpack.

She struggled out of the straps and took off running again, her hand sliding to her thigh. She glanced behind her. The bobcat that had tackled her seemed to be staggering to catch up.

Natalie continued to run. She grasped the handle of the machete and slid it out of the sheath as she felt the warm breath of something unreal on her neck. She didn't look—she just let out a yell as she swung back with all her might.

She heard the scream, felt the slight resistance as her blade met flesh for the briefest of moments, but she didn't look back. She skidded around the corner of the hallway, pulling the gate closed behind her. She ran across the main chamber, past the old Jeep, and kept running. Her legs pounded along the concrete corridor, her arms pumped, and all the while dark shadows chased her in her peripheral vision.

She rounded the corner too fast and crashed into the wall. She could hear the barking, the baying of the wolves behind her, and then she heard the thunderous roar of a bear.

Natalie swallowed as she felt along the tunnel wall for balance, forcing her legs to move. Each time they attacked her, they taxed themselves, but she didn't know how long she could stand their onslaught. Her thigh muscles were burning. Sweat ran down the side of her temple, and she slashed with her machete, hearing the pained howl of a wolf this time as her blade caught him. She lifted her other hand to the silver lariat at her neck, giving the quick twist-and-jerk movement that undid the intricate knot. She swung it out wide, using it like a whip to lash at the shadows. The ghosts disappeared in a puff of black at the contact, only to rematerialize moments later.

"Natalie!"

She ran toward the sound, panting harshly as the corridor inclined. She could see a lone figure standing in the opening, arms outstretched. *Lucien.*

The dark shadows overtook her toward the end and she sobbed as the massive door started to close. She smashed into a wall as a furry figure hurled itself against her. She raised her machete, felt something warm and wet splatter her shirt, and the wolf sagged to the floor then disappeared in a dark puff of wind. She swung the lariat around, trying to clear a path through the shadows that were surprisingly substantial.

She lurched forward, forcing herself to run, to lash out at anything that reached for her. She screamed as a claw ripped at her side and she launched herself through the narrowing gap.

Lucien caught her before she hit the ground and the door swung shut behind her.

Lucien scooped up Natalie, hissing at the contact of silver against his flesh. He glanced down. She clutched her silver chain in her fist. While he watched, she looped the chain twice around her neck with trembling fingers, her eyes wide and panicked as she tried to fight him off.

"Easy, minx, I've got you," he whispered. It took a conscious effort to keep his voice low and calm in the face of her panic. He could feel her shaking in his arms. She was hurt. Her clothes were torn, blood seeped from various cuts and grazes. Now was not the time for explanations, though. He had her, she was safe. He could stop mashing this situation with the night his mother died and simply focus on Natalie, on keeping her safe.

A shot rang out and Lucien ducked, hissing as the bullet grazed his shoulder. Silver. Damn it, these folks were beginning to piss him off. He ran across the trail and jumped off the edge, sailing through the air. His grip tightened on Natalie, who turned and wrapped her arms around his neck. She screamed when she realized they were falling.

Eyes focused on the ground rushing up to them, Lucien landed in a clearing, his knees and ankles absorbing the force of their landing. He backed up, ran, and jumped again, leaping down the side of Mount Solitude at a speed that the humans simply couldn't keep up with. Trees, branches, leaves—all whizzed past them in a blur. He heard another shot ring out, heard the bullet thunk into a tree several yards to his right. Natalie buried her face in his neck. He wanted to ask her to drop the machete that rested flat-side against his chest, but he didn't want to slow down.

He needed to get Natalie to safety. That desire burned inside him, driving him with each twist, each leap, each step he took. Several leaps later, he landed at the base of the mountain and raced through the undergrowth toward his car. He reached the edge of the clearing and hunkered down low, listening. Nobody was guarding his car. His lips tightened. The fools probably thought he and Natalie would never get off the mountain.

He jogged over to the car and jostled Natalie slightly as he pressed the button on the key in his jeans' pocket. He opened the door, placed her gently on the passenger seat and grasped her hands, pulling at them until she finally let go and he could release his neck from her grip. He slammed the door, raced around and in minutes was speeding down the mountain road toward Devil's Leap. It was the middle of the night now, and most of the lights had been turned off, with only the occasional bar or streetlamp shedding a glow into the darkness. He didn't slow down, just sped through town and took the turn for the interstate.

It wasn't until they were on the blacktop, the ride smoothing out, that he glanced over at Natalie. She was trying to pull her gloves on, but she was shaking so badly she couldn't fit her fingers into the sleeves. She hadn't put her seat belt on. He leaned over and pulled the belt across her body and clicked it into place. She was mildly distracted by that, then her gaze slid back to the gloves and he could see her frustration, her confusion. Damn it, what the hell happened? He glanced in the rearview mirror. Nobody was following them.

"Are you hurt?" He pulled the car over to the side of the road and kept the engine idling, just in case.

She shook her head slowly, but from the stunned look on her face, he could have asked if she was female and she'd probably give him the same response. Damn it, she was scaring the crap out of him.

"Natalie, are you hurt?" He twisted in his seat and reached for her, pulling her shirt sleeves up. His heart hammered as he looked for her injuries. He had to help her. Her arms were bloodied, yet when he gently stroked, the skin beneath was smooth. Her shirt was splattered with blood. He swallowed, especially when he saw the ragged, bloody fabric on the side. He lifted the shirt, despite her halfhearted protest, and sucked in his breath.

She had a nasty, deep cut, but even as he watched, he could see the skin slowly closing, healing, until all that was left was smooth, taut skin. What the hell? She wasn't a vampire, though, and she sure as hell wasn't lycan. But she could self-heal? He remembered the conversation they'd had back at her house, how she'd tried to end her life but nothing had stuck. Now he could see why. She was immortal.

He grasped her hand. It was cold and he could feel the tremors deep inside. She was shaking like a leaf. He gently helped her drag on her gloves. He was relieved that, despite being hurt, she looked like she was going to be okay. Physically. The scent of blood wasn't quite so strong anymore, now that her injuries were healing. He raised his hand to her face, turning her to him. Her eyes shocked him. The hazel color almost consumed by dark gray, they looked hollow. Haunted.

"You left a few things out, didn't you?" he murmured softly, gently.

She nodded, her eyes brimming with tears. He wanted to roar; he wanted to rant—but not at her. He wanted to go after what had dared strike her, cut her, bleed her—and rend it limb from limb. He wanted to destroy what had frightened her, what had damaged her, but he didn't know what that was. He'd seen her run toward him, her eyes wide with terror, flinching as she was cut. He'd seen her being thrown against walls, watched as she'd wielded her machete and whipped her lariat around like some sort of warrior—against the night air. And he'd never felt more helpless, or more enraged, as he'd watch her get hurt. But while ranting and raging would definitely make him feel better, it wasn't what was desperately needed at this time. It wasn't what Natalie needed. He exhaled, dredging up some calm from God only knew where.

"Mind telling me what happened?" He kept his tone low and soothing, injecting what he hoped was the perfect amount of mild curiosity.

Her mouth opened and it looked like it took a couple of attempts before she managed to make a sound.

"I—I saw the ghosts," she whispered. A tear fell, tracking slowly down her cheek, and his heart cracked at the pain and grief he saw in her face. Then her words registered and he tilted his head, his brow dipping.

"What?"

"The ghosts. I saw them." She licked her lips and took a deep breath as she met his eyes, all vulnerable and unguarded. "I—I see dead people, Lucien. All the time."

He digested her words for a moment. Ghosts. Dead people. Oo-kay. Not quite what he was expecting. "We need to talk, but not here. We're going back to the roost. I know we'll both be safe there."

It said so much about her current state that Natalie didn't protest or try to launch from his car at his words. She meekly nodded and rested her head against the car seat.

He turned back in his seat and drove the car onto the

road. Dead people. *She sees dead people. Of course she sees dead people. Because that's completely normal. Not.*

Chapter 13

Natalie followed Lucien through the hotel reception area. She hadn't balked when he'd driven into the tunnel. Strangely, after what had happened on the mountain, staying at a roost didn't bother her as much as it should have. She still wore her machete strapped to her thigh, and she could see the other vampires eyeing it assessingly. That's okay, let them try. She still had her custom-made lariat lash around her neck and the knife in her boot, but more than that, she had the man walking alongside her. He'd waited for her. He hadn't left. She'd fallen into his arms and he'd whipped her away from danger. She'd heard the shot, felt him flinch. He'd put his body on the line to keep her safe. Now, here, she trusted him to keep doing that, to keep her safe.

Although he did seem to be operating a little on autopilot. She guessed he was still trying to process what she'd divulged in the car. She touched the shirt she now wore. She was still wearing her gloves, could only guess at the feel of it. It looked soft, comfortable. It was Lucien's. He'd insisted she take her shirt off. It was ripped and bloodstained beyond repair, and would act like an invitation to the other guests staying at the roost. His shirt felt warm and soft against her skin, and had smelled like him, all sexy male. She glanced under her lashes toward him. He'd left his jacket back on the mountain, along with his pack. Now he strutted through reception shirtless, looking like some fierce warrior god who was ready for a fight.

A tall man with brown hair stood behind the reception desk, talking to the attendant. When he looked up, his eyebrows rose as he watched them walk by. He then pulled out a card from the supply packed neatly on the desk, typed something into the computer and flicked a keycard across the space. Natalie watched as it spun through the air. Lucien caught it effortlessly, not even slowing as he escorted her through the lobby.

The cool light shone silver on his skin, and his eyes glowed red at some of the vampires in the lobby as they stared at Natalie. She noticed all of them avert their eyes in the face of Lucien's stare. He looked…intense. Battle-ready. She knew it; she could see it. He looked fierce and resolute. He guided her into the elevator and stood in front of her, arms folded, glaring back into the lobby and preventing any other vampire from entering the elevator, if they were so inclined. None of them seemed to have a death wish, though, so when the doors closed it was just her and Lucien inside. He stood with his back to her, eyeing the gauge above the doors. She eyed his back. All smooth skin, she frowned when she noticed a red gash on his shoulder. It looked painful. Although it was healing, it was doing so at a slower rate than she'd expect. She placed her gloved hand on his shoulder blade.

He stilled at her touch, then turned his head, but not enough to meet her eyes.

"You're hurt," she whispered, not sure how to hide her concern.

"It's just a graze. Silver bullet. Takes a little longer to heal." His words were clipped, but his tone was gentle.

He really had put his body on the line for her. "Thank you," she murmured.

He turned to face her, a light frown marring his handsome features. His blue eyes were troubled as he met her gaze. He opened his mouth but hesitated. He reached for her, pulling her against him, and enfolded her in his arms against the warmth of his muscled chest. Her eyes widened in surprise as he hugged her tightly and lay his cheek on her head. She could hear his heart beating against her ear, could smell him, all manly musk from the hike and their escape down the mountain. She hesitated then slid her arms around his lean waist and hugged him back. He was so warm, so strong. So... protective.

He held her that way, his hand caressing her shoulder in small circles, an oddly comforting gesture, until the elevator dinged and the doors slid open. She tilted her head, expecting him to step back, but he remained where he was, eyeing her. The doors started to close and his hand shot out. His bicep bunched as he prevented the doors from closing, and he eventually stepped out, his hand sliding down her arm to clasp her hand. He didn't say a word, and she found it hard to read him, to figure out what exactly was going on inside his head. He hadn't said anything about her ability to see ghosts, but she didn't get the impression he was ignoring it. No, Lucien Marchetta was quietly assessing the facts and would discuss it when he was ready. Well, if he didn't want to talk about it, that was fine by her. She couldn't believe she'd admitted it to him in the first place.

They walked, hand in hand, to their room. As soon as they were inside and the door was closed, Lucien led her to the sofa and took one of the armchairs opposite her. She eyed him. He really was a gorgeous man. Broad shoulders, smooth skin, and muscles that rippled with his every move. Not that she should be noticing this at all.

His expression was calm, his tone mild. "Now, where were we? Oh, yes. Ghosts. You were saying?"

Okay, so apparently he was ready to discuss it now. She took a deep breath, regretting her lapse from before, but he shook his head, as though he could see her trying to figure a way out of this conversation.

"Oh, no, you don't. Tell me. What do you mean by ghosts? And what happened back there?"

Did he realize he was sitting there without a shirt? And he expected her to concentrate? Okay, so maybe she was treating that gorgeous chest as an easy distraction, a way to avoid talking about something she found really difficult to talk about. Knowing Lucien, though, he wouldn't be satisfied unless he got to the heart of the matter. She sighed.

"When I... When I died, something...happened." She shrugged. "I'm not quite sure what, but when I was revived, I could see people that nobody else could." She folded her arms, her mouth turning down at the memory. "Initially, when they told the press I'd died, they had to hide me somewhere... When I started to speak to people who weren't there, they hid me in the psychiatric ward."

She smiled bitterly. "My injuries healed, my white blood cell count went up. I was the first person to be cured of this type of cancer, and they thought I was going mad due to the trauma of losing my parents." She shrugged. "To be honest, they weren't too far off the truth. I was a mess when I realized they were truly gone and I was left. I had cancer as a kid. We all thought I'd die before them. I'd never once considered that I might outlive them." She took a deep breath. "Do you…do you know how many people die in those wards? How many ghosts walk the halls of a hospital?" She shuddered as she remembered that time.

"You…see ghosts," Lucien repeated carefully. As though he was considering the insane idea might actually have merit.

She nodded. "I know how crazy it sounds, but sometimes if I touch an object, it's like waking up any ghosts attached to it."

His gaze dropped to her hands. "The gloves." It wasn't a question; he was just stating a simple fact as he put the facts together.

She nodded. "Yeah, it helps minimize contact."

"What is it like? I mean, when you see a ghost?" He looked around the room. "Are there any here, now?"

She smiled, surprised by the humor that tugged at her lips. "Uh, no. That book is in the car—"

"That book? Our book? *Our* book has a ghost?" He leaned forward, surprised.

"Yes. Her name is Courtney, and she was a student who was studying the poem when her school bus crashed." Natalie winced. She'd had a nice little chat with Courtney back in Westamoor.

"Is she…is she an angry spirit?" Lucien asked hesitantly, and then rolled his eyes. "I don't even know what I'm saying. Spirit, ghost—how does this all work?"

Well, at least he wasn't calling her all kinds of crazy. That was a good start, right? Natalie rubbed her arms and her brow dipped. "I'm not quite sure," she admitted. "I thought I understood, but…" She took a deep breath. "Okay, so people die. Sometimes they must go on to some sort of happy place, whatever that might be. Other times, they may attach to something, or someone… They get confused and hang around what's familiar, I guess." She carried around her mother's locket, on the off chance she might actually see her parents again, but as yet that hadn't happened, may never happen.

Lucien's eyes narrowed, his blue gaze glittering as he tilted his head to the side. "Is there a ghost at the institute?"

Her cheeks warmed. "Yes. His name is Rupert, and he's very sweet. He died of a heart attack during one of his lectures, way before my time."

"He threw the book at me, didn't he?" Lucien stated, leaning his elbow on the armrest of the chair.

She tried not to stare at the play of muscles across his chest.

"He's a little protective, sometimes," she acceded. "He's also been a ghost for so long, he's learned a few tricks. But when that book hit you in the face, it wasn't Rupert. That was…unusual."

Lucien's eyebrows rose. "*Another* ghost?" He frowned. "What do you mean 'unusual'?"

"Most ghosts can't move anything. Rupert has learned a few tricks, but that's because he was a professor of occult studies and has spent all of his time trying to figure out how to communicate from beyond the

grave. Ghosts are—" she gestured with her hands, trying to find the right word "—ethereal. Insubstantial."
She nodded. Then frowned. "Mostly."

"Mostly?"

"Well, other than Rupert, Grace Perkins is the only ghost I know who could control an object's movement." She winced. "She's the one who hit you in the face with her diary. You pissed her off by reading it."

"Officer Pumpkin?" Lucien glanced warily around the room.

"And because you couldn't get her name right," Natalie sighed.

"She's the one who told you about the bunker, isn't she?"

Natalie nodded. "Yes."

He nodded then leaned back in his chair, and she got a good look at his naked torso, the smooth skin rippling over a washboard stomach. Her mouth dried. She forced herself to remember— *this is Lucien.* The guy who used to read her bedtime stories, who sat with her teddy bears and played tea parties, who wasn't there for her when she needed him—like he'd promised—and who'd later threatened Ned Henderson and everyone else she cared for. She shouldn't be noticing how his pecs dance when he gestured with his arms or how temptingly low his pants rode. Geez. She must be in shock from the mountain. Shock made you lose all sense of rationality and self-respect, right? Shock could make you horny…?

"What happened at the bunker?" he asked her quietly.

Oh, wow. Way to kill the mood. She rose from her seat, rubbing her arms briskly. She couldn't get warm, damn it. She felt so chilled. Shocked. "It was horrible," she whispered.

Almost immediately she felt warmth at her back. Lucien's arms enveloped her, pulling her back against his chest. He wrapped his arms around her, as though trying to share his warmth. It stirred a heat within her, something that was at once comforting and comfortable but also stimulating, as though her senses were finally awakening after a prolonged slumber.

"I was really worried about you," he said, his voice husky. "I didn't know what was going on..."

She swallowed, staring at the black-and-white artwork on the wall. Her arm muscles clenched as she remembered the corridor, those dark shadows, the pain...

"Ghosts aren't supposed to be substantial. Those ghosts—they fed on emotion, I think. Fear and anger—*their* fear and anger—made them strong." She thought about the horrific information she'd read in the reports. If even a fraction of that was true, she could see why they were so angry.

"They tortured them, Lucien," she whispered, her eyes welling with tears as she remembered that teenage boy's report. "What they did in that bunker to the shadow breeds—it was too cruel. There are a lot of ghosts down there, Lucien. A lot of angry, violent ghosts." She didn't like vampires or werewolves, but she'd never considered abuse of the breeds as an appropriate reaction. She would defend herself when necessary, but she wouldn't actively look for ways to hurt them.

"They hurt you." He rubbed her arms and she relaxed under his gentle caress.

"Yeah, I was taken by surprise. I think something really bad happened down there, Lucien. Worse than the experiments. I've only seen human ghosts, but down there, there are vampires, shifters…" She shuddered as she recalled the growl of the bear, the claw ripping into her…that boy with the missing hand. "They are angry, but I sense that they have good reason to be."

Her eyes widened and she spun to face him. He jerked his head back to avoid being whipped by her hair.

"I almost forgot—I think I found something," she said.

He gaped at her for a moment then shook his head. "Natalie, you were hurt. You're done."

"No. There might be a flower—"

"A flower?" Every time he thought he got close to a cure for his sister, there was a setback and another bloodied bunny dangled in front of him to chase. But this time, Natalie had been hurt.

"Okay, maybe more like a weed, found in the desert. We could—"

"No, Natalie. No more. Do you have any idea what I was going through outside?" he said to her, his voice low and harsh. His hands rose to grip her shoulders, his lips tightened. "I could hear you screaming inside, Natalie, and I couldn't get to you. I was stuck outside because of that damn witch barrier spell and, for all I knew, you were dying inside. Do you have any idea what that did to me?" he finished on a pained whisper, his eyes touring her face. "I thought I was losing you, all over again."

His hands rose to cup her cheeks as he lowered his mouth to her lips.

* * *

Her lips were so soft, so gentle, beneath his, Lucien thought. He heard her gasp and he seized the opportunity, sliding his tongue between her lips. His hands delved into her hair, the strands sliding between his fingers like ribbons of silk.

He thought he'd lost her again, back there. He'd been paralyzed by fear. Fear for her. It had stirred up so much anger and pain, hearing her cry out, and him not being able to help her. He'd felt trapped in a vortex, reliving that night of his mother's death. Right now, though, with her safe in his arms, he felt relieved, calmer, stronger than he had in a long time.

He kissed her, taking his time, his hands tangling in her hair, destroying the remnants of her ponytail as he angled his head to kiss her deeper. Holding her, kissing her, he could convince himself she really was safe, really was okay.

There was a discrete knock at the door, one that he was fully prepared to ignore, but she started in his arms. Stiffened. He moaned. Damn it. Whoever was on the other side of that door was going to cop hell from him.

He ended the kiss slowly, pressing gentle kisses against her pouting lips. She wasn't fighting him off, wasn't trying to withdraw from him. That encouraged him, but it also confused him. Each time they'd kissed, he'd been injured. This time, though, she wasn't throwing him across a room, and no ghosts were hurling books at him. No, she'd kissed him back. He raised his head to look at her directly. Her eyes reflected desire warring with confusion, with skepticism. Yeah, he could relate to that.

The knock sounded again, a little louder, a little

firmer. His lips tightened and he let her go. He strode over to the door and peered through the peephole. He felt his shoulder muscles tense. Damn it.

"You might want to go to your room for this," he said, turning briefly to glance at Natalie. She stood there in the sunken living area, all beautifully tousled, her lips swollen. God, just looking at her made him hard as a rock.

Not a reaction he wanted to experience with this particular person at the door, though.

She folded her arms, frowning. "Are you seriously trying to send me to my room, old man? That's not going to happen."

He sighed. Shrugged. Winced at the slight pull of skin at the bullet graze in his shoulder. "Fine, your choice. Don't say I didn't warn you, though."

He opened the door, keeping hold of it as he leaned against the doorjamb, effectively blocking the entrance to the vampire standing on the other side.

"What do you want, Enzo?"

Enzo stood there in his dark suit, with his dark hair slicked back, his brown eyes gazing past him into the room. "I'm here for an update for your father."

Lucien leaned forward slightly, using his bulk to shield the room from the guardian prime's gaze. "If there was something to tell, I'd let you know. For the last time, scram." He started to close the door but Enzo's fist slammed against the timber.

"Why were you up at Devil's Leap?" the guardian asked in a silky tone.

Lucien's eyes narrowed. "Hmm. I know for a fact that you didn't follow us…" He'd taken measures to avoid that very thing, including using Heath to distract

Enzo when he was leaving. Realization dawned and his lips pursed. "There's a tracking device on my car, isn't there?" God, how could he have been so dense? No wonder Enzo was able to find him everywhere.

"Tell me what you found—and why Devil's Leap?"

Lucien realized Enzo would have only been able to track him to the car park at the bottom of the mountain and wouldn't know where they'd gone from there. He wouldn't know about the bunker. He heard Natalie move behind him, sensed her approaching until he could feel her presence behind him. His gaze remained on the guardian, though.

"Devil's Leap saw some heavy shadow breeds traffic before The Troubles," Lucien stated brusquely. If he gave Enzo something, maybe the guardian would leave them alone. "We were just checking the area to see if there was something we could use."

"And did you? Find something?"

Lucien kept his expression neutral. For some reason he wasn't ready to share anything with this vampire, with his father. Natalie had mentioned some sort of weed, but, really, that could amount to nothing.

He shook his head as Enzo narrowed his gaze on Natalie and demanded, "What did you find?"

He heard her contemptuous snort. "I don't owe you any explanations." She moved away. "I'm going to bed."

"I second that." Lucien smiled at the guardian and started to close the door.

Enzo's eyes flashed red. "If she's unable to give us anything, she's outlived her usefulness."

Lucien stilled. Natalie halted in the sunken living area and he heard her swift intake of breath. Lucien met the vampire's eyes with his own determined gaze.

"She's not a loose end to be tied up, Enzo. She's helping us, and she's under the protection of the Nightwing
Vampire Prime," he said in a moderate tone.

Enzo tried to step forward but Lucien blocked him.
The guardian glared at him. "If you found something—
if she knows anything—we have to protect that information."

Lucien's eyes narrowed. "Whatever happens, at the
end of this, Natalie will be free to return to her life,
untroubled by any of us," he told the guardian. "I don't
know what my father expects, but that will be the reality."

"We are talking about a cure for a lycan's bite," Enzo
said in a low voice. "How do you see that working? If
it's not kept secret, everyone will want it. The other
vampire colonies will fight us for it. The lycans will
fight to destroy it. The witches and humans will want
to destroy it, too. We have to protect it."

"What are you implying, Enzo?"

"If anyone else finds out what you may have found,
or be close to finding, they will try to take that cure
off you, or prevent you from finding it altogether. We
can't let that information get out. If she has nothing to
offer, she needs to be silenced."

Lucien ignored the sound Natalie's machete made
as she drew it from her sheath. He shook his head in
disbelief. "Has this been my father's plan all along? If
that was the case, I've spoken to many people about
this search for the cure. Is he going to kill them, too?"

Enzo shot him a deadpan glance and Lucien's shoulders sagged as realization hit. "He's already done it,
hasn't he?" Horror filled him at the implications. "My

father has killed people whose only crime is that they spoke with *me*." He shook his head. "That's barbaric."

Enzo shrugged. "Your father can't be blamed if those people met with accidents..."

"It's wrong," he responded, aghast his father would operate in such a way. And now they wanted to "silence" Natalie? For *helping* them? No, damn it.

He leaned forward. "I know that I'm a temporary fill-in to the vampire prime post until my sister recovers," he said, "but believe me when I say that if you mess with me on this, you mess with Nightwing, and my father's name will not protect you from my wrath." He let his eyes flash red.

"Your father was right to send me to watch—" Enzo sneered "—this is your mother all over again."

Lucien resisted the urge to punch his father's guardian square in the face. "This has nothing to do with my mother, and you'd do well never to mention her name in my presence again. I have a tendency to lash out. You've been warned. Now, run back to Papa. This conversation is over."

He pushed Enzo out of the doorway—admittedly with a little more force than necessary, but he did enjoy the surprise on the guardian's face when he flew across the hall and crashed into the wall opposite. Lucien slammed the door shut, locked it and then watched through the peephole as Enzo picked himself up and dusted himself off. The guardian glared at the door, the muscle in his jaw ticking, and then he stormed off down the hall.

Lucien eyed the crack in the plaster left behind by the guardian. He'd ask Heath to put it on his tab.

He turned to find Natalie staring at him, a slight

frown on her face. "What did he mean with that crack about your mother?"

"Nothing," Lucien muttered as he stalked across the room toward his bedroom. "We should probably get some sleep."

Natalie shook her head. "No, that vampire was ready to tie up this little loose end, as you so nicely put it, so I want to know why. What did he mean this was your mother all over again?"

Lucien looked over at her. She'd planted her feet, hands on hips, chin up—just like she'd done that night when she was twelve and insisted she really was well enough to visit the Marchetta night garden.

The night his mom died.

"My father blames me for my mother's death."

Chapter 14

The admission brought forth old hurts and he stalked toward one of the bedrooms in an effort to distance himself from them, if only by shutting down the conversation. Natalie's hand flashed out, catching his arm, her expression confused. "Why would he think that?"

"Because maybe I *am* responsible for my mother's death." It had been several years since the event but, even now, the pain and guilt weighed heavily on him. Her hand slid from his arm. He didn't think she noticed the retreat, the physical withdrawal…but he did.

"But—your mother died in the Nemuritor Ball fire, didn't she?" Natalie said, her brow wrinkling. It had been a horrific tragedy. The ball had been held in the historical ballroom on Pier Sixty-One, and the whole pier had burned that night. "You couldn't have killed your mother. You were with me that night."

He looked away. "I'm going to bed." He wasn't going to discuss this with her. He strode into the bedroom, flicking the light switch on as he went. The bedside lamps turned on, giving his room a subdued light over the bed, the rest of the bedroom still hidden in gloom.

"Lucien, please, why does your father think your mother's death is your fault?"

Damn it, she'd followed him in. He gestured to the door but she pointedly ignored him. He sighed. "Leave it alone, Natalie. It happened so long ago, it's water under the bridge."

"Well, apparently not," she stated, walking further into his room. "Not if your father's guardian thinks it's happening all over again. What does he mean?"

"I don't want to talk about this. Let's just get some sleep and I'll drive you home tomorrow night." He leaned over and pulled the covers back on the bed.

"That was the night you took me to your night garden," she said.

He whirled on her, angry that she was pushing, prodding him for information he didn't want to give. Angry for the memories the conversation was stirring up. The guilt. The pain. "I'm not talking about this with you."

She didn't even blink, damn it. Her chin rose. "Why not? I could go to your father, explain to him—"

He laughed in derision. "Explain what? That the reason I snuck out of that ball and left my mother to her socializing was because I had promised to take some sick little twelve-year-old to visit our night garden?"

He instantly regretted his words as dread crept into her gaze. "What?" she asked, her voice low and hoarse.

He closed his eyes briefly. Damn. He'd never wanted this conversation with her—with anyone. He hadn't even told Vivianne. He rested his hands on his hips and sighed.

"I'd promised to take you to our night garden, so

once Mom and I arrived at the ball and she'd settled into her cozy group of friends, I snuck out. The plan was to take you for that visit, see you safely back home, and then return to my mother's side, hopefully without her noticing my absence." His lips tightened over his teeth in a bitter smile. "They locked all the exits and then set the fire. If any of the vampires had managed to escape, they would have ended up in the harbor."

He winced. Trinity Harbor was a saltwater port, and highly corrosive to vampires. The vampires who had managed to jump from the burning building had died an excruciating death in the water as the salt ate at their skin. He could still remember arriving at the scene, aghast at the flames shooting into the night sky, cringing at the screams of the vampires trapped within. He couldn't get in to save his mother, the flames too hot, too high, too volatile. Those screams still haunted him…he'd never quite managed to escape the nightmare of his imagination. Those dreams of what his mother must have experienced still occasionally caught him by surprise.

He shrugged, trying to mask his pain behind a pragmatic front. "My father feels that I shouldn't have abandoned my mother when she most needed me." And he'd been trying to make up for that ever since.

Natalie folded her arms around her middle and turned away from him. "I'm so sorry," she said finally. He frowned. Her words carried sympathy, but they were also heavily laden with guilt. He shook his head as he came up behind her, his hands rising to rest on her shoulders.

"It wasn't your fault, Natalie. Nobody was ever

brought to justice for that attack on the vamps, but you had nothing to do with it."

"But I took you away from your mother," she said in a voice that was so soft, so full of remorse, it was almost childlike.

"Well, as you pointed out before, if I'd remained, I would have died along with her," he said, pushing away at the guilt. Ever since that night he'd tried to make it up to his father, tried to compensate for abandoning his mother, as his father put it. He'd become very protective, fierce, even, when it came to taking care of his family, of their interests. He'd successfully built up a division of the Marchetta empire that easily swamped its previous success. His father had changed, though. Vincent Marchetta had sworn vengeance against the lycans, the party everyone suspected guilty of the deed but could not prove responsible. His father had been working against them ever since.

"You left for the west coast after that." Did she realized she'd swayed toward him? He slid his hands down her arms and gathered her close, his hands resting lightly on her hips. He should focus on the conversation. But she was wearing his shirt and looked so damn sexy in it...

He blinked. "I did." It had been for the best. His presence was an irritant to his father, a reminder that for every day Lucien lived, his departed wife did not. While Vincent still viewed his actions that night as abandoning his mother at her most vulnerable moment, of betraying the Marchetta family in the worst possible manner, he'd stopped short of disowning him. Everyday since, Lucien had tried to make it up to his father. He'd worked his butt off on the west coast. Now, with

Vivianne in the state she was, if he didn't find a cure, he feared his father would blame him for her death, too. But despite his father's plans, and his desire to support his father, he couldn't allow Natalie to die simply for trying to help them. He would never support that. She was becoming far too important to him.

She shook her head and he felt the strands tickle his chin. "And now your father blames you for her death. I need to see him, explain to him—I'm so sorry."

He was stunned. She was concerned—about *him*. She wanted to go to Vincent to defend him, to try to repair that relationship. That realization overwhelmed him. She'd said she didn't like vampires—or werewolves, and really, he was in total agreement with that one—but now she felt sympathy, guilt and regret—for *him*. Ever since his mother died, he'd tried to protect those he loved, and now this woman wanted to protect him. A wave of possessiveness swept through him. He couldn't let her walk away when this whole thing was over, damn it.

He buried his nose in her hair, closing his eyes and inhaling. Her scent, that sweet spice—innocent invitation—curled inside him, awakening a fierce sense of protectiveness and a healthy dose of hot arousal. "You do realize you're in my room, next to my bed..." His voice emerged from his throat in a low rumble.

"Do you—?" Her voice came out all breathless and whispery. She cleared her throat. "Do you want me to leave?" Her words were polite, but she tilted her head to the side, exposing the delicate line of her jaw and neck to his lips.

"I don't think I can let you go," he said, his voice rumbling against the tender spot just behind her ear.

Both physically, in the now, and metaphorically, in the future, he didn't think he could let her go. Not willingly. Not without a fight. He felt her tremble in his arms. He pressed a kiss at the spot where her ear, jaw and throat converged in a creamy column. He was conscious of using lips instead of teeth. He didn't want to spook her.

"You—you might have to," she murmured huskily, leaning her head back against his shoulder. He smiled against her skin and gently lifted his cotton shirt, moving nice and slow until he could run his fingers across the bare, smooth skin above the waistband of her jeans. Her stomach muscles clenched beneath his touch and he saw her lips part on a sexy little gasp.

He used his other hand to grasp her hair and turn her head gently toward him. Her eyes were all beautiful golds with streaks of gray. "Never," he whispered, taking her lips in a possessive kiss.

Natalie closed her eyes and moaned, and Lucien's tongue slid inside her mouth to rub against hers. His hand tightened in her hair and her stomach dipped as he caressed her abdomen. His hand was beneath her shirt.

Heat swept over her and she relaxed against his chest. His body supported hers, his groin cradling her buttocks, and she could feel his cock hardening, lengthening, pressing into her cleft. Her breasts swelled and she arched her back as his fingers danced over her skin, rising beneath the shirt. Her heart pounded heavily in her chest.

She slid one arm up over her head, sliding her fingers through his hair, her other hand lowering to rest on the side of his hip. All the while his tongue toyed with hers, licking, gliding. He tilted his head, changing the angle, deepening the penetration.

She moaned again, barely recognizing the sound as her own. Her nipples pebbled and she shuddered when he trailed his finger softly across the skin just below her lace bra. Good grief, the man was touching her so delicately, so teasingly, and she felt ready to combust. Her heart pounded even faster and she pressed herself against him at the same time she arched into his touch.

His hand trailed over the top of her bra and he hissed, jerking against her. He lifted his head, his blue eyes glittering with carnal desire. "Perhaps we could lose the chain?" he suggested in a whisper against her lips. She realized she still wore her lariat chain around her neck. She slid her hand from his hip up her body, watching his gaze as he watched her movement. She skimmed over her breasts and he closed his eyes briefly.

"You're driving me crazy," he muttered then met her gaze again. She smiled as she touched the silver around her neck. Natalie hesitated. She'd commissioned this particular piece of jewelry not long after leaving the psych ward, and had grown used to its weight and the security it offered.

He dipped his head close to hers. "I'll never hurt you," he whispered.

"I know," she whispered back. She gave the unique twist-and-jerk motion and the chain slid from her neck, pooling onto the floor. She trusted him. She couldn't explain why, not logically, but inside, where it mattered, she did. She trusted him.

And it had nothing to do with the mounting sexual tension coiling inside her.

His lips took hers again and she gasped in delight

as he cupped her lace-covered breast with his hand. He let go of her hair, his hand dropping to her waist, pulling her in closer as he rubbed his cock against the cleft in her buttocks.

She writhed in answer, her core growing damp with her desire. She trembled. Despite the fact he wore no shirt, they still didn't quite touch skin to skin except where his hands skimmed her body beneath his shirt. One hand pulled down the cup of her bra, the other unfastened the button of her jeans. She moaned into his mouth as he slid her zipper down. Tormentingly slow. She reached behind her, sliding her hand between their bodies until she could feel the hard ridge of flesh pushing against his jeans.

He growled softly, the sound possessive, primitive, and he ground against her. He tore his lips from hers, kissing his way across her jaw to her neck. She trembled as his fingers slid into the opening of her jeans, beneath the lacy edge of her bikini briefs. She was so hot, so damp, her breaths coming in hot pants.

"Maybe we should—" She moaned as his finger parted her slick folds. She had no idea what she was saying, all thoughts whirling away like smoke in the wind.

His tongue flicked out along the line of her throat and he grasped her chin, tilting her head to give him more access. "Maybe we should," he said in agreement. He kissed his way down her throat as he toyed with her, his finger rubbing her clitoris.

"Uh-huh," she panted as the tension coiled within her. Sensations were bombarding her, his strength holding her up as he played with her. Her breasts swelled, her back arched. So much. Too much. She trailed her hand down his zipper. He felt so hot, so hard, throbbing through the denim and metal.

"That's it," he whispered against her, his hand sliding down to cup the breast he'd freed. He gently pinched her nipple and clitoris simultaneously, and she sucked in her breath, her eyes closing as that coil tightened further.

"Luc," she gasped as he circled her slick flesh. Her knees trembled and he slid another finger inside.

"Let go, minx. Let go." He cupped her breast, lifting it as he teased her clitoris again in a taunting little pinch, and this time those sensations burst inside her. She tilted her head back and cried out as the orgasm tore through her with surprising force, hot and ferocious.

Chapter 15

Natalie sagged in his arms, trembling. He felt ready to explode, but grappled with his desire. He wanted to thrust into her, to bring her more pleasure, to bring him some release. And if it were any other woman, he would have. But this wasn't any other woman, this was Natalie. It was too soon. They may not have fully shared their intimate attraction, but things were now different. She'd gone into that bunker, alone. To help save his sister. She hadn't had to. When he'd been barred she could have just shrugged, turned around and gone home, her end of the deal fulfilled. But, no, she'd risked her life for his personal mission, and had been injured in the process.

When he made love to Natalie—and that's what it would be, love, not some quick, brief physical interlude— he wanted her to be as fully conscious and accepting of the consequences. When he made love to her—and, yes, when, not if—he didn't want there to be any regrets, any recriminations, any retreat.

He smiled as he enveloped her in his arms, caressing her, soothing her sexual euphoria. There was no need to rush this. When they did it, they would do it right. He had no intention of walking away from her, not now. Not ever. But she'd been hurt by his breed, and he wasn't about to risk a future with Natalie by pushing her before she was ready. He could wait. Need bit at him. It would be excruciating, but he'd wait. He held her until her trembles subsided, then swept her into his arms to lay her gently on the bed. She cupped his face, meeting his gaze with a stunned yet satiated expression, her lips swollen from his kisses, her skin flushed.

"What about you?" Her voice was husky and skittered along his raw nerves. She trailed her finger across his lips and he caught it in a playful nip, then kissed it softly.

"Soon," he promised as he leaned down to kiss her on the lips. She sighed into his mouth and it took all of his control not to strip them both and finish what he'd started. He levered back from her, smiling at her heavy-lidded gaze. "We have plenty of time."

"But—" she protested.

He shook his head. "Soon," he promised again. He untied the straps of her sheath and placed it on the bedside table. He trailed his hands down her long, slender legs and removed her shoes. His eyebrows rose when a blade fell out of one of the boots.

"Protection." She sighed the explanation as she stretched on the bed.

"You can now add me to that mix," he told her quietly. He eyed her, his mouth drying when he took in her relaxed pose. Unbelievably, she was still pretty much clothed, although he must have lost some of his shirt buttons. The fabric parted to reveal her smooth, toned stomach, the fly of her jeans opened to reveal the top of her soft-pink lace panties. He swallowed as his cock throbbed. Plenty of time, he reminded himself. Good things come to those who wait, although those who wait don't necessarily come. His hands curled. Plenty of— okay, he had to leave before he joined her on that bed.

"Sleep," he whispered and backed out of the room. She watched him, blinking slowly as he retreated. She was asleep before he closed the door.

"So, where is Grace now?"

Natalie winced as she focused on her laptop, the scenery flashing past her as Lucien drove back down to the desert. The sun was setting and the hills and valleys were bathed in golds, crimsons, blues and indigos. She had convinced Lucien to detour into the desert on the way home.

"She's back at the bunker." She answered Courtney's question, glancing briefly over her shoulder. Courtney folded her arms and pouted.

"I liked her," she said in a sulky tone.

"What's going on?" Lucien asked, checking the rear-view mirror.

"Courtney is going to miss having Grace around," Natalie explained, trying to avoid eye contact with him.

"They talked to each other?"

"You told him about us?" Courtney exclaimed, leaning forward.

"Uh, yes." Natalie answered both of them and kept her gaze on the screen on her lap. It still felt a little weird, talking so openly about something only she could see and hear, and had kept hidden for so many years. It felt a lot weird, sitting in the car beside the man who'd given her so much intimate pleasure and had left her to sleep it off, acting as though it was completely normal to touch a woman deeply and then just walk away.

Didn't he want...her? Didn't he want to...with...her? Sure, she'd been, uh, satisfied, but he hadn't. She'd seen his arousal, heck, she'd felt it—but he'd walked away. Did he not find her attractive...enough? Didn't he want to go there with her?

Sex, she told herself. Sex. Why couldn't she even think of Lucien and sex in the same sentence? She fanned herself a little.

"Do you want me to adjust the air-con?" Lucien offered, glancing at her for a moment. His gaze dropped to her neckline and out of habit her fingers rose to toy with the lariat chain at her neck. His eyes heated, trailing over her, and she shook her head as she turned back to her screen.

"No, no, that's fine." And completely mortifying. "Thanks."

"Did you guys do it?" Courtney asked suddenly.

Natalie whipped around to face her. "What?" she gasped.

"What?" Lucien asked, darting around to stare at what would be an empty backseat for him.

Courtney shrugged. "You guys keep staring at each other without letting the other see. You're barely talking, but it's not like last time. You remind me of Stacy Borden and Greg Shingles after they did it. It was so obvious."

Natalie's mouth opened and closed for a moment. She didn't even know where to start with that. Her mouth dropped open again.

"Now you look like a fish," Courtney stated.

She shut her mouth with a snap then took a deep breath. "No."

"No what? What is she saying?" Lucien asked, his brow dipping in frustration at not being part of the conversation.

"Nothing," Natalie snapped. She turned to face the teen. "How old are you?"

"Oh, old enough to know how these things work," Courtney said with a little head waggle, her ponytail bouncing gently.

"How old?" Natalie persisted.

"Fine. Fourteen," Courtney said, tilting her chin in challenge.

Natalie had dealt with enough students to know when one was stretching the truth. She stared the ghost down. Courtney eventually dropped her gaze. "Soon. I'll be fourteen, soon," she muttered. "But that doesn't mean I don't see what's going on here. You and he are together now, and you abandoned Grace."

"No and no," Natalie stated, wagging her finger. "First, we're not—" She stopped, realizing that Lucien was sharing his attention between her conversation and the road, and second, that she was about to share more than he needed to hear. "It's not like that," she stated firmly. She didn't know what had happened back at the roost—well, she *knew*, she'd been a willing participant…oh, so gosh-darn willing… She blinked. Cleared her throat. From now on, whatever happened at the roost stayed at the roost. "And I didn't abandon Grace," she said in a softer voice. "There were things— ghosts—in that bunker, that she was involved in the making of. I think, really, that perhaps she needs to be there, too." Ghosts didn't kill other ghosts—they were already dead, so it wasn't like the ghosts there could do Grace any harm. But those experiments, the torture. Maybe there was a way Grace could work through her death by facing what had happened during her life, and possibly help the others trapped there.

"I'd like to go back there and exorcise those ghosts," Lucien muttered.

Courtney blanched and Natalie sighed. "I think we should leave it alone. I don't know what happened in that bunker, or why it's been closed and abandoned for so long, but I think it should stay closed."

Courtney was staring at the back of Lucien's head as though she was waiting for him to spin around and somehow hurt her.

"I'm sure Lucien didn't mean exorcising you, Courtney," she said, giving him a meaningful glance.

Lucien frowned. "Uh, no, Courtney. Not you. You just keeping on ghosting, girlfriend."

Courtney's cheeks pinked. "Did you hear that? He called me girlfriend." Courtney sighed as she leaned back in her seat. "He's so dreamy."

Natalie rolled her eyes as she twisted around in her seat to face the front. They were just cresting a hill, the desert valley unfolding below them.

"What did she say?" Lucien asked, amusement making his tone light and teasing. Attractive.

Natalie frowned crossly. "Nothing." What the hell was wrong with her? Had she forgotten what that vampire had done to her all those years ago? Confusion twisted her in one direction then the other. She'd spent the last four decades hating vampires, avoiding vampires, running from vampires, and then Lucien steps back into her life and she was traveling with him, staying at vampire roosts and kissing him and…more.

She glanced at the map on the laptop. "We have to take the next turn on the right." She'd woken up—alone and mortified—and promptly buried her nose in the laptop, following up on some of the information she'd spied in Dr. Morton's reports.

"Tell me again why I'm not taking you straight home?" Lucien asked. She could hear the doubt in his tone. She didn't know what to say to him. Should she offer encouragement? In truth, she was drawing a rather long bow with this.

"Doc Morton had some interesting notes in his office. They were testing all sorts of treatments—" She frowned. No, treatments wasn't the right word. "Weapons." Better. "They found something that could neutralize wolfsbane." She turned the laptop around so he could see the screen. "*Lupinus ignis*, a rare flowering plant found in various pockets within the Red Desert."

Lucien checked it briefly before turning back to the road. "Pretty."

Natalie knew he was being sarcastic, but she had to agree with him. Clumps of flowering stalks, with purple blossoms bearing a deep red spot on the tip of the petal, reminiscent of the sweet pea. Very pretty.

"Well, they found they could make a tincture from the leaves and it could neutralize wolfsbane in humans and werewolves."

"But wolfsbane doesn't affect vampires," Lucien pointed out. "And Vivianne hasn't been infected with wolfsbane."

Natalie sighed. "I know, but if it can negate the affects of a poison that works on lycans, it might possibly have some qualities that can work with the lycan toxin. Maybe. At the moment, anything that neutralizes anything lycanistic is on the table." She shook her head. "I have no idea," she said to Lucien, "but it's something we didn't have before. Or did we? Have you tried *Lupinus* on your sister?"

Lucien shook his head. "No, we haven't, and you're right. It's better than nothing." He looked over at her and flashed her a smile, one that was tinged with sadness and a little resignation. Her eyes widened. He was losing faith.

"Hey, we'll find something. If this doesn't work, we'll try something else. You need to turn here," she added, gesturing to the turnoff. She frowned, glancing around. The sun was now below the horizon and darkness was encroaching. "There are no signs here, no territory markers. How can we seek permission for access?"

She started to type rapidly into her computer. The last thing she wanted was a vicious breed going all territorial on them. If they didn't have permission, the landholders could sanction them for trespass. Maybe even kill them, depending on their mood.

Lucien glanced through the darkening dusk. "I think this is still Eventide territory. Heath's family have the foothills and a portion of the desert."

She frowned. "Uh, RTDB shows this area as being ridgewalker territory."

Lucien shook his head. "No, that's got to be wrong. They were wiped out before The Troubles. I believe this would still be Eventide, and Heath won't mind."

"Yeah, well, if any of his vamp staff come at us, I'm so throwing you in front of me."

"Oh, I don't mind being in front of you. It has its perks." His words came out all low and rumbly and suggestive. Her cheeks heated and out of the corner of her eye she saw him smile. She really wasn't used to Lucien being flirty. It was…disturbing, but in an exciting, thrilling kind of way.

She closed her laptop and placed it back in her tote. She wondered if the ridgewalkers were related to the young man who had been tortured up on Mount Solitude.

The twin beams of Lucien's headlights cut large, powerful swathes through the inky nightscape.

She glanced out the window. "*Lupinus ignis* grows on the leeward side of a hill, right at the base where the water collects. I guess we just look for hills." The road they were on lined the base of the foothills, entwining through dunes and rock formations. Occasionally she saw darker shadows. Caves. Not many, but enough to make her wary. Coyotes, bobcats, cougars—she hadn't seen any since they'd turned off the interstate, but assumed they had to be around. Bobcats, especially.

"Well, which side is the leeward side?"

Natalie bit her lip. "I guess it's opposite to the windward side," she said, trying not to smile.

"See, I could never figure that one out. What if the wind changes direction?"

She shrugged. "Well, it's like moss on a tree, I guess."

"Yeah, I don't follow."

"Well, moss generally grows on the north side of a tree. How does the tree know which direction its facing? Same as those hills."

Lucien slid his gaze to hers. "You're kidding."

She started to chuckle. "Yes, but I had you going."

They drove along for a while. Lucien drove slow enough that she could peer into the blackness. They were so far off the interstate, there were no lights. No streetlamps. No windows in the dark that hinted at some form of civilization. Fortunately, Lucien had asked Heath for some snacks for the road. She turned toward the basket on the floor behind her seat. "Want something to eat?"

"Sure."

She wrestled the basket over the console between the seats and perched it on her lap. She lifted the lid, her eyebrows rising when she realized it was a cleverly camouflaged cooler.

She found a couple of raw steaks that admittedly had her mouth watering. She couldn't help but smile. Whoever had packed the cooler knew what they were doing. Fruit. Raw steaks. Cooked chicken-salad sandwiches and, if she wasn't mistaken, a very substantial supply of choc-chip cookies. Raw, freshly butchered meat was a good staple for a vampire, with blood still present in the flesh. She hadn't fed a vampire her blood since the night she'd died, and had no intention of changing that small personal rule, not even for Lucien.

She handed him one of the steaks and the smell of the meat called to her. Lucien had ordered room service back at the roost, but he'd ordered her childhood favorite for her—pasta alfredo. She'd been surprised, and oddly touched, that he'd remembered that about her, and hadn't wanted to break it to him that she now preferred red meat, and lots of it. One of the side effects of returning from the dead, apparently. She nibbled on her own raw steak.

"You eat steak? Raw?" Lucien asked, his surprise evident.

She nodded. "Love it. It's like an energy shot for me, ever since I died." She paused. Good grief. That had come out like part of a casual conversation. She'd never spoken so offhand about that night. How could she be so dismissive? Ever since she'd told Lucien about her death, though, it didn't seem to bother her as much. She realized some of the anger had dissipated, leaving behind it a well of grief and sadness. She blinked. She realized she'd carried that anger with her for decades, and hadn't even recognized its weight until it was lifted.

Lucien eyed her and the steak assessingly. "Interesting."

Natalie shrugged and they ate in silence. A memory of her and her parents in a car on some long road trip to a distant clinic surfaced in her mind. Her mother turned to hand her some sweets, while her father mock protested, and started a candy war in the car. She blinked a couple of times. That was the first time she'd thought of her parents in years without the screams and blood. She sniffed then peered into the cooler again to distract herself. She retrieved a water bottle and grimaced as she held out a blood bag. "Thirsty?"

"Yeah, thanks." He used his teeth to pull off the lid on the injection port and then sucked at the liquid like a juice box. She contented herself with the water bottle, staring out the window as they drove along.

"Not sure if we'll be able to spot these plants in the dark," she muttered. "Maybe we need a drone to fly out here during daylight, or something." She'd used drones in a couple of her archaeological trips.

"Oh, sorry, I forgot your sight is limited," he murmured and flicked a switch on the dashboard. The windows flickered briefly and Natalie gaped when she realized she could see outside the car almost as though it was daylight. It was all varying shades of green, though.

"What is this?" she asked, curious.

"Night-vision mode. I also have thermal mode, but I figure we'll find what we want with—"

A loud bang interrupted him and the car swerved. Natalie braced herself against the passenger door and the dashboard as Lucien quickly brought the car under control and slowed, pulling over to the shoulder.

"Stay here, I'll check it out." Lucien was out of the car before she could argue.

She folded her arms. "Go to your room, stay in the car…" she muttered. Should she tell him that she was quite competent with changing a blasted tire?

Lucien ducked his head in the driver's open window. "One of the rear tires is flat. Sit tight, we'll be right in a jiffy." He went and opened the trunk, and she heard him remove some items from the cavity. Then he was lost from her sight.

She sat for a moment, then shifted in the seat. She grimaced at the pins and needles in her feet. Now would be as good a time as any to get out and stretch her legs; they'd been driving for a few hours.

She opened the door and stepped out, her breath gusting in the cool night air. She glanced around. It was so silent, so still, out here in the desert at night. She glanced at her watch. It was coming up to midnight. Sun was due up in just over six hours. Should they push on or start to head back? Lucien would be stuck in the car if they did proceed…

She started to walk along the length of the car. Lucien peered over the trunk of the vehicle. "I won't be long."

"That's okay. I wanted to get some exercise before we took off again." She started to walk toward him, rubbing her arms. The desert night air was quite chilled. Lucien frowned in concern. "You should sit in the car, you'll be warmer."

For a moment his care warmed her. But then she realized he was looking at her as someone who needed to be cared for. Not like an equal, but like when she was a sickly kid. Natalie frowned at him. "I don't have cancer anymore, Lucien. I won't catch a chill or anything. You can stop babying me."

His surprise at her remarks made her uncomfortable and perhaps just a little bit guilty. She may have spoken more harshly than necessary. She turned away from him and started to walk toward the front of the car. She heard him swear softly.

"Get in the car, Natalie," he called gently to her.

She shook her head. He had to realize he couldn't tell her—

"Get in the damn car, Nat," he said urgently, and she could hear the speed with which he was spinning the wheel brace on the wheel nuts.

"I'm fine—"

A rock skittered in the darkness and she halted. She cocked her head, listening intently. Lucien rose from where he'd hunkered down toward the rear of the car and threw the damaged tire into the trunk, slamming the lid.

"Car. Now." His words brooked no argument and she turned toward the passenger door.

A low growl rumbled through the night air. The

hair on her arms rose, her eyes widening as she jerked around. She fumbled with the latch of the car door and then a shadow moved.

She froze, eyeing the dark shape coming out of the night. It growled again, eyes glowing amber, and her heart stuttered. That was a werewolf. She'd recognize that sound anywhere. She'd heard it that night her mother and father had died, had heard it as it stalked her, pounced on her, tore into her shoulder.

"Nat."

She couldn't move, couldn't respond. Visions flashed through her mind as the creature stepped closer and she could make out its features from the cabin light of the car and the headlights. Its eyes shone golden. Its fangs gleamed. Its hair was a matted dark gray. Her heart pounded. Her muscles spasming all over, fighting against whatever quagmire had her in its grips, fighting against the need to pee.

She trembled, frozen. This wasn't like the bunker in Mount Solitude. Despite the pain, the lycans there had been ghostly. Painful but not invulnerable. This—this was the real deal. She flinched as the lycan snarled, its lips curling back to reveal the saliva dripping from its teeth. Just like when it had stood over her all those years ago. It actually enjoyed the fear it created in her.

She couldn't move, not with this horror slide show on repeat in her mind. Almost as though she'd stepped outside of her body, and everything slowed down, she watched as the lycan hunkered down, muscles bunching, eyes eerily golden in the darkness. It launched at her and her muscles stiffened. She couldn't move, couldn't even scream as the werewolf attacked.

Chapter 16

Lucien vaulted over the car, incisors lengthening and a harsh growl erupting from his throat. He clenched his hand into a fist and swung at the lycan as he landed in front of Natalie. He connected with the werewolf's shoulder, heard the satisfying crunch of bone breaking, felt it give beneath his fist as the werewolf stumbled off course.

The lycan whirled on him, teeth bared, lips curled back. Lucien stood, feet planted shoulder-width apart, fists up and ready. He flashed his eyes, anger coursing through him. This damn mutt had tried to hurt Natalie.

The werewolf sprang toward him and Lucien felt a claw rip his arm as he twisted out of the way.

He grasped a hank of fur in both hands and threw the lycan. The lycan's body thunked against the car then rolled off the hood to land on all paws. The werewolf was large by any standard, and Lucien could see the shoulder he'd broken was already mending, the caved-in section smoothing out. Lucien frowned. The wolf had accelerated healing powers. Well, that just made things a trifle more challenging.

Lucien raised his fists in a boxer's stance, shifting from one foot to the other. Out of the corner of his eye he saw Natalie shift along the side of the car, her face pale, eyes wide, but he didn't shift his focus from the lycan.

The werewolf hunkered down, his fur rising along the back of his neck, and Lucien showed him his fangs. The lycan might be big, ugly and harder to kill than most because every injury knitted before the next blow could be landed, but he had no intention of losing, of putting Natalie in danger.

The wolf sprang at him and Lucien ducked, landing a blow in the werewolf's soft underbelly as he sailed over him. He heard the light whimper as the wolf landed, but didn't give the lycan time to recover. He launched himself at the werewolf, tackling him, latching on to the beast with his teeth, and he heard the wolf howl as the metallic taste of warm blood filled his mouth.

He kept landing blows, dodging out of the way as the wolf twisted, his teeth snapping. Lucien gritted his teeth as a claw slashed across chest and had to dodge another paw that came close to unmanning him. He shoved at the snout that was dangerously close to him, exposing the lycan's neck. He raised his head to bite, but the werewolf anticipated the move and sprang off him, racing toward Natalie.

"No!" Lucien bellowed, white-hot rage flooding him. He rolled to his feet and bolted after him. Natalie clutched at the door handle, fumbling with the latch with shaking hands. Lucien leaped just as the werewolf reached her and all three crashed to the ground in a twisted heap of lashing limbs and snapping teeth. Natalie's scream was cut short and Lucien smelled fresh blood. The realization Natalie was hurt gave his anger strength.

The wolf had Natalie pinned beneath him, jaw widening, and Lucien thrust himself between them, roaring as the lycan's teeth clamped down on his shoulder. He pushed back and both he and the werewolf tumbled backward. The lycan snapped at him again, teeth tearing into his right biceps. The pain, the immediate comprehension of the consequences, sent Lucien into a frenzy. He bit down, his jaw tightening, a warm wetness splattering his chest as he bit through the werewolf's jugular.

Slowly the agonizing clamp on his arm loosened and the wolf collapsed on him as he bled out. Lucien grasped his neck and twisted, then wrenched with all his might, grimacing as he felt bones pop, muscles tear and the head separate from the body.

He shoved the bloodied, torn mess of a corpse off of him. "Heal that, you bastard," he rasped. He sat up, wincing at the pain in his left shoulder and right biceps. The muscles felt like they were on fire. Damn it. He'd been bit.

He looked over to Natalie and saw her still form on the dirt road. He rolled to his feet, staggering over to her. His blood trailed down his arms and as he lurched in front of the car the headlights picked up the black fluid trailing down his skin. He swallowed. That didn't look good. His blood wasn't black. He closed his eyes briefly. The lycan toxin. It was already distorting his blood.

He blinked as the road dipped and curved around

him. He squinted beyond the twin beams of light. The windshield was like a snowflake, all pretty fractures. So pretty. He staggered around to Natalie and fell to his knees beside her. Blood stained a rock near her head, her face pale and still. He reached out and rested his trembling hand against her chest. His shoulders sagged as he felt the slow, regular thud of her heart. Unconscious, not dead. Thank God.

He patted her gently on the cheek, wincing as his torn muscles protested the movement. "Hey, Nat." He tapped her lightly again, but it was hard to keep his balance, the desert was beginning to dip and roll around him. "Come on, minx. Wake—"

The road rolled up and hit him in the face, embracing him in darkness.

Natalie's eyes flickered open. Her head throbbed in time to the pulse in her aching neck and a heavy weight lay across her, making it difficult for her to breathe. She winced, blinking. Where the hell was she?

She tried to shift at the weight on top of her. It was warm and bulky. Solid. Her eyes widened as she twisted her head, grimacing at the pain the movement caused her. She gasped when she saw Lucien's unconscious face. He was slumped across her, arms out, as though trying to protect her, even in his senseless state.

She pushed him off her and sat up. He didn't stir. He was still alive, though. She winced as she carefully examined him. His one shoulder was torn and his other arm was looking pretty nasty, too. She frowned. They looked like bite marks, but the blood vessels radiating from those bites were turning black. His veins down one arm were turning dark gray under his skin.

She glanced around then flinched when she saw the werewolf—or rather, what was left of him. Oh, God. She looked at Lucien's wounds again. He'd been bitten by a werewolf and it was the lycanthrope toxin spreading through his system.

Natalie ripped at his shirt, tearing the fabric into strips. She bound his wounds firmly and he groaned softly but didn't come to. She ripped at her own sleeves, using them to wrap tightly around his arm in an effort to slow his circulation and hopefully slow the toxin.

She'd never personally seen the effects of a vampire suffering from a werewolf bite, but she'd read plenty of case studies. The toxin caused fever and hallucinations. Violent hallucinations. The victim was racked with excruciating pain as sepsis set in and was then tormented both physically and mentally before muscles contracted, causing agonizing spasms that resulted in broken bones and eventually liquefied organs and death. It was a horrific way to die.

And now Lucien would suffer horribly then die. Her fingers shook at the realization and she glanced around. The sky was lightening, going from dark gray to light. The sun would rise soon and both she and Lucien were out in the open. If she didn't get him under cover, they wouldn't have to worry about the lycan toxin, the sun would turn him to ash.

The car. Tempered glass. He'd be safe inside it. She opened the door and realized Courtney cowered in the corner, eyes wide with fright.

"It's going to be fine, Courtney, but I have to move you, sorry." She grabbed her tote and raced to the trunk, dumping it inside next to the flat tire and tire jack Lucien had thrown in earlier. She closed the trunk then hurried over to Lucien. She rolled him onto his back and his eyes fluttered open.

"Oh, hey, minx." His voice was weak, but still warm and tender.

"Hey, yourself," she said back to him and gave him a reassuring smile. "I have to move you, Luc. Sun's up soon, so need to get you someplace dark, okay?"

He nodded. "'Kay," he murmured then groaned as she grabbed him by his arms and raised him effortlessly over her shoulder in a fireman's lift.

She carried him to the car, gently laying him on the backseat. She pushed his long legs in and closed the door, then raced around to the driver's seat. It wasn't until she was inside and starting the ignition that she realized the windshield was cracked and a chunk of glass lay on the passenger seat.

She hit the steering wheel in frustration. She could barely see out front, but worse, it would provide no protection to Lucien when the sun rose. They had to find someplace dark, and quick. She eyed the horizon. It was already turning light shades of orange and pink.

A cave. That's what she needed. She remembered seeing the mouth of one a couple of miles back and hoped to hell there weren't any lycans or shifters hiding there. She twisted, raising her leg to kick out the glass panel so that she could see beyond the dashboard. The glass splintered as it fell to the ground, the tinkling absurdly musical in the predawn air. She pressed her lips together as she put the car into gear and spun the wheel, creating a cloud of dust as she drove back along the road.

It took another twenty minutes before she found what she was looking for and she turned the car in that direction. The vehicle bounced and dipped as she drove off-road, aiming directly for the cave entrance. Lucien groaned in the backseat and she winced. She couldn't begin to imagine what his injuries felt like, the pain he was experiencing.

She swerved to avoid a boulder, coughing on the dust and dirt that flew in through the windshield frame. She wiped at her eyes as she pulled into the dark opening. The headlights cut through the darkness. She slammed her foot on the brake as a low outcropping leered toward her and the vehicle came to a shuddering halt, millimeters away from the rock taking off the roof of the car.

Natalie glanced around. The light was brightening at the crest of the distant hills and she gauged the distance from lip of the cave. They weren't in far enough. She got out of the car and jogged to the rear door. In moments she had Lucien over her shoulder and was running further into the cave. The shadows darkened toward the back and she made a beeline for it, puffing as she jumped over rocks and boulders. She dived around a natural curve in the rock wall as the sun's rays peeked over the hills, lancing through the cave behind her with a determined reach.

Lucien groaned as he hit the ground, but Natalie sagged with relief as their little pocket of the cave remained in a cool, dark, nondestructive shadow. She leaned back against the wall and gazed around. No lurking lycans or creepy little cougars. Great. She swallowed then leaned over Lucien, shifting him into a more comfortable position. His forehead was beaded with sweat and she peeled back his collar, wincing. The lycan toxin was spreading from his shoulder, worming its way through the veins of his neck. She pressed the back of her hand to his forehead. He was burning up.

For the first time she could appreciate Lucien's panic. She could understand his determination to find a cure for his sister, the worry and the dread that went with it, as she was experiencing it, too. Lucien had been bitten by a werewolf—while protecting her, damn it. He was dying.

His eyelids fluttered and he gave her a shaky smile. "Hey, minx."

"Hey, Luc." She cupped his cheek, returning his smile with a shaky one of her own.

He swallowed. "Do you know how long I've hoped you'd call me that again?" he whispered hoarsely.

"Shh, don't talk. Rest," she said. She made an effort to move away but he caught her hand, halting her.

"We both know this isn't something I can recover from," he said hoarsely. His blue eyes bore a sadness and regret that was devastating.

She shook her head, tears filling her eyes. "I refuse to give up, Lucien."

"Stop, Natalie." He chuckled, his voice a soft rasp. "It's ironic, that in trying to find the cure for my sister, I fall prey to the same condition."

"No. This is my fault," she whispered fiercely.

Lucien frowned. "How do you figure that?" His tone was incredulous.

"You were trying to protect me, Lucien."

He made a noise that sounded like a snort. "Natalie, if I hadn't dragged you across the desert, forced you to stay at roost surrounded by vampires, exposed you to pathologically enraged ghosts and then driven you into that desert, you wouldn't have needed the protection."

He shook his head weakly. "No, this is all on me." His mouth turned down at the corners as his gaze swept over his face. "I just wish I had more time with you."

She shook her head. "Don't talk like that, Luc. We'll fix this."

Lucien laughed then winced at the pain. "Natalie, there is no fixing this." He coughed, then groaned.

She pulled away from him and darted back to the car. She riffled through the contents of the cooler. There was another blood bag, another bottle of water in here somewhere—there. She removed the contents and jogged over to him.

"Here, have some of this." She ripped off the lid on the tubing and held the injection port to the blood bag up to his lips. He dipped his head forward and took a sip, then sagged back against the rock wall.

She laid the bag on his chest, within close reach of his lips. "I'm going to find that damned *Lupinus* plant. I'm going to make you a tea and then we're going to take that cure back to your sister, okay?"

He gave her a resigned look. "Give it up, Natalie. I'm dying."

She clasped his face with both hands, leaning down to glare at him. "I'm not ready to lose you yet," she told him, realizing belatedly the sincerity of the statement. "Not again."

He closed his eyes. When he opened them, the crystal-blue irises were darkened with devastation. "I'm sorry, Natalie," he whispered. "I'm sorry for not being there for you."

She smiled as a tear ran down her cheek and she had to face the truth at last. "Don't. I was looking for someone to blame, and you were the easy target," she told him. "I couldn't accept that bad things happened. It was easier to carry around my rage for you than to face the truth." She shrugged, tears streaming down her face. "I couldn't make those responsible pay for what they did to me, to Mom and Dad. That made me so angry, I had to direct it somewhere."

Lucien shook his head, opening his mouth to argue, but she held a finger to his lips. "No, hear me out. If I blamed you, then I couldn't blame me. If it was your fault for not being there, then it wasn't my fault for dragging them out of the house in the first place. But, really, those two monsters, they'd been killing together for some time. If they targeted my family, I don't think there is anything anyone could have done to prevent what happened to us, short of killing *them*." She sniffed then brushed at the tears on her cheeks. "So, really, Luc, you need to rest, while I go track down those blasted plants. We will fix this." She tried to infuse as much confidence as possible, for his sake, and for hers.

She retreated from him and he shook his head urgently. "Natalie, no."

She shook her head. "Let me do this, Lucien."

He subsided against the rock wall, his blue eyes glittering in the darkness as he gazed around the cavern. He considered her words and then his lips lifted in a sad smile. "Thank you."

She returned his smile and turned, jogging into the larger cave toward the car. She hesitated at one point, thinking he'd uttered something. Had he just said goodbye? She refused to return the farewell, shying away from the permanence of the phrase.

In moments she'd reversed out of the cave, heart

pounding as she squinted against the daylight. She needed to find those damn plants. She prayed to God they worked.

Chapter 17

Lucien cracked his eyelids open. The cave was wavering around him and he felt like he was slowly burning from the inside out. His head rolled back against the rock wall. A shadowy figure stepped forward and he blinked.

"Vivianne?"

His sister knelt by his side, giving him an angry look. "What have you gone and done now, Luc?"

A lump grew in his throat as he stared at his once-beautiful sister. Now, though, her skin was gray, her blood vessels black, her eyes black. "I'm sorry," he choked out. "I tried—"

Her expression hardened. "Well, you didn't try hard enough, did you? Papa was right. You don't deserve to bear the Marchetta name. You're a pathetic excuse for a brother, you know? Leaving me to die in extreme agony while you go gallivanting off with your sickly little slut."

He shook his head, dismayed at her reaction. "Please, I'm sorry, Vivianne. I'm sorry I couldn't help you."

"Well, sorry doesn't really help, does it? Not when

we both die. It should have been you in that ballroom fire, you know? Mother died because of you."

He squeezed his eyes shut. "Stop it!"

"Why, because the truth hurts? Mom died because of *you*, Lucien. You've killed Mom and now you've killed me. The best you could do is put the rest of us out of our misery and die."

"No!" he bellowed, eyes flashing as he glared into the darkness. He blinked, panting. Where was she? He squinted into the darkness. Shadows, light, but no Vivianne. He collapsed against the rock wall behind him, exhausted. Oh, God. He swallowed. She wasn't there. Hadn't been there. He'd imagined it. He was beginning to hallucinate. He moved his arm, groaning as fire, hot and painful, lanced through his shoulder and down his arm. He held up his hand. The veins stood out, nearly black. He clasped the blood bag and raised it to his lips. He hoped Natalie didn't come back. Not until he was gone. He didn't want her to see him like this. Didn't want to hurt her. Maybe he should hide? Crawl somewhere else to avoid her?

A rock skittered across the floor of the cave. He froze, heart pounding. He could hear it. The soft pad of paws across the dirt. A low growl rumbled through the cave. The hair on the back of his neck rose. He kept his gaze glued to that rocky outcropping, muscles tense. A puff of steam, like an exhalation in the cold air, drifted around the wall. He shifted closer to the wall behind him, wincing with effort. A snout appeared, fangs visible and dripping with saliva. His own incisors lengthened as the werewolf that had bitten him prowled around the corner.

Rage at the audacity of the wolf rolled over him and

bitter hatred fogged his brain. He'd done this to him. The lycan's eyes glowed golden in the dark cave. Lucien flashed his eyes then heaved forward as the wolf attacked. They rolled on the ground, wrestling and growling. Lucien screamed in rage as the wolf bit his hand. He grabbed hold of the lycan's snout, wrenching back and feeling, hearing, the neck snap. He glared down at his hands, only to find them empty.

He panted in confusion, gazing wildly around. Where did he go? Where did that stinking mongrel of a fleabag go? A sickening dizziness swept over him and he blinked. Slowly. So tired.

"Lucien," a voice whispered to him in the darkness. A familiar voice. Sweet, soft. He opened his eyes to stare at the little girl in the hospital gown who knelt by his side. She had an IV line hooked up to her chest, the port beneath her gown, and he stared, fascinated, at the red fluid inside the tube.

"You don't look so good," she said, touching his forehead lightly.

"I lost a fight," he said, wheezing with laughter. He was in a bad way. He needed blood to heal.

"I should call a nurse," she said, looking around. He glanced around, too, eyes widening when he realized he wasn't in a cave anymore but in a hospital room. There was something oddly familiar about it. The little girl reached for the call button, but he covered her hand with his.

"Don't," he said in a gentle voice.

"But you look sick, too," she said.

He eyed her curiously. He could smell illness in her. He couldn't drink from her; her blood was tainted. He had to disregard her as a potential food source. He smiled, hiding his frustration. "What's your name?"

"Nina. What's yours?" The girl tilted her bald head in curiosity.

"Lucien."

"What's wrong with you?" she asked him. Nothing like a direct question from a kid. Where did he begin? He'd lost a fight with Mikhail Petrowski, and his father would be furious.

He gestured to the IV. "I need blood, just like you."

Her eyebrows dipped and she eyed him intently for a moment. She slid her hand beneath the neckline of her gown and he heard a little click and pop. Crimson bloomed on the fabric of her gown near her shoulder, and she withdrew the IV line from her chest, offering it to him. Blood dripped over her fingers, the tantalizing scent fogging his brain, and he had to clench his muscles to stop ravaging the girl, sick or not.

He leaned back against the wall. "What are you doing?" he asked hoarsely.

She offered it again, stepping closer. "Take it. You need it." Her eyes traveled over his body, his blood-stained clothes. "I think you need it more than I do."

He shook his head. "I can't." If he took blood from an ill kid, what kind of monster did that make him?

Nina sighed. "I'm dying," she stated matter-of-factly. "They don't think I know, but I do." Her eyes welled with tears. "I lost my hair. I hurt. And chemo makes me sick. Everyone tries to hide it from me, but I know. It's not working. I can't see my friends, I can't go out and play…" She sniffed and lifted her chin. "I'm dying. I can't be fixed. But you can be. Take it."

He was touched by her gesture in a way he hadn't

been for years. He wanted to reach out and pat her in an attempt to make her feel better—an instinct he couldn't actually remember having—but that just seemed awkward. He crouched so they were on eye level.

"I owe you one," he said softly. "And a Marchetta always pays his debts."

She frowned. "What's a Marchetta?"

He chuckled, the sound surprising him. He didn't laugh often. "I'm a Marchetta. What would you like in return for this?"

She narrowed her eyes as she met his gaze. "Will you play a game with me?" she asked hopefully.

He gaped. "You could have anything, and you want to play a game?"

She shrugged. "My parents don't want me to get too tired, so I don't get to play much." Her nose wrinkled. "But I'm not dead *yet*."

He laughed, low and husky, then nodded. "Fair enough. A game. Although I think I get the better end of the deal," he told her.

"Two games," she added hurriedly.

He smiled. "As many games as you want," he told her, and she nodded.

"Deal." She offered the IV line again and he held it to his lips and sipped.

Something bitter and acrid filled his mouth and he coughed in disgust.

"Shh, drink it up, Luc."

A hand gripped his chin, lowering his jaw, and more of the foul-tasting liquid entered his mouth. His chin was raised and he was forced to drink the concoction.

He blinked and Natalie's face swam into focus.

"Nina," he gasped.

She gazed at him, worried. "Natalie," she corrected.

"Uh, yeah, sorry. Natalie," he repeated. He grimaced. "God, that blood tasted disgusting."

"It wasn't blood, Lucien," she said, concerned as she surveyed his face. She touched his forehead then his cheek with the back of her hand. "I found the plants and made a tea. I found an arroyo a ways off the road."

His heart hammered in his chest. "You found it?" he murmured, amazed. She smoothed some hair off his forehead and nodded. "I did. You're going to be fine, now rest." He noted her tone was more hopeful than confident.

He closed his eyes, smiling. "You're my saving grace," he whispered as he let the dark wave claim him again.

Natalie glanced at her watch again then turned back to her patient. Lucien was sleeping fitfully, muttering away. How long would it take for the antidote to kick in? It had been just over three hours since she'd forced it down his throat. She shook her head. Not once had she ever expected to see Lucien in this state. For an undead, he was so full of life, so vibrant. Even now his broad shoulders and biceps suggested strength she knew was rapidly depleting.

She touched his forehead again, jerking her hand back. Hell, he was on fire. She hoped that was a sign of a reaction, somewhere; that the *Lupinus ignis* was doing its job.

She glanced back toward the cave entrance. It was midday, the sun high overhead, the rest of the cave cool and dim. As soon as the sun set, she'd haul Lucien back into the car and hightail it out of there, before any more shadow breeds came for a visit. Not that they were bound by night, like the vamps were, but it was blistering hot out there. She didn't think any of them would be interested in picking a fight in this heat.

"I will *kill* you for what you did to her," Lucien roared as he sat up and Natalie started, turning back to him. His eyes glowed red as he glared at her and his incisors lengthened.

"Hey, it's okay, Luc. It's just me," she said in a soothing voice.

"Your sick vampire friend isn't here to protect you, but don't worry, I'll track him down, too," he snarled.

Natalie's blood chilled in her veins as she realized he didn't see her, didn't know where he was. She swallowed. "What…what do you mean?" she managed to ask.

"Your biggest mistake was thinking you could get away with killing her," he rasped, his voice low and gravelly. "She was very important to me—you took her from me." His eyes took on a dull, soulless look. "And for that, you die." He reared toward her.

Natalie dodged him, staring in shock as he collapsed at her side, unconscious again. Did he…did he mean the werewolf who'd killed her? She frowned in confusion. She had seen the reports of that particular lycan's body being found, viciously attacked, but she'd assumed it had been his accomplice who'd done the damage. But… had Lucien tracked him down and killed him? It certainly seemed that way.

She rolled him on to his back and one of his buttons popped, revealing more of his chest. She gasped, ripping the rest of his shirt open. Oh, God, no. His torso was turning gray, the veins black. A lump rose in her throat. The plant wasn't working. Tears filled her eyes at the realization and she lifted his head to cradle his upper body in her lap.

His eyelids flickered and she stiffened as he looked up at her. Relief relaxed her shoulders when she saw the cool blue shade of her friend and not the blood-red predator. His features were haggard as he stared up at her and shook his head.

"Natalie?" His voice was uncertain, as though he wasn't sure if he could trust his eyes.

She nodded, smoothing back his hair. "Yes, it's me."

"You need to leave me," he said, his voice a dry croak. She leaned over to grab the bottle of water but he stayed her hand. "No. Listen to me, Natalie. I—" He coughed, the hacking sound harsh within the cave. "I'm getting worse. You need to go."

She shook her head. "No, I'm not going leave you," she whispered stubbornly.

He closed his eyes briefly, as though pained. "You need to. I'm dreaming. I don't know what's real and… and what's not. You need to go, before I hurt you."

"No, I'm not leaving you, Lucien."

"Luc," he demanded, and she smiled.

"Luc."

"I'm ordering you to leave," he said, frowning, injecting his voice with more strength.

"You keep ordering me to do things as though you think I will," she said gently, smiling down at him. "I—I can't leave you, Luc. I'm not ready," she told him honestly.

A tear welled in his eye and he took a deep, shuddering breath. "I'm losing it, Natalie, and I couldn't bear it if I hurt you. I never wanted to hurt you."

"Shh—"

"You keep shushing me as though you think I will," he shot back, a weak smile teasing at his lips. Then his expression grew serious. "I'm sorry. I'm sorry for threatening your friends. That was not good of me. Please. I dragged you out here, I put you in danger. Forgive me?"

"Stop it," she cried softly, tears running down her face. Lucien was always so confident, so cocksure, and him seeking forgiveness rammed home the reality of the situation in a way nothing else could. "There's nothing to forgive you for, but if you think you need it, it's yours. I forgive you."

He closed his eyes for a painful moment. "Thank you," he whispered. Then he opened his eyes, meeting her gaze with a determined jut to his chin. "My father—he wants to kill you," he rasped. "He wasn't always like that. You need to know that." He took a shuddering breath. "I've tried to fix what I broke." He rubbed his lips together. "Promise me you won't go home."

She shook her head, clenching her jaws together to prevent her sobs from leaching out.

He grasped her hand with surprising strength, his gaze fierce. "I have money in the car. Enough money for you to start your life over ten times. That's what you do, Natalie. You run, and you don't let my father or Enzo find you. I need you to be safe." He shook her hand. "Promise me," he hissed. "Let me do this right, just once, Natalie. Let me protect you."

This time she couldn't hold back the sobs as she leaned over and hugged him. "I don't want you to die," she wailed.

His hand smoothed her hair. "Shh. I don't want to

die, either," he admitted. "I wanted to save my sister. I wanted my father to forgive me." He tugged gently on her hair and she tilted her head back to meet his gaze. "I wanted forever with you," he whispered, tears rolling down his cheek to mingle with the perspiration. "I'm so sorry I didn't get that with you. I love you, Natalie."

"I love you, Luc. Stay with me," she sobbed. "Please, stay with me." She stroked his cheek and he closed his eyes, turning his face into her touch. "Please, just until sunset. Stay with me."

"I'll try," he promised, although his eyelids fluttered as though too weak to lift. "I love you," he sighed. Then grimaced.

Natalie sat up, anxious as his back arched. His eyes opened, flashing red, his incisors lengthened and he growled, the agonized sound echoing through the cave.

He rolled off her, twitching as his muscles spasmed. She shrieked as she heard the bones pop, break. He convulsed, his voice emerging from his throat in a gutteral roar that was unrecognizable. He lay on his stomach, growling at her, lurching toward her.

Natalie scrambled back as he advanced, heart thudding in her chest as she realized Lucien's vampiric nature had consumed him. There was no sign of humanity in his eyes, just manic bloodthirst. She sobbed, hustling along the rock wall as he tried to crawl after her, growling and whimpering as another spasm racked his body.

He arched back on his knees, arms raised, and she heard the ripple effect of his vertebrae cracking. Blood seeped from his nose and ears, and she covered her mouth, sobbing almost hysterically as he took a slow, painful breath and collapsed.

The red glow diminished until the crystal-blue irises

stared up at her. His mouth opened a couple of times. She reached for him, then drew back. But when she realized it was Luc, she went to him.

"Love..." His mouth formed the word "you," but no sound emerged from his lips as the life drifted from his eyes.

Natalie screamed, her hands fluttering. No, no, no! The sound reverberated in her mind.

"No, Luc, please," she cried. She took a deep breath, calming herself. No. This wasn't happening. This couldn't happen. Not to Luc. "You can't die," she murmured, patting his cheek. "You're a vampire. Vampires don't die." She slapped his cheek harder, but his eyes stared sightlessly up at the ceiling of the cave. "No, no, no, this can't be happening." She patted him on the chest. "Come on, wake up. Wake up." She rocked on her knees, panic coursing through her.

"What do you need? What do you need?" She glanced wildly around the cave. The bottle she'd used to hold the *Lupinus* tea was empty—fat lot of good it did. "What do vampires need?" Blood. Blood. Blood bag. She rose on her knees then slumped down when she saw the flat, emptied sack on the floor. No. This can't be happening. She shook her head as hysteria began to build in side her. No, not Luc.

She reached for him again, her pale skin such a contrast to his marbled complexion. Because she had blood pumping through her veins. She glanced at her wrist for a brief moment, and all the possibilities sprang into a logical chain of events in her mind, all within the blink of eye. She didn't hesitate. She placed her wrist against Lucien's lips and pressed against his incisors, hissing at the pain as she slowly punctured her skin against his teeth.

Blood seeped into his mouth and she squeezed her arm, as though trying to squirt blood from veins and into his throat. When the red fluid coated his lips and tongue, she drew back, holding her breath. Waiting.

Waiting.

It took several long, apprehensive moments before realization dawned on her. It wasn't working.

Lucien was dead.

Tears tracked down her face and she lay next to his body, her head on his chest as she cried.

Chapter 18

Her muscles were stiff and sore. She blinked slowly, her eyes itchy and irritated as she gazed blankly at the wall opposite, watching the colors change, the shadows lengthen. How long had she'd lain there? Hours.

She didn't care. Wasn't interested in going anywhere. Where could she go? She sure as hell couldn't go back home. Where did she want to go? Anywhere without Luc just didn't hold any appeal. Her eyes watered again. No. She didn't want to leave Luc. She was warm and cozy right—

She blinked. Warm? Warm! Luc's chest was warm! She jerked upright, her jaw dropping. His skin was pinking. She placed her hand on his chest, leaning over to peer down into his blank eyes.

"Luc?" She leaned closer. "Luc?"

Lucien gasped, eyes widening as he sucked in a breath, and she felt the small boom in his chest as his heart started again.

She gaped and stared as Lucien blinked, awareness slowly creeping into his eyes as he sucked in another breath, and another. He sat upright, effortlessly, his star-tled gaze meeting hers before flicking away to survey the cave, before finally coming back to rest on her. She stared at him, stunned.

He grabbed her, pulling her to him and enveloping her in a bear hug.

"Oh, my God," she gasped in disbelief. "What?" Words failed her, but his warmth, the beat of his heart…

"I love you," he whispered, pulling back to kiss her in quick, hard kisses. His hand delved in her hair, "I love you," he kept saying as he kissed her forehead, her tem-ple, her cheek, along her jaw. "I love you, I love you."

"I love—" Her words were cut off as he pressed his lips to hers and kissed her thoroughly. She kissed him right back.

He trailed his lips along her jawline to that sensitive spot below her ear. Heat flooded her, but she was too confused as emotions ripped through her. "Wait, wait," she said breathlessly. "Let me look at you."

She drew back and with one swift yank tore the rem-nants of his shirt over his broad shoulders and down his muscled arms. His smooth shoulders and unscarred arms. He chuckled as she pushed and poked at him, in-specting him.

"I don't understand," she breathed, her eyes wide with wonder as she caressed the defined musculature of his shoulder and collarbone.

He held up her wrist and licked at the dried blood there. His eyes blazed. "I don't either, but I'm not ask-ing questions," he said as he pulled her to him.

She braced her hands against his chest—that fabu-lous, gorgeous, healthy chest. "No, wait." She pulled his lips back. "Show me your teeth," she ordered.

He laughed, but he acquiesced, lengthening his incisors.

"You're still a vampire, then," she stated.

He frowned. "Of course I am," he said, perplexed. "What else would I be?"

"Do you feel different?"

He slid his arms around her, caressing her waist and back. "I feel great," he answered in a deep voice. He waggled his eyebrows suggestively.

Natalie frowned, despite the heat curling inside her. She looked at him intently. He looked temptingly cheeky, crazy-hot seductive. Normal—if you ignored the fact he'd been dead, like *really* dead, for the past few hours.

Just like she had been, until she was revived in the ambulance and then woken up in a hospital—after being bitten by a werewolf, and with vampire blood in her veins.

Exactly like she'd been... suspicion, doubt, hope—all bombarded her with a sense of anticipation.

"Come with me," she said, rising and dragging him with her.

"Natalie, I'm good," he said, tugging her toward him and planting a hot kiss on her lips. She almost gave in to sensual temptation, but something was...different. She pulled away and tugged him along. He laughed as he followed her out into the larger cave, but he stopped laughing when she stepped into the light of the waning sun. He followed, then jerked back, frowning.

"Natalie, I just cheated death. I'm not going to barbecue myself."

She grabbed his hand, raising it to the sunlight, and held on as he attempted to pull back again.

His eyes rounded as his skin shone pink in the sunlight. There was no burning, no smoke. No sizzle. He lifted his gaze to hers and she could only describe his expression as flabbergasted.

"You're a daywalker," she said softly, almost afraid to speak too loudly in case she jinxed it. "Just like me."

Lucien turned his hand over, watching as the light caressed his skin for the first time in centuries. His jaw dropped. He never— How—? What the *hell*?

He reached for Natalie's wrist. He'd woken with her blood on his lips, on his tongue, and it had been such an adrenaline rush. It had curled inside him, like a live wire to his heart, and had sparked a desire so hot, so consuming, even now, in the face of this revelation, he was so hard he could barely think straight.

"It's your blood," he stated hoarsely, meeting her gaze. Her brow dipped in confusion. "Your blood cured me, Natalie." He knew her selfless action had cost her dearly, considering her experiences with vampires. Wave after wave of emotion hit him. Gratitude. Humility. Protectiveness. Possessiveness. Love.

Tender warmth rose within as he realized just how much that single action meant. She'd trusted him. She'd trusted him in a way that went beyond anything he could have hoped for, and it humbled him. He reached for her, lowering his lips to hers with a delicate, subtle pressure. God, she was stunning. She took his breath away. She leaned in toward him, and that acceptance, that welcome, registered in his brain, and his heart. She'd saved him. Again. His heart hammered in his chest. For her.

Her lips parted beneath his, and he slid his fingers

into her hair, dragging her toward him. He kissed her, and his cock hardened. Throbbed.

She moaned into his mouth, the sound not a protest, but a surrender. This time she didn't try to push him back to assess the secrets of the universe. Her mouth opened beneath his and he slid his tongue inside, rubbing against hers. He grasped her hips, lifting her, encouraging her to wrap her legs around his waist. He walked back to where she'd parked the car just inside the cave. The light from the setting sun bathed them, the heat glorious against his bare chest. He sat Natalie on the hood of the car and started kissing her in earnest, relishing the exquisite sensations. There was something new, something blossoming inside him, as though it wasn't just his body awakening, but his very soul.

She trailed her hands over his chest and he moaned against her lips. To feel her touching him, no reservations, was such a heady experience. He nipped at her lips, his hands sliding to the buttons of her blouse. Starting from the top, he began to slide them ever so slowly through the holes, caressing the skin he revealed with each button he undid. He managed about three before she gave him a soft growl of frustration and yanked the rest of the shirt open.

He chuckled against her lips, delighted she was as eager for him as he was for her. He parted the cotton fabric, sliding it back off her shoulders, and took a moment to survey the treasure he'd uncovered.

She wore the same soft-pink bra as last night. He could see the rosy nipples, like dusty shadows behind the decorative cover, and almost lost it right there. He wanted to be inside her, he wanted to take his time. He wanted to dance. He wanted to leap. He wanted everything. Right here, right now, with her. He dipped his head, nipping at the tightening bud through the lace, and she trembled in his arms, throwing her head back on a gasp.

His hands circled her and undid her bra with efficiency. Her shoulders rose as she shrugged the straps down her shoulders, and he pulled it off her, dropping it to the side as he stared down at her.

"You're perfection," he said, cupping her breasts.

She sighed at his touch then reached to caress him, trailing her hands over his nipples. "You're not so bad yourself," she breathed, her eyes surveying his body. She caught her lip between her teeth and he almost combusted on the spot.

He lowered his head to flick at her nipple with his tongue, and she arched her back, pressing her breast into his mouth. He obeyed her silent urging, drawing the peak into his mouth, lowering her onto the hood of his car. He sucked on her nipple and palmed her other breast possessively. She was so damn beautiful, so reactive, so full of life in his arms.

He released her breast with a pop and then turned to her other breast and laved it with similar attention.

Natalie's fingers slid into his hair, clenching as he tugged on her nipple. The tightness of her grip sensitized his scalp and sent electric shocks to his cock. She tasted so good, felt so good... He gave her nipple one last nip that had her jerking off the car, then kissed his way down her flat stomach, undoing the clasp of her jeans as he went. He slid the zipper down and her stomach rolled like a dancer's as he ran his tongue across her navel.

"I need you," she panted as she writhed beneath his mouth.

"I need you, too, minx," he murmured, scraping his teeth gently down her lower abdomen. He grasped the waistband of her jeans, as well as her panties, and started to slide them down her body. She lifted her hips to help him and he tugged them off her body, kissing her thighs gently as he did so.

He returned to that juncture between her thighs and her scent, that heavenly, desirable musk, flooded his senses. Everything was heightened. Smell, taste, touch—even those sexy little pants she made as she arched under his caress. She was so damn beautiful. He couldn't have imagined it would have been like this with her, so consuming, so overwhelming.

He slid his thumb between her legs. Her eyes flew open in surprise then closed in bliss as he stroked her.

"More," she demanded, all feminine sensuality as her thighs parted beneath his caress.

He smiled. "Bossy little thing, aren't you?"

Her eyes flashed at him. She opened her mouth to give him a tart response but then gasped as he flicked her clitoris. "Oh, yes," she sighed, her head tilting back, her neck arching.

She was the sexiest woman he'd ever had the fortune to see in the throes of passion, and his cock pressed uncomfortably against his jeans.

He leaned forward, dipping his head to kiss her intimately, and she damn near shot off the car. He clasped her thighs with a strong grip, holding her beneath him, and she tugged at his hair. He rubbed his tongue against her, enjoying her scent, her taste. He made love to her with his mouth, trying to ignore the throbbing demand of his cock. He wanted to please her. He wanted to drive her insane with lust, just as she had him, but most of all, he wanted her to find joy with him. He flicked his tongue against her clitoris, then slid a finger inside her. Over and over, he played with her, he pleasured her. He ran his teeth gently over her nubbin. She arched beneath him, keening, as her muscles contracted around his finger, and he lifted his head to smile at her.

"I want you," she moaned. He dipped his head again and flicked his tongue teasingly, but the act backfired on him, filling his mouth with the flavor of her pleasure, driving his lust to a painful level. He fumbled with the button and fly of his jeans, hissing as he carefully lowered the zip of his erection.

"I want you, too, minx," he rasped, stepping up to her. He delved his fingers through her curls, parting her, and slid home.

She gasped, her eyes widening as she met his gaze, and he caressed her clitoris. He watched her come apart, head thrown back as another orgasm swept over her, clenching around him. It took every ounce of control to stay still, until eventually the sensations were too much and he moved, thrusting into her, over and over again.

She trembled beneath him and he could feel her spasm inside, contracting around him. It went on and on, the sensation unlike anything he'd ever experienced, until it, too, became too much and he felt his own release race up from that hot spot at the base of his spine, racing up over his scalp and driving any thought from his head as he gave in to it.

Natalie shuddered on the hood of the car, stunned as she slowly became aware of her surroundings again.

Lucien met her gaze and leaned down to kiss her languidly, his chest pressing against hers. She relished his weight, arching against him gently as she wrapped her arms and legs around him, kissing him in the afterglow. He sighed against her lips and rested his elbow on the hood of the car, cupping his head with his hand.

"God, why did we wait so long to do this?" he asked, marveling.

"I don't know." She giggled.

His eyes widened and he pressed his hips against hers.

"That feels good," he purred, and she felt herself getting all hot and damp again at his sensuality. "Do it again."

"Do what?"

He trailed his hand up over her hip to her ribs and she giggled. "That," he rumbled, closing his eyes as he thrust against her.

She gasped at the sensation as she felt him hardening inside her. "Already?"

He groaned as he rocked against her. "Making up for lost time," he murmured, capturing her lips. This time he made love to her gently, tenderly, and she discovered that quiet little fireworks were just as pleasurable as the big bangs.

The sun had set by the time they'd taken a change of clothes from their bags in the trunk of the car and gotten the car back on the road.

Natalie smiled as Lucien turned onto the interstate and headed toward the vampire roost. He planned to borrow a vehicle from his friend, Heath, and they'd drive to his sister to feed her some of Natalie's blood.

Natalie tilted her head back against the seat, the wind

playing with her hair. Lucien reached over and grasped her hand, raising it to press a light kiss to her fingers. He couldn't stop touching her, and she liked it. A lot. He wore a charcoal gray T-shirt, his arm muscles were toned beneath the short sleeves. She just wanted to climb into his lap and strip him bare again. She watched the scenery pass in a blur.

She'd lived the last forty years surrounding herself with colleagues and acquaintances. She'd never let them get close, never shared her secrets, never really connected with anyone except on a perfunctory level. In less than a week, Lucien had smashed through those barriers. It wasn't until he had that she'd realized the small things she'd missed so much but hadn't noticed until she had them back again.

Just the act of sitting next to someone, sharing space with them, touching them. Holding hands… A small thing, really, but the companionship was both familiar yet new. Thinking of someone else, of putting another person's needs before your own—it was…refreshing. They'd seen so much—life *and* death—it was as though she'd gone through the worst possible scenarios with him and gotten those experiences over and done with, and now they had a chance for the good moments.

The trip back to the roost seemed to go much faster than the trip out to the desert. Lucien turned into the tunnel and her fingers tightened in his. He rubbed his thumb over her knuckle as he drove up to the portico.

"It's going to be fine," he told her, his voice low and husky. She nodded and smiled, relieved that yet again he was by her side. Lucien gave the keys to the valet and then escorted her up the steps. She had to sidestep a little as Lucien's friend strode out of the grand entrance, reading a sheaf of papers. Heath's eyes widened as he neatly avoided trampling her.

"Whoa, hey, sorry. Didn't see you there." He glanced quickly over his shoulder then gave her a polite smile. He raised his eyebrows when he saw Lucien's car in the drive. "Dude, what happened to your car?"

Lucien grimaced. "We bumped into a werewolf," he said then snapped his fingers as though remembering something. "Oh, and you know those ridgewalkers? They may not be as gone as you think they are."

Heath pursed his lips. "Well, that's not something I wanted to hear."

"No, I expect not. Can I borrow a car to get back to Irondell?" Lucien asked. Natalie watched the exchange with interest. Both handsome men, both carried a grim air around them, but were entirely relaxed in each other's company.

Heath nodded then glanced over his shoulder again. "Hey, you might want to go around—"

"Lucien!"

Lucien stiffened next to her and Heath winced. "Sorry, tried to warn you."

Lucien shifted, gently nudging her behind him as an austere-looking gentleman stalked out of the hotel entrance, his expression impatient. The guy who had tried to come into their room the night before accompanied him, and Natalie shifted closer to Lucien. She'd never been introduced to the man, but she'd seen enough images in the news reports to easily recognize Reform Senator Vincent Marchetta.

"Hello, Father," Lucien said in an even tone.

Chapter 19

Lucien kept his expression cool as his father approached. He had to battle the need to run up to the man and hug him. His father would probably want to send him to a psych clinic for an evaluation if he did. What the hell was he doing here? He let Enzo see his irritation. Tattletale. A horn sounded at the gate and Heath gestured to the lobby.

"Perhaps you'd like to make use of one of the meeting rooms?" his friend suggested. "We need to open the gate." He turned to Lucien. "I'll look after your request and have it delivered immediately," he said meaningfully.

Lucien nodded gratefully and followed his father into the hotel lobby. He couldn't stop staring. Since waking up in the cave, some things had crystalized for him. Namely, the importance of family, of loved ones. At one point, he and his father fit into both categories. He knew his father's anger, his coldness, his unreasonable demands and expectations all stemmed from the pain of his wife's death. Since then, Vincent had tried to do everything within his power, within the law and without, to destroy the lycan population. Lucien had tried to do everything within his power to obtain his father's forgiveness. Perhaps it was time to mend that connection. It was just one of the relationships he planned to improve. He eyed Natalie. So many relationships he wanted to work on...

"Well, what have you to report, Lucien?" His father's words were brusque as he stalked across the marble floor.

Lucien frowned. "Not here."

Vincent sighed in exasperation as he halted and turned to him. "Your sister's condition has deteriorated so much already. I don't have time for polite pleasantries. Are you going to stand back and let your sister die, too? What have you found?"

Yes, he needed to work on the relationship, but so did his father. He was sick of being treated like a lackey instead of a son. He realized his father wasn't the only one to carry anger with him. Yes, he hadn't been there with his mother when she'd died—and he carried enough guilt and regret to sink a battleship on that score—but he hadn't set the fires, he hadn't lined all the exits with silver to prevent an escape. He bore guilt for not saving his mother's life, but he wasn't the one who'd killed her, damn it. He didn't know what he had to do to make his father see that.

Lucien stepped closer to his father. "Keep your voice down," he growled softly, eyeing the other vampires in the lobby and the bar area. Most carried on with their business, but some had stopped to take note of the conversation.

Vincent smiled tightly. "Fine, let us speak in code. Did you find what you were looking for?"

Lucien pressed his lips together. He wanted to tell his father no, tell him to leave, but that wouldn't be in the spirit of improving relationships. Instead he gave his father an infinitesimal nod.

Vincent hadn't expected that response as he allowed his surprise to show for a brief moment. "Really?" His father eyed Natalie. "Apparently, I didn't give you enough credit." He gazed assessingly at his son.

"Where is the cure?" his father asked softly.

"It's safe," Lucien responded.

Vincent's eyes narrowed. He didn't like not controlling the situation, Lucien could tell. "Enzo."

Enzo's eyes flashed and his fangs lengthened as he stepped toward Natalie.

Lucien braced a hand against the guardian's chest.

"Where is the cure?" the guardian asked in an obvious attempt to intimidate.

"Back off, buster," Natalie snapped, and Lucien's eyebrows rose at her feisty manner. "I *am* the cure."

Ah, damn. Lucien winced. He could understand Natalie's desire to put his father's guardian in his place—oh, he could so understand—but she'd picked a risky way to do it. He glanced around the lobby. Yep. They were now the center of attention. "Let's go. Now."

He turned toward the entrance but halted when two vampires approached, their eyes glowing. They'd heard the exchange. Hell, probably every damn person in the lobby had heard the exchange and now knew Natalie was the cure for a lycan's bite.

He pulled Natalie behind him as the vampires launched toward them. His teeth lengthened and suddenly Enzo was at his side as they took on the attackers. He dodged the first punch, grabbed the vamp's neck and twisted. The vampire hit the ground with a thud and Lucien turned to take on his next opponent. He shoved Natalie behind a white marble column, staying her hand when it rose to the silver lariat chain around her neck. He shook his head. If she tried to fight them, she became more of a target, and with this many vampires, could wind up getting hurt. If they believed she was the cure, that could ensure her safety.

He ducked a punch and lashed out with a kick. Enzo dispatched a couple of vampires, and Lucien had just enough time to notice Heath running in the front door, his face grim as he saw what was happening inside the lobby of his hotel.

More vampires came out of the bar, their eyes locked on Natalie.

"Son, let me help. Enzo and I can get her out of here, if you and Heath can hold them off long enough," Vincent offered urgently.

Lucien gritted his teeth, his gaze meeting Natalie's as he caught the kick aimed at his solar plexus and twisted, popping the ankle of his assailant and throwing him to the ground. She shook her head slightly as she peered around the column.

A vampire snuck up behind her and, before Lucien could do or say anything, grabbed hold of her hair. Natalie squealed, clutching the hand. She stomped on his foot, punched him in the groin, and then did this neat little dip-and-twist thing that had her turning under his arm, hand still attached to her head. He heard the arm break from where he was, heard the vampire scream, only for it to be cut off when Natalie rammed his head into the marble column. He slumped to the ground, unconscious.

Lucien didn't want her hurt and although she possessed a strength that rivaled most, there were too many vampires here. After nearly losing her at Mount Solitude, then dying on her in the Red Desert, he wasn't prepared to put her in any further danger.

"Think of Vivianne," his father urged, stepping out of harm's way as a vampire came barreling past. "She needs the cure."

Lucien growled. Damn it. He had to choose between his sister's life and his primal need to protect Natalie. Well, maybe he could have both. If Natalie went with his father, she would be removed from this situation and his sister would receive her cure.

"Go," he called out, jerking his head toward the door.

She blanched. "You want me to leave? With your father?"

He eyed his father. "He'll look after you," he said loudly, and his father nodded his agreement. "Go, save Vivianne. I'll come as soon as I can."

Enzo grabbed her arm and pulled her toward the entrance. Heath smashed a vampire in the face, pushing him out of their way as Vincent followed closely behind. Lucien watched as they ran out of the building, Natalie glanced over her shoulder, her expression worried, before Heath stepped in front of the door and caught a pursuing vampire in a headlock, effortlessly snapping the man's neck and tossing him off to the side.

Natalie allowed herself to be tugged along, running down the steps toward a waiting limousine. Vincent climbed in first and Enzo pushed her in, quite roughly, actually, and followed close behind, slamming the door and yelling instructions to the driver. Natalie fell back against the seat as the driver took off with a squeal of tires and the gate to the tunnel started to open.

"That will buy us some time," Enzo stated as he settled on the seat closest to the door. "Any vamps who come out while the gate is open will be vaporized."

Natalie weaved over to the seat that ran along the length of the vehicle, grasping a seat belt to prevent being thrown around the car.

"Good, then we can relax," Vincent said and smiled at Natalie. "Make yourself comfortable, dear."

She buckled herself into the seat belt, bracing her hands against the leather on either side of her. She looked up just in time to see Enzo withdraw a gun. She didn't even have time to scream before she felt a familiar burn in her side and she grasped instinctively at the cartridge protruding from her skin. She pulled it out and held it up to look at it. She had time for one thought before the haze took her under.

Another friggin' tranquilizer.

Lucien grimaced as he snapped the vampire's neck and let him fall. His shoulders sagged as he gazed around the lobby. There were bodies strewn everywhere.

Heath stalked over, an unconscious vampire slung over his shoulder. He dropped him unceremoniously on a pile of bodies by the bar entrance.

The discrete beep of a phone echoed through the lobby. "Rafferty's Roost, how may I help you?"

Heath turned and gave his receptionist a thumbs-up.

"Love your work, Kayla." He turned back and surveyed the mess, then gave a low whistle. "That was fun."

Lucien stretched his neck. He had to agree. Since he'd awoken in that cave, he felt so damn alive, so hyper, and this had been a good way to work off some energy. Although working it off with Natalie was far more pleasurable. "They're all going to wake up with sore heads tomorrow."

Heath shrugged. "At least they'll wake up. Come on, let's grab a drink."

"Just a quick one, then I have to go meet Natalie."

Lucien followed him into the now empty bar and sat on one of the stools as Heath vaulted over the bar.

"Whiskey, bourbon or cognac?"

"Whiskey."

Heath poured them both a measure, then picked up his glass. He tilted his head. "Man, this is going to be an expensive visit for you." He chuckled.

Lucien nodded. "Yep, but Natalie got out safe, that's all that matters."

Heath nodded. "Good for you." He gazed through to the reception area and all its unconscious occupants. "Well, here's to a good rumble at Rafferty's," he said. He tipped his head back and swallowed the contents of his shot glass.

Lucien followed suit, enjoying the slow burn down his throat, then frowned. "Sorry, Heath. I didn't plan for this."

Heath shrugged as he poured them each another drink. "Hey, shit happens. Although I'd dearly love to know how my reception got turned into a fight club."

Lucien shook his head. "Dad didn't want to go to a meeting room. He wanted to discuss what I'd managed to turn up, right there in the lobby." He gestured casually past the pile of vampires still out cold. He sighed. "I'll pay for the damages. Just put it on my tab." He clinked his glass against Heath's and they both drank the shot of whiskey.

Heath bared his teeth at the fiery liquid, then lined the glasses up again for another shot. "I'll put it on your father's tab," he said, sloshing the whiskey into the glasses and then placing the bottle on the bar with a clunk.

Lucien frowned as he accepted yet another drink from his friend. "Why my father?"

Heath eyed him intently. "Because he was in this bar not two hours ago talking it up with that goon he calls a guardian, and they were making no secret of the fact that you were out there looking for a cure for a werewolf bite. Drink."

Lucien drank, then thunked his glass down on the bar. "Why would dear old Dad do that?" he wondered aloud. His father was a Reform senator. Keeping secrets and being discrete was second nature to him.

Heath shrugged. "Not my dad, not my problem." He leaned his forearm on the bar. "Although, any other vampire would have to think twice about taking on the Marchettas if even a werewolf bite can't hurt them... Hey, you don't think he was trying to start a fight, do you?"

Lucien shook his head. "No," he said, but he drew the word out slowly as he thought about it, gazing at the bar. His father's actions screamed irresponsible, which wasn't necessarily a word he'd associate with his father...but to do that intentionally? That was harsh. Cold. Now *that* sounded like his father. But why? Then he realized, and he felt like such a fool. A naive, gullible fool who'd just put his lover in harm's way.

He looked up at Heath. "He wanted to separate us."

Heath's eyebrows rose. "Us? As in that pretty little 'helper' of yours?" he said, tweaking his fingers as though to parenthesize the word. "I've never seen you that way with another vampire, let alone a human. You love that chick."

"I do, and now my father has her, and fully intends to kill her when she outlives her usefulness."

"And what might that be?"

Lucien looked at his friend, trying to gauge how much he should tell him. After his assistance in getting Natalie out of the roost and away from a whole posse of marauding vamps, he felt maybe he could trust him with the truth.

"It's about the cure. For Vivianne."

Heath frowned. "You found something?" His eyes widened. "You found the cure?"

"Natalie *is* the cure."

Heath gaped at him for a moment then poured another shot. "Something to celebrate."

Lucien shook his head. "No, my father is just as much a threat to Natalie as these vamps here. I have to stop him." Just the thought of Natalie being alone and at the mercy of Enzo, working on his father's instructions, was enough to ignite a slow, simmering pot of rage inside him. Lucien was off the stool and halfway to the door when Heath whistled. He turned around and caught the keys Heath tossed to him.

"Take my car. It's parked in the drive," his friend

said, and Lucien nodded. He leaped over the pile
of vamps just outside the door. "And no dings or
scratches, okay?"

...said, and ducked quickly. He leaned over to help
Owens fit... before the door. And perhaps if
he just...

Chapter 20

Natalie stirred, her eyelids flickering. White. Dark.
White. Dark. Each time the white lasted a little longer
until she could open her eyes without them drifting
shut again. She stared up at the ceiling. So much white.

Her head throbbed and her mouth tasted like she'd
dined on ash. She tried to sit up, but something stopped
her. She looked down, frowning in confusion. Her legs
and arms were strapped to a bed and there were a number of needles stuck into her skin. An IV port, connected to a cannula that had been inserted into the crook
of her elbow, led to a little blood bag seesawing in a
cradle scale. Her other arm was connected to a fluid
drip. Her frown deepened as she glanced around the
room. What the hell had happened? For a moment she
thought she was back in that psych ward, when seeing
dead people seemed weirder than being cured of cancer and coming back to life. She racked her brain, trying to make sense of the jumble inside.

The last thing she could remember was fighting the
vampires at the roost and running out to the limousine

with Lucien's father and—Enzo. The dart, the pain in her side, the scary rush of darkness...she remembered.

She struggled against the restraints, gritting her teeth as the needles pricked and a little alarm sounded on one of the beeping machines next to the bed.

The door burst open and a man in a white coat rushed in, relaxing when he saw her trying to jostle the restraints. "I wouldn't do that," he cautioned, hastening over to her. He switched off the alarm and went to check on the IV line. He checked her cannula and she hissed when he adjusted the needle inside her arm. "See, we don't want to knock anything out."

He glanced down at her. "You're a very interesting test subject, Ms. Stewart."

"Segova," Natalie corrected then winced as speaking made her feel like she'd swallowed razor blades and they'd caught in her throat.

"Oh, we know who you are," he said, reaching for a jug and a glass with a straw on the table by the bed. He poured some water, then held the straw to her lips so she could slake her thirst. She eyed him as she sipped. His hair was graying at the temples, although he still had a youthful face. Handsome, if you liked freaky doctors. "Easy, there. Good girl. That will be the sedative wearing off. Not to worry, though, we've got you hooked up to a line and I can increase the dose. We thought we'd take it easy for the first donation."

She shot him a dark look as he withdrew the straw and placed the glass back on the table. Donation implied free will on the part of the donor. She jerked at the restraint on her arm again.

"Let me go," she said, relieved the words emerged smoother, louder. Firmer.

"No can do. Sorry," the doctor chirped as he leaned over to pick up the chart at the end of her bed. "You are quite the find, Nina."

"Natalie."

He sighed then inclined his head. "If that's what you'd prefer to be called. He lifted a page of her chart. "Your blood is like one serious hot mess. Did you know that? We've got markers for lycanism, vampirism, humanism and just a little nullification. There is damage, but the cells repair on a biochemical level. Truly unique." He tilted his head. "You had cancer, didn't you? When you were a kid? Chemo? Radiation therapy? That could explain the distortion. When you died and were revived, you deviated from the norm on so many levels."

This guy knew way too much about her. It was creepy. She gazed around the room. Apart from her bed and the machines she was hooked up to, there was nothing else. No windows, no other doors except for the exit. Again, just like that damned psych ward.

"Where am I?"

The doctor smiled. "The Marchetta estate. Our very own research facility. Oh, by the way, we're running some tests on your blood—obviously we're not going to give it to Vivianne if there are going to be detrimental effects. Then, once we've assessed the success of that test, we'll start harvesting properly."

Her blood chilled in her veins. "Harvesting?"

The doctor nodded. "Why, yes. You might be a deviant breed, but you're also a gift, Natalie. Your blood can help so many."

Her chin dipped and she glared at him. "Did you just call me a deviant?"

The door opened and Vincent Marchetta walked in. His eyebrows rose when he met her gaze.

"Oh, our patient is awake."

"I'm not your patient. Let me go." She snarled. She didn't care if this man was Lucien's father, he was being a class-A douche.

"I can't, I'm afraid. You're far too valuable. If what my son claims is true, you've just given me quite an advantage among the vampires—and against the mangy mutts. The good doctor here believes your blood can be quite an effective vaccine for my breed."

Natalie shook her head. "No. I don't give my permission. Let. Me. Go."

Vincent raised his eyebrows. "Permission?" he asked in a silky tone as he stepped toward the bed. "Consider this a down payment. My wife is dead because of you." His words came out with barely leashed rage. So civilized yet with suppressed violence.

She gaped at the man and he smiled, his fangs lengthening as his eyes flashed briefly in warning. "What? You think I don't know what my son does? Who he sees? He couldn't lose a fight without me knowing before it happens. He certainly couldn't visit a pathetic little human girl in the burbs without my allowing it. Do you think I don't know where he was when his mother died? That I didn't make it my business to find out? Imagine my surprise to see you pop up on the Marchetta radar again, forty years later."

"Lucien won't allow this," Natalie insisted. "He'll come looking for me."

Vincent gave her a pitying look. "Oh, you actually think he cares for you. He tracked you down with the intention of using you, my dear. Of getting what we need out of you. You saw him back at the roost. He gave you to me. To save his sister. When it comes to his family, his loyalty will always trump any misguided romantic notion."

Natalie blinked, trying to mask her hurt at his words. They echoed what she'd wondered as he'd agreed with his father back at the roost. Back in the cave, when he'd thought he was dying and that the cure they had wasn't effective, he'd told her not to trust his father, and to run. Now, with her blood proving to be an effective remedy, she found herself strapped to a bed with a needle in her arm and Lucien nowhere in sight.

"I don't believe you." The words didn't come out with the conviction she'd intended and Vincent Marchetta smiled.

"Yes, you do. You're not normal, Natalie, or Nina, or whatever the hell you want to call yourself. You're a deviant, a freak of nature who's finally discovered her purpose is to serve others."

He turned to the man in the white coat, as though bored with the conversation. "How long?"

The doctor glanced at his watch. "Well, we're at the eight-hour mark now, so we'll be introducing the antidote to the test subject within the hour. Would you like to watch?"

"I would," Vincent said, nodding. "I have some things to attend to, so I'll return later, Dr. Morton."

Natalie's gaze flicked to the doctor as Vincent left the room. "Dr. Morton?" she asked, a chill creeping over her.

He smiled as he jotted some notes on her chart and placed the pen in the folder's clip. "That's my name."

Her mouth dried. "Uh, any relation to the Mortons in Devil's Leap?" She kept her tone casual.

Morton hesitated, then put the folder down next to her on the bed as he gave her his full attention. "Why yes, as a matter of fact," he said silkily.

She mentally calculated the time frame. "Great-grandson? Great-great-grandson?"

He shook his head. "No, I'm the real deal," he told her, and smiled. She flinched when his incisors lengthened.

"You're a vampire?" she whispered, aghast.

He nodded. "I know, quite ironic, isn't it? Nasty accident at the lab. I spent so much time researching how to kill a vampire, now I spend my time researching how to preserve one. You know, we're not nearly as invulnerable as people think."

He frowned at her as he picked up the folder and placed it in the tray at the end of the bed. "How do you know of me?"

"Uh, we have a mutual friend," she muttered. "Grace Perkins."

"Ah, Grace. She was my first. You always remember your first, don't you?" he admitted, touching his tongue to his fang. He grimaced. "Admittedly, I was quite rough with her. I've since learned a little finesse."

His watch beeped, distracting him. "Well, time to check on our test subject."

A dark suspicion bloomed in her mind. Vivianne was a vampire, bitten by a lycan. Based on Morton's past history, had he forced a werewolf bite on a vampire? Maybe there was someone out there willing to be Morton's lab rat. She wasn't one of them.

"Are they a volunteer?" she asked.

Morton turned in surprise at the door. "What?"

"Your test subject. Did they volunteer?"

He gave her a patient look. "We like to replicate scenarios. In usual circumstances so many factors need to be considered—adrenaline, cortisol, heart rate and so on. We try to make it as realistic as possible." He smiled. "Now, you need your rest. I'll check in later."

She remembered the teen back at Mount Solitude, his injuries… "What about the werewolf?" she asked.

Morton smiled. "Oh, we'll keep him a little longer. He's a fine specimen for further experiments."

The door closed and Natalie lay there for a moment. The room was silent except for the beeping of the machines monitoring her. She trembled. The room was cool, but it was the loneliness that ate at her, that settled into her bones like an arthritic ache. A tear rolled down her cheek. She'd thought Lucien loved her. He'd told her he loved her. Was it delirium that had spurred those words? He'd let her go so easily.

To help his sister.

She glanced around the sterile room. He'd given her up for this. Had their whole time together been a sham? One long con to manipulate her into this very spot? Another tear tracked down her cheek. Hours ago she'd been so happy, she'd felt…*loved*. Cherished. Protected. For the first time in decades, she'd had a real friend. Someone she'd confided in, someone she'd shared intimate secrets with, she'd shared her *body* with, and to whom she'd given her heart.

She stared at the ceiling, trying to pull back the tears. As a kid, she'd been lonely. She was that sick kid who'd had to stay in bed while the other kids had played in the street. Then she'd met a dark angel in a hospital ward and suddenly wasn't so lonely anymore. After her parents died, she'd been lonely again. She knew she was different…what had Morton called her? A *deviant*. Her lip curled. She'd felt so alone, and that dark angel had returned and had cracked her reserve, pierced the shield she'd hidden behind.

A soft sob escaped her lips and she clamped her mouth shut. Losing Lucien, or the *ideal* of Lucien, was as bad, if not worse, than when she'd lost her family.

She was so sick of being vulnerable to vamps, of being hurt by them, by Lucien. She'd trusted him, damn it. And now she was part of some sick blood harvest for the very breed that had once killed her. She was sick of being a victim, of being betrayed. She was sick of being a *deviant*.

Most of all, she was sick of being underestimated.

She palmed the pen she'd slipped out of the medical folder and slid it between the straps of her restraint.

Lucien stormed into his father's home office.

Vincent stopped talking to Enzo and frowned at the interruption.

"Where is she?" he said through gritted teeth.

His father waved a hand. "She's fine. She's resting." Lucien darted over to Enzo and grasped his neck, twisting until he heard the snap. The vampire hit the floor before his father could blink. His father gave him an exasperated look.

"Really, Lucien? Don't you think that's a little over-dramatic?"

"Just be thankful I've only broken his neck and not killed him, after that little stunt you pulled at Rafferty's. Oh, and by the way, you now have at least three colonies on their way over here to try to catch this miracle cure you've just broadcast to all and sundry. I've sent a call out for reinforcements. Now, where is she?"

Vincent sighed. "Downstairs."

"Down—" Lucien clenched his teeth. "You put her in your *lab*?"

His father's lab conducted research on weapons, but he'd never been down there. Knowing his lover was down there, being treated like a patient—or worse, a test subject—infuriated him. How could his father treat her that way?

His father frowned. "Where else do you expect me to house a medical miracle?"

"Her name is Natalie and she's a person."

"But her name was once Nina, was it not?" His father's voice was quiet. Mild. Too mild.

Lucien's eyes narrowed. "You...know about her? About what happened to her?"

"I know everything, Lucien. I know you used to visit her. Play games with her..." He shrugged. "Personally, I couldn't see the appeal, but really, some of my friends had sons who were into drugs or those underground bloodfests. My son was playing board games with a kid. I wasn't going to quibble. But then your mother died..."

Lucien gazed up at the ceiling for a moment, trying to reach for that patience, that new-life-new-attitude philosophy he'd decided upon at the roost. Now he understood how his father could treat Natalie that way. When it came to his wife's death, his father tended to lose sight of his scruples. "She wasn't part of that," he said quietly.

Vincent smiled grimly. "Well, you were with her and not with your mother, saving her from that massacre."

Lucien's lips tightened and he stepped closer to his father's desk. "Let's follow that line of logic, shall we?"

His father opened his mouth, but Lucien shook his head. "No. This conversation is a long time coming. Let's suppose I was in that ballroom. What do you think the outcome would have been? Really? With all the other able, capable, strong vampires in that room, what do you think I could have done that they didn't?"

"You could have saved her!" his father roared, his fist landing on the three-hundred-year-old desk with such force the wooden surface cracked. "You could have saved her."

"Really, Dad? Silver, everywhere. Salt. Fire. That's pretty much the holy trinity for killing vamps. Fifty-three people died in that fire, because fifty-three people couldn't find a way out. If I was there, it would have been fifty-four." Lucien shook his head, sorrow pulling at his lips. "When I told Natalie that I was with her that night, do you know what she wanted to do? She wanted to come and talk to you, to apologize."

Vincent's eyes flickered and he looked away for a moment. "You lie."

"No, Dad, I don't. She lost her family, she lost her parents, and when she heard about your loss, the first thing she wanted to do was reach out to you, to offer some comfort—and that was *after* she learned you wanted her dead as soon as she outlived her usefulness."

Vincent shook his head. "She is the reason your mother is dead."

Lucien threw up his hands in frustrated exasperation. "You can't have it both ways, Dad. You can't punish me for Mom's death and then punish Natalie for the same thing. What about you? Or Vivianne?"

Vincent went still. "I beg your pardon?"

"Well, by your definition, I wasn't there, so I'm responsible. Natalie, who wasn't there, is responsible. Vivianne wasn't there. Is she responsible, too? What about you? You were away on a business trip. Are you responsible?" Lucien was stunned as the words popped out of his mouth. He'd never spoken to his father in such a manner before, but now that he'd said it, things started to make a little more sense.

Vincent's face grew mottled with rage. "Hold your tongue," he bellowed as he swept around the desk. "How dare you?"

"No, Dad. How dare *you*?" Lucien punctuated the word by pointing at his father's chest then curling that finger into a fist. Maybe he'd gone a little too far. He hoped to God this new-life-new-attitude thing worked, otherwise he was in for a reprimand from his father. And they were vampires, so that could last several lifetimes.

His father's eyes flashed red and his incisors lengthened. "You little—"

"Son. I'm your *son*, Dad. I'm your son, who lost his mom, and not a day goes by that I don't mourn her, that I don't miss her, that I don't grieve for her, that I don't wish I could take her place, and *she* could be here, arguing with you. I lost my mom, but that night I also lost my father and got a bitter, angry, vengeful stranger instead."

Vincent halted and his eyes dimmed a little. "She shouldn't have died," he rasped.

Lucien could sense the shift in mood. He took a cautious step closer.

"No, she shouldn't have. None of those vampires

should have died that night. But they did." Lucien's eyes began to itch a little and he rubbed his lips together as he finally realized what his father needed to hear. "I'm sorry, Dad. I'm sorry I wasn't there for Mom."

Vincent's shoulders sagged, his body seeming to collapse in on itself in desolation. "I loved her."

"I know," Lucien said softly. "We all did."

Vincent lifted his gaze and for the first time Lucien saw beyond the cold, aloof mask to the sheer devastation of a man who'd lost the woman he loved. Vincent grabbed him and hauled him close, hugging him tightly to him.

"I'm sorry, son," he whispered against his neck.

Lucien closed his eyes and hugged his father back. Hard. "Me, too." After a moment he sighed and pulled back. "Now, let's go get the lady I love, and wake up Vivianne."

His father shook his head stubbornly. "I can't let you take her, she's too valuable."

Well, there went that chick flick moment. "She's not a commodity, Dad," Lucien argued, frowning. He stepped back, astonished his father could still look at her like that after the moment they'd shared, the hurdle they'd both jumped. The truth they'd both faced.

"You don't understand, Lucien. She can help our breed," his father stated, his chin going up.

Lucien recognized that stubborn chin lift. "Let her do it of her own free will, Dad."

"This is something that can help us in our fight against the lycans," Vincent said, shaking his fist. "Their one advantage is that a single bite is fatal to vampires, and we can eradicate that."

"Not like this, Dad."

"Yes, exactly like this. If her blood can really cure a lycan's bite, we can produce an anti-venom, perhaps even a vaccination."

Lucien's eyes rounded. "We don't have the quantity for that, Dad. What are you going to do, hook Natalie up to a blood bag and just keep swapping them out?"

His father's chin lowered, just a little bit, as he glanced away, just briefly. "Well…"

Lucien clapped his hand over his mouth, his eyes wide. "Oh, my God," he said, the words muffled behind his palm. He lowered his hand. "I was being sarcastic. Have you—? Did you—?" Anger filled him at the realization of how far his father was prepared to sell his soul in his mission to exact vengeance against the breed who'd killed his wife. Lucien shook his head.

"Mom would not want this," he said forcefully.

"Your mother's dead," Vincent barked.

Lucien turned away, shaking his head. "I can't even look at you right now." He held up a hand to stop whatever ludicrous argument his father was about to come up with to justify this horror. If he wasn't a damned one, he'd pray to some god for patience.

He turned to face his father. "Do you want to know how we learned Natalie's blood was the cure, Dad? Hmm?" He scratched his cheek. "I got bit."

Vincent frowned. "What?"

"That's right, Dad. I was bitten. By a werewolf. In the Red Desert. Do you want to know how I survived being bitten by a werewolf in the Red Desert—a werewolf, by the way, that shouldn't bloody be there?" His hands dropped to his hips as he paced in front of his father.

"Natalie hauled my butt out of the sun. Then she

went looking for some pokey little weed in the sand, because that's what we thought would work—only it didn't." He grimaced. "I went through it all. The fever, the hallucinations…" He gestured in the general direction of his head. "I was pretty messed up. I'm not sure, but I may have tried to attack Natalie. But she refused to leave me, Dad." Lucien strode up to his father, angry at what he'd done to a woman who didn't deserve that kind of treatment.

"She stayed with me, and then she fed me her blood—and you have to understand, that was pretty major for her, considering she'd been murdered by a vampire. She gave me her blood."

He lifted his hands out. "And that saved me. She. *Saved*. Me. Just like she saved me when she was nine years old. She gave me her blood." He held up two fingers to his father, his eyes narrowed. "Twice.

"But not only that, she was prepared—and *willing*—to come back and save Vivianne, and you've locked her up in some research lab." He shook his head in disgust. "Tell me how that honors Mom or Vivianne? Tell me where she is."

"We need her blood, Lucien."

Lucien's hand fisted. He wanted to punch his father so damn hard right about now. He was so angry, but that anger was masking hurt, and he hurt so badly now. "Tell me, Dad. If it was Mom in that lab downstairs, would you leave her there? Because I can't leave Natalie there." He turned away then paused to look over his shoulder. "I expected better of you."

It was the same words his father had said to him

the night his mother had passed away, and he saw the flinch, saw the anger in his father's eyes. He turned and walked out on his father.

Chapter 21

Idiots, Natalie thought as she looped her silver chain twice around her neck. They'd left her with her jewelry. She slid her sneakers on. She'd found her clothes in the bottom drawer of the table beside the bed. The bastards had taken her knife, though.

She glared down at the IV still attached to her arm. Once she took that out, an alarm would sound and Dr. Morton and maybe more would come running through that door. She steadied herself. She'd have to make a run for it.

She eyed the blood bag in the cradle. She refused to be a reduced to a vaccination. She picked up the bag and detached the IV from her cannula. The alarm triggered on the machine. She smiled grimly, her movements efficient as she closed off the cannula and IV lines. After spending years in the health system, she could look after her own injections and IV in a pinch.

Within seconds she was out the door, the alarm receding as she bolted down the hall.

She could hear shouts at one end of the hall, could

see shadow figures running toward the corner, so she abruptly changed direction. She ran along, but could hear them behind her, getting close to that corner. As soon as they rounded that bend, they'd see her.

She skidded to a halt and burst through a door, wincing as she closed it behind her as quickly and as quietly as possible. She leaned against the door, panting, peering into the dim room.

"Well, hello there," a deep voice rumbled from the shadows in a corner. A shadow emerged, a tall, broad-shouldered man with dusty blond, close-cropped hair and sunglasses. He was dressed all in black. Black jeans and boots, black T-shirt, black leather jacket and gloves.

She jerked at the lariat, the chain sliding from around her neck. She looped it twice around her palm, and slid the blood bag into the back of her jeans before raising her fist in a defensive stance.

"Back the hell up," she said in low voice.

The man's eyebrows rose over his sunglasses and he held his hands up, palms facing her, as he stopped walking. An alarm sounded, it's strident peals echoing down the hall. He tilted his head.

"For you, I presume?"

She nodded. "Yes. I'm very dangerous, so I wouldn't come any closer if I were you." She swallowed. She was stronger than most, but this guy was…big.

He nodded. "Oh, I can see. Positively lethal." He smiled. "But I should warn you, silver doesn't have any effect on me."

She frowned as she tried to back up closer to the door. She could hear the footsteps as staff ran along the hall outside. "You're not a vampire? Or a werewolf?"

She said the words quietly as she peered at him. He looked rough and just a little dangerous himself.

His jaw dropped for a moment, then he pressed his lips together, clearly offended. "I'm going to pretend you didn't say that," he said. He gestured toward the door. "Relax, I'm not one of them."

"Yet, you're here… Why?"

"I have…" The man hesitated, as though searching for the right word. "I have a duty that I need to fulfill here."

"Who are you?" she asked, still poised to fight.

"Oh, where are my manners? Dave Carter, witch extraordinaire, at your service," he said, giving her a courtly bow. "And you are?"

"Natalie Segova."

His face lit up. "Oh, Professor Natalie Segova." He took the glove off his right hand, extending it toward her. "Hey, I'm a big fan. I read your article on the mystical relevance of Egyptian burial practices, great stuff."

Her brow dipped as she shook his hand in an automatic response. "Uh, thanks. I think."

This was so weird. He cocked his head as he clasped her hand. "Wow. You're…interesting."

She tugged her hand free. Was he trying to read her? She knew some witches could. She eyed him suspiciously. "You don't look like any of the witches I've met."

He grinned as he slid his glove back on. "Oh, I can assure you, there are no other witches like me." Then he frowned. "Why are you here? I mean, I guess it's got something to do with Vivianne Marchetta, but why are you here, hiding?" The alarm continued to peal. Irritatingly so.

Her eyes narrowed. "Why would you think I'm here for Vivianne Marchetta?" she asked. How closely associated was he to Vincent Marchetta and Dr. Morton? Lucien?

"Well, I told Lucien about your field of study. I thought there was a chance you may have come across something in your research that could help Vivianne."

Her lips pursed. "So, you're the reason I'm here."

He stared at her for a moment and she found looking at his sunglasses a frustrating block to trying to gauge his expression. All she could see was herself reflected in the lenses. And why was he wearing sunglasses in a dark room, anyway?

He folded his arms, his leather jacket creaking with the movement. "Why do I get the impression there's some tension here?" he said, lifting his chin to the door and the alarm and confused staff in the hall.

"Maybe the alarm gave it away—"

A knock sounded at the door behind her and she started.

In a flash, Dave had stepped up to her, covering her mouth with his finger on her lips. He shifted her to the side, gave her a cautioning waggle of his finger, then opened the door, pulling it wide so that she was effectively hidden from whomever might walk inside the room.

"I thought I told you all I wasn't to be bothered?" Dave said harshly, his features stern. Natalie would have trembled, if there was enough room between the wall and the door to do so.

"We apologize for the intrusion," a woman's voice answered. "We've got a patient on the loose. A little addled, I'm afraid. Quiet dangerous. We're doing a room check." Natalie heard a footfall and through the crack between the door and wall, she saw a tall blonde woman, dressed in a black uniform, step inside the room.

"Are you kidding? I'm trying to rest, to save my energy to help your vampire prime's sister, and you're wanting to search my room because you've lost a patient?" Dave barked.

The female guard hesitated. "I apologize, Mr. Carter—"

"Apologize to your prime when I'm too drained to perform any more spells," he said through gritted teeth. He stepped to the side, effectively concealing Natalie behind his large form. "Look. There is nobody here except me and you."

The guard held up her hand as she backed out of the room. "I apologize, Mr.—"

"Just make sure it doesn't happen again," Dave snapped and slammed the door in the woman's face. They listened at the door, and Natalie sagged in relief when she heard the woman's boots retreating down the hall.

"Now," Dave murmured, folding his arms and leaning against the door, blocking off any attempt for Natalie to leave. "Can you please explain to me how the professor of occult studies who I recommended has wound up as a 'patient' in Vincent Marchetta's research lab?"

Natalie gave him the condensed version.

Dave swore softly then dipped his chin. "So, what do you want?"

"I want out," she said softly. "Will you help?"

"You don't need my help."

She gestured to the door and the guard beyond. "It appears I do," she whispered back.

His head tilted from side to side, as though he was weighing his options. "You'll owe me one," he said in warning.

She'd be happy to pay whatever price he demanded if he got her out of this nightmare. She nodded.

He nodded once. "Fine. It so happens I'm free at the moment, anyway."

"Where is she?" a familiar roar echoed down the hall and Natalie's breath caught. Lucien. And he sounded pissed.

She flattened herself against the wall, her eyes wide. Lucien had sacrificed her for his sister, now he was helping the guards find her. To put her back on blood donation duty?

Dave gave her an exasperated look. "Not all Marchettas are the same, Natalie. Vivianne didn't ask for this, and while she may be a bitch on wheels when she's not in a coma, she wouldn't have condoned any of what has happened to you. Lucien can be a tool, I know, but he does seem to have a streak of fairness running through him." The witch dipped his head. "Okay, you may have to look really deep to find it, but he values a promise. Remember that."

"Why are you defending them?" she angrily whispered at him.

Dave pulled a face. "I wouldn't normally, but I have to be fair and give credit where it's due," he whispered back. He shook his shoulders, as though trying to shake off something creepy. "Ugh, can't believe I said that about vamps. I need a shower."

"Where is she?" Lucien bellowed down the hall again.

She flinched when she heard a body hit a wall.

"We're looking for her now, sir." Footsteps could be heard running down the hall. "She escaped—"

"She shouldn't have been here in the first place," Lucien snapped. "You had no right to hold her."

Natalie's eyes widened. Dave looked at her for a moment and then they both pressed their ears to the door, listening intently.

"But your father—" The words were cut off on a gurgling gasp.

"My father does not give the orders here. I am your vampire prime. I release Natalie Segova, do you hear me? She is free to leave, and you and the rest of the guardians will not harm her. Do you understand?"

Even though the words were uttered with such menace, with such suppressed violence, they stirred a soft warmth that bloomed inside her like a rose in the sun.

"Yes, sir," the female guard choked out.

Natalie clutched her chest, a smile tugging at her lips. Dave leaned closer. "Told you," he whispered.

Natalie opened the door and peered out into the hall.

Lucien's head whipped around, his eyes red and incisors extended, but his aggression retracted the moment he saw her.

"Natalie," he breathed, dropping the guard to the floor without a glance.

Lucien ran toward her, wrapping her in his arms. "God, I was so worried about you." He kissed her on the forehead. "I'm so glad you're okay." His heart pounded in his chest and he closed his eyes, chin resting on her head, as he held her. He just wanted to hold her.

"I'm so sorry," he whispered. He pulled back to gaze down at her, cupping her face. "I had no idea what my father intended," he told her. "There is no way I would have let you go if I had known."

She stared up at him and he could see the dark, haunted shadows in her eyes. "I thought... I thought you'd left me, again," she admitted in a hoarse whisper. He closed his eyes against the guilt her words sparked. He couldn't blame her. He caressed her cheek as he stared down at her again. "I'll never leave you again, Natalie. You're stuck with me now."

He lowered his head, infusing his kiss with all the solemnity, all the promise and resolve he possessed. She opened her mouth to him, and he sighed as he deepened the kiss, his tongue tangling with hers as his passion for this woman in his arms awoke.

"Get a room," a deep voice interrupted them.

Lucien frowned as he lifted his head. Dave Carter. "What are you doing here?"

"I'm on vacation. What do you think?" the witch responded, rolling his eyes as he turned to stroll down the hall.

A chill of worry crept over Lucien's shoulders. The last he'd heard, Dave had been trying to boost the suspension spell his sister was under. "Vivianne?"

"Hanging in there. She's stubborn." Dave cast a casual glance over his shoulder. "That trait runs in your family."

Lucien looked down at the woman in his arms. She had the power to save his sister. Saving Vivianne's life had been his life's mission for the past eight and a half months. It had been what he'd lived and breathed, what had kicked him out of bed in the evening. He'd blackmailed Natalie. He'd put her in some risky situations. She'd saved his life in such a brave action that he was still humbled by it. And as a result his family had abused her. Hurt her. Held her against her will.

He couldn't ask any more of her.

"Come on," he said quietly, clasping her hand. "Let's get you out of here."

The decision pained him, but the relief in her eyes did a little to assuage the guilt he now wore like a mantle.

They walked to the end of the hall. One wall was glass, revealing an empty lab with various supplies and equipment. He frowned. Maybe it was time he paid a little more attention to what was going on down here under the main house. They turned the corner. Lucien walked toward the double swing doors that were the main entrance to his father's underground facility, but halted when the doors burst open. Enzo ran through, pausing when his eyes met Lucien's. Vincent wasn't far behind.

Lucien shook his head. "Don't."

"Ah, Lucien…?" Dave called.

Lucien looked over his shoulder. More guardians were jogging down the hall. Some wore the uniform of his father's guards. Some wore casual clothes—his own Nightwing guardians. And some guy in a white lab coat.

"You can't take her, Lucien," his father called to him. Enzo stepped closer.

"You can't stop me, Dad." He was furious. Vincent was creating an internal war between his guards and the Lucien's Nightwing guardians. "What do you think you're doing? You were once Nightwing and now you're fighting against your family?"

"I'm doing this to *protect* our family," Vincent growled, his eyes flashing red in rage.

"Her blood works," Dr. Morton called out, and Vincent nodded.

Lucien heard Natalie shake out the chain she normally wore around her neck, and it made a soft ringing sound as the links snapped together. He'd seen her use it before, back at that facility in the mountain.

Dave held up his hands. "I think we can all take it down a notch and—"

Enzo growled, eyes flashing as he leaped at Lucien. That action was like a signal to the rest of the vampires and all of them sprang at the trio in the middle.

Natalie lashed out with her silver chain and the vampires screamed as it sliced through their skin and bone with laser-like precision.

Lucien caught Enzo, fists clenched, and they went down fighting. Out of the corner of his eye he saw Dave land a few punches that made jaws break and heads spin.

Natalie ducked and darted like some little crackerjack ninja, her chain lashing out like a whip. He saw her grab both ends and charge at a vampire, changing direction at the last moment by bracing her leg against the wall and leaping over him. She twined the chain around his neck and gave it a vicious tug. The vampire's eyes widened as the chain sliced cleanly through flesh and bone, separating his head from his shoulders.

Where the hell had she learned that?

He grunted as a stray kick caught him in the solar plexus and then he felt Enzo's muscular arms slip around his shoulders and grab his chin. *No.* He tried to remove the hand from his chin. All it would take would be one swift jerk to break his neck and this fight would be over by the time he revived.

Natalie saw the move, recognized it for the impending kill it was, and she screamed in rage. Lucien gaped as his lover's eyes flashed bright silver. She launched herself at Enzo, tackling him.

Enzo thrust Lucien away, where he fell into the waiting arms of two guards.

"No!" Lucien roared as Enzo caught both of Natalie's hands, preventing her from using the chain on him. They crashed to the floor in a twist of limbs. Lucien struggled against his father's guards as Natalie cried out in pain. Enzo trapped her legs beneath his own and smashed her wrists on the floor until she dropped the chain.

Lucien lashed out with his feet, connecting with one of the guards behind the knee. The guard went crashing down, dragging Lucien and the other guard on top of him. He roared, eyes flashing red as Natalie screamed again, but this time her scream was different. There was so much rage contained in it and she used the only weapon left to her disposal. She reared up and bit Enzo savagely in the neck.

Chapter 22

Natalie felt her teeth puncture skin, tasted the warm flood of blood on her tongue, and it was as though a haze of red descended upon her. She heard Enzo bellow in pain, but it was as though the sound came from a distance. Power coursed through her, awakening and sharpening her senses. She could feel the hairs on her arms lift, her muscles contract. Then she felt a bone pop.

She screamed, stunned and a little afraid of what was happening to her, but the sound that erupted from her through was a guttural growl. She felt as though hot rods were emerging from her upper jaw. She clenched her teeth against the burn as her body twisted and jerked, and Enzo's neck snapped.

She tilted her head back and roared as a slow burn radiated down her arms and out of her fingertips. She lifted her hands up, staring in stunned amazement as sharp claws protruded from the ends of her fingers. Energy unlike anything she'd ever experienced flooded through her and she rolled to her feet with graceful agility.

A vampire sprang at her and she lashed out, her claws ripping through his abdomen. He fell to his knees and she struck his face, turning to face the next vampire before the first one's head hit the ground. More vampires leaped toward her and it was as though everything slowed down, as though time paused to watch what she'd do next.

Her movements quick and efficient, she neatly dispatched three before the rest could back off. She bared her new fangs, a low growl emerging from her throat. Those in uniform turned and ran.

Dr. Morton caught her eye as he shakily loaded a tranquilizer gun. She shook her head. Nuh-uh. No more tranqs.

She sprang at him, knocking him to the ground. His eyes glowed red at her attack and his incisors lengthened as he raised the gun and leveled it at her.

She flexed her claws and sank them slowly into his chest. His eyes widened and he howled at the pain as her claws kept going, until she could feel his heart beating in her hand.

"What was it you said...'we all remember our first?'" Her voice came out as a rough, husky rumble. She smiled at him grimly. "Forgive me. I'm a little rough, but in time I'm sure I'll acquire a little finesse." He stared at her in horrified realization. She pierced his heart with her claws, preventing it from beating any more.

Natalie rose and turned to face the stunned collection of vampires in the hall. She saw Vincent Marchetta's shocked face, and her eyes narrowed. She stalked toward him, casually flinging a guard out of her way as though shooing a fly. Vincent backed up, but she grasped his neck and thrust him against the wall, lifting him with one hand until his feet were dangling three feet off the ground. He was making a gurgling sound.

"Call off your guards," she hissed.

Eyes wide, he nodded, glancing at the uniformed guards. She could sense them backing away warily, and looked over her shoulder to make sure they'd let Lucien go. They had. She turned back to the man who'd planned to place her into a blood slavery for the rest of her life.

"Your son loves you, so I won't kill you. But for the last time," she said in a low voice, "I do not give you permission." She flung him to the floor. "Don't make me regret letting you live."

She took a deep breath, consciously willing her heart to slow down, and it was as though there was a relaxation of tension throughout her body. Bones creaked, shrinking back into place, and she could feel her fangs and claws retract. Wow, that was an interesting sensation.

A movement in the hall caught her attention. Morton drifted up from his body, his face taut with anger.

"You fool," he snarled. "We could have done so much."

Black shadows flickered around him and Natalie squinted, trying to make out was happening behind the doctor's ghost.

Her eyebrows rose as Grace Perkins flickered briefly before fully manifesting behind Morton. Her shirt was clean, her badge shiny. Beside her stood the teen ghost who'd attacked Natalie in the mountain facility. But he looked different. Before he'd looked gaunt, starved. Now he looked fit and strong, and—Natalie gasped—

whole. More shadows flickered to life, more figures from the facility now whole again.

She met Morton's gaze. "I think some folks want to say hello," she said, lifting her chin to indicate behind him.

Morton frowned and turned, then screamed as all those he'd tortured and murdered charged at him. He twisted, trying to fight them off, but grew weaker, more ethereal, until he disappeared in a puff of inky vapor.

One by one, the ghosts left behind brightened. Natalie had to put her hand up to shield her eyes as each of the spirits flared into a ball of blinding light, drifting peacefully up to the ceiling and beyond. Grace was the last to go. She smiled, mouthing the words "thank you" as she waved goodbye, her presence shifting into golden light before disappearing.

Natalie turned back to the vampires, startled as they all stood, stunned. Lucien stepped forward, his expression awed.

"Did you see that?" she breathed.

He nodded, smiling as he embraced her, and she relaxed into his strength. "I saw everything."

She smiled, looking over his shoulder. Dave leaned against the wall and casually gestured to the bloody mess in the hallway. "See, I told you. You didn't need me." He held up a finger. "But you still owe me."

Lucien held the woman in his arms, quietly stunned, ferociously proud. He glanced back at the surviving guardians in the hall, at his father. They all wore the same astonished expressions. What they'd seen here tonight—he couldn't explain it. Natalie had become... something. Not a vampire. Not a werewolf. Something...other. Teeth like a vampire, claws like a were-wolf, with the noble heart of a human warrior queen. A crossbreed.

Natalie raised her head. "Where is your sister?" she asked.

His eyes widened and he shook his head. "You don't have to—"

"I know." She smiled. "I want to."

He glanced around the hallway. "Even after—"

"Even after."

He took a shaky breath, overwhelmed at her gener-osity, her kindness. "This way," he said, and lead her down another hallway. Dave followed.

He opened a door and led her into a softly lit room. A glass coffin sat atop a gurney. He gazed down at the woman sleeping inside. Despite the black marks mar-bling her skin, the gray tone of her complexion, she was still beautiful. Since Dave had placed her under the suspension spell to delay the spread of the lycan toxin in her system, Lucien had marveled that his lively, feisty sister could look so peaceful and tranquil. He'd give anything to have her frown and bitch at him again, though. He glanced at Natalie. He'd given his whole heart.

Dave unlocked the lid and lifted it, then placed his hand on her forehead. A soft glow, barely seen, caught as it was between the witch's palm and his sister's head, cast a shadow across Vivianne's features. Dave with-drew his hand and looked at Natalie.

"I've lifted the spell. It's up to you now."

She was staring at the other side of the coffin, her brow dipping. She shook her head and he peered into the shadows of the room. "What is it?"

Natalie blinked. "I'm not sure. I thought I saw someone." She shrugged. "It's nothing," she said to him, giving him a reassuring smile. She stepped forward and Lucien's brows rose as Natalie removed a blood bag from the waistband of her jeans. How the hell had that not been destroyed in the fight?

Natalie removed the lid from the injection port and held the bag to his sister's mouth, letting some of the liquid drop onto her lips. She stepped back, looking at Lucien. "I'm not sure how long this will take. For you, it was a few hours, but you'd progressed further—"

Vivianne's eyes flew open and she arched her back as she drew in a deep, shuddering breath.

Lucien watched in awe as black veins slowly disappeared and her skin returned to its normal olive-toned hue.

Vivianne coughed, her eyes wild and confused, and she gave Dave and Natalie startled looks before she finally saw him. Recognition and relief flared in her eyes, and Lucien smiled at her. She stared at him, taking in his disheveled appearance, the cuts and bruises. She coughed again, then frowned at him.

"You look like hell, bro," she rasped, and he laughed as he reached down to hug her.

"It's good to see you, too, sis." It felt so good to hold his sister again, to feel her warmth and strength, her vitality. He looked at Natalie, who tilted her head as she watched, a smile on her lips.

"Thank you," he said huskily, sincerely, and she nodded.

Vivianne turned to look at Natalie and Dave. "Who are you?"

Lucien put his arm around Natalie's shoulders as

he made the introductions and explained to Vivianne briefly what had happened.

After several long minutes Vivianne shook her head, her long dark hair shifting with the movement.

"I think this is going to take several re-tellings to digest." She gazed around the room, a frown marring her brow. "I can't believe Dad had this place right under my nose." Her lips pressed together. "I think it's time we held a family council." She seemed to be distracted, her attention caught by something in a darker corner of the room. She squinted, then blinked, shaking her head.

"What's wrong?" Lucien asked.

"Is someone there?" Vivianne shook her head as though confused. She pressed her fingers to her temple. "I think I just need to recover a little," she murmured, closing her eyes briefly.

A blast echoed from above and dust filtered down from the ceiling.

Lucien's shoulders sagged. Seriously? Could they not catch a break?

"What's that?" Natalie asked, concerned.

Lucien's lips tightened. "Dad wanted to spread the word that we had a cure for the lycan toxin as way to flex his muscles over the other vampire colonies. I think they want in."

Natalie closed her eyes briefly and Lucien grimaced at his father yet again causing trouble for Natalie. "What are we going to do?" she asked wearily.

He rubbed her shoulders. "We fight. I'm not losing you, Natalie. Never again."

Another blast shook the foundations and Dave frowned. "Well, if you're going to fight, I'd suggest you start before they flatten this place."

Natalie clutched Lucien's arm, her eyes wide. "Wait—Dr. Morton had a vampire down here, and a werewolf. We need to free them."

Vivianne's lips curled. "I'll kill the werewolf myself."

Natalie shook her head. "No. I've seen what this doctor can do. Nobody deserves that. You need to free anyone down here."

Dave nodded. "I'm on it."

"Hey, I said—"

"I know what you said, Ms. Marchetta, but you seem to be misunderstanding. I don't take orders from you," Dave said, grinning, and jogged out of the room.

"Come on, let's get you both out of here," Lucien said. If their home was under attack above ground, he didn't want his sister or the woman he loved to be trapped beneath it.

He lifted his sister out of the coffin and then slung her arm over his shoulder to help her walk. She was a little shaky on her feet—to be expected after spending eight months in a suspended state, he supposed.

Natalie took her other arm and slung it over her shoulder, and together they half ran, half carried Vivianne through the halls.

"I have to get something," Natalie said as they passed the lab. She ducked out from under Vivianne's arm and ran inside the room to a fridge. She scanned the contents, then pulled out a vial of blood. Lucien frowned.

"What are you doing?"

"We need to sort this out, once and for all," Natalie panted as she ran back to help him with Vivianne.

"What?"

"Enzo was right, back at the roost," she said. "He

said that vampires, lycans and witches won't stop until either they have the cure, too, or there is no more cure."

Lucien's frown deepened in consternation. "What are you planning to do, Natalie?"

She smiled over his sister's head. "Trust me."

They emerged into a battlefield of a ballroom. The Marchetta mansion had been breached, and vampires were fighting vampires. Vivianne insisted on walking in under her own steam. Lucien lowered her arm and Natalie followed suit.

When they stepped into the room, though, the growls and screams slowly died down, and all eyes turned toward them. Everyone knew that the Nightwing Vampire Prime, Vivianne Marchetta, had been attacked by a lycan. Now she stood before them, eight months later, fully recovered. She'd been cured.

Vincent gaped, stepping hesitantly toward his daughter, as though not sure if he could truly believe that she really was going to be okay. When the realization sank in, all of those inside the ballroom turned to focus on Natalie. She swallowed. So many vampires. All so desperate to get a piece of her.

Enzo had been right. Vampires would want her blood as a protection. Lycans and witches would want her dead for the advantage she gave the vampires. She couldn't do this anymore. If she somehow got out of this situation, she'd spend her whole life running, hiding, looking over her shoulder. She'd lived that for the last forty years, and she didn't want to do it anymore. She glanced over Vivianne's dark head to her handsome brother—the man who'd defied the father he'd so desperately wanted to please, to save her.

She wanted Lucien. She wanted him with all her heart, and she wanted the freedom to live with him and love him every day without the threat of capture or torture hanging over their heads. Just like in the desert, when he'd risked his life to save hers, when he'd given up a part of himself to protect her, she was prepared to do the same. She glanced at Lucien. He eyed her warily and perhaps with a little bewilderment.

"Do you trust me?" she asked softly.

"Implicitly."

"Do you love me?"

His lips lifted in a soft, tender smile. "Always."

She nodded then turned to the vampires gathered in the ballroom.

"I know what you want and—" she took a deep breath, knowing what she was going to say would not be well received "—you can't have it. You can't have me. This is my body, my choice. I will not be a target anymore."

A rumble began, as those in the room talked among themselves. The rumble started to grow as protests were shouted.

Natalie opened her senses, calling forth the power in her body. She could feel her eyes flicker and suddenly she could see more details. Everything seemed sharper, clearer. She lengthened her incisors, feeling that slow burn through her jaw, the same in her hands as she drew out her claws. She hissed gently as her muscles spasmed and bones popped and grew, just a little, until she stood before them. She threw her head back and roared. Some of the vampires closer to her stepped back.

She reached into her pocket and gingerly withdrew the vial of blood. There was a number on the label—

relating to one of Morton's test subjects, no doubt, but it also clearly stated "Null."

Lucien started when he saw it, but she flashed him a glance.

Trust me, she pleaded with her eyes. His jaw clenched, but he didn't step toward her. She pulled the lid off the vial, then drank the blood, grimacing at the too salty flavor. She forced it down her throat. God, no wonder nulls weren't fed upon. They tasted disgusting.

Almost immediately, her stomach cramped and she clutched her abdomen. Her bones ached then cracked as they returned to their original state, and she cried out in agony as her muscles tremored, her claws and fangs retracting so fast it was like hot pokers sliding beneath her skin. She screamed at the pain that lanced through her, all over, as though a rough tidal wave of thumb pricks was washing over her, drowning her. She fell to the floor, writhing, flinching, as a new wave of pain hit, so hard so fast, it left her breathless.

"Natalie!" Lucien raced to her side and dropped to his knees, his expression anxious as he stared down at her.

"I'm okay," she rasped and his eyes closed briefly with relief. He helped her to sit up, then stand, and she shivered. Maybe her body was going into shock. That would be expected. She sagged against him, his strength holding her up as she glanced around the damaged ballroom.

The vampires stared at her in stunned dismay. She swallowed as she felt sweat bead her brow. "You can all go home now," she called out, and wavered a little on her feet. Lucien wrapped his arm around her waist, supporting her. "There is no more cure." She clapped a hand over her mouth as her stomach heaved, gulping down the bile that rose in her throat.

"Did you hear me?" she yelled at the crowd. "There is no more cure. Go home."

She sagged against Lucien and the world spun as he lifted her into his arms. She had a vague impression of the vampires stepping back to allow him passage as he carried her through the ballroom, and then everything went dark.

Chapter 23

Lucien propped his head on his elbow as he stared down at Natalie, asleep in his bed. Late-afternoon sunlight streamed through the window and bathed his bed. It was a unique experience for him, lying in his bed in the sun. He eyed the woman next to him. She'd slept for nearly sixteen hours, and he'd been by her side for every one of them. He'd been so damned worried. Her temperature had flared and she'd rested fitfully. He'd kept her cool with damp cloths on her face and ice chips on her lips. Her fever had broken in the early afternoon, and she'd slept soundly since. He glanced over at the pile of bags just inside the door. Heath had had one of his staff drive them back from the roost. He didn't want to unpack them, though.

His father had visited, a fact that had surprised Lucien. Natalie wasn't an asset to the Marchetta family anymore. His father had sat with him for a little while, and although they hadn't talked—Lucien was still way too furious with him—there was something different about the old man. Maybe it was having Vivianne come back from the dead. He didn't know, but something had cracked that cold block of a heart inside his chest.

Lucien's lips curved. Occasionally he could hear Vivianne's raised voice downstairs as she organized repairs to the mansion. His sister was back from the dead and letting everyone know it. He still hadn't told her about the daylight side effect. He was looking forward to showing her, though. He'd happily handed back the Vampire Prime title to her. He smoothed a lock of blond hair off Natalie's forehead. His sister was alive, all thanks to this woman. He dipped his head to kiss her bare shoulder. He hadn't really thought past saving his sister. He'd assumed he'd go back to work on the west coast, but he no longer felt the desire to prove himself to his father. Maybe it was time to think about what he was really interested in, what really mattered to him.

Whatever he did, he'd be doing it with Natalie. He couldn't see his life unfolding any other way.

Natalie's eyelashes fluttered and she yawned as she opened her eyes, stretching languidly beneath his sheet. Her eyes caught his and they widened, the varying shades as complex and as beautiful as the woman herself. She smiled at him, all lush and sleepy and sexy as all hell.

"Hey," she murmured as she rolled over to face him.

"Hey," he responded, leaning forward to capture her lips in a tender kiss. He brushed her nose with his. "How are you feeling?"

"Good." She peeked under the covers, her eyebrows rising. "Why am I naked?"

He nodded. "You were burning up."

She eyed his body. The sheet was draped low over his hips and he saw the appreciation flare in her eyes as she took in his chest and the part of his hip that was exposed. "And why are you naked?"

"Then you got the chills." He gestured between them. "Sharing body heat," he explained. "I was a complete gentleman. I only peeked a little." She had a beautiful body, but at the time he'd been more worried about the fever, about how the null blood would affect her, and whether she would wake up at all. He pressed his lips together. "You had me scared," he admitted. He scooped her close, pulling the sheet up to warm her shoulders.

She smiled. "I thought you trusted me."

His arms tightened around her. "With my life. I just wasn't expecting you to nullify your gift."

Her smile faltered. "Do you mind?" Her gaze lowered to his collarbone. "I mean, that I nullified my blood?"

He tucked his finger under her chin and tilted her face up so he could meet her gaze. "I love you," he murmured, dipping forward to kiss her briefly on the lips. "I don't care if you're vamp, lycan, null—hell, you can even be part witch for all I care—I didn't fall in love with your blood, or what it could do for vampires. I fell in love with *you*, with your heart, with that fascinating brain of yours, the way you think… I fell in love with your romantic streak, your curiosity…"

He cupped her cheek. "You have such a big heart, so brave, so generous, so giving of yourself." He smiled. "I didn't stand a chance."

She persisted. "So, you don't mind that I'm not some special cure that could protect you from death?"

He frowned. "You're special to me, just for being you. Besides, I don't intend to die. Ever." He kissed her again and his cock stiffened as she kissed him back. He trailed his lips across her jaw to her neck.

"But the other vampires—they know I can't help them anymore?"

"Trust me, word has spread about the crazy human chick who fed herself null blood and killed off any supernatural elements in her body."

"Does that…does that bother you?" she asked, but he grinned against her skin. She sounded distracted. He inhaled, drawing her scent in, relishing the warmth and soft curves nestled against his body.

"I want my forever with you, Natalie," he told her huskily. "Do you think you could put up with my family?"

She sighed, arching her neck against his lips. "As long as we don't have to live with your father," she said.

He nodded as he gently bit her earlobe. "We'll go hunting for a place tomorrow," he murmured.

"So soon?" She moaned as he kissed his way down her neck, pulling at the sheet as he went. He rolled her over onto her back, staring down at her.

"I want forever with you to start right away," he told her. "If that's what you want…?" Did she still feel the same way about him as he did her? She'd told him she loved him back in the cave, but so much had happened since then, so much hurt…

She arched an eyebrow. "And if it isn't?" Her voice was low and flirty with challenge, and his lips curved as he trailed his hand down her body to the delta between her thighs. He slid his fingers through her curls. She was warm and dewy already.

"Then I'll just have to convince you," he said, sliding his fingers into her slick channel.

She arched her back, thrusting her breasts high, and he leaned forward to take a jutting nipple into his mouth. She moaned as he stroked her, his finger caressing her clitoris. He sucked on her breast, drawing her nipple deep into his mouth, letting her scent swirl around him. He closed his eyes, feeling his cock harden painfully as she writhed against him. He toyed with that secret pleasure spot between her thighs, swiping over her nub and away, only to return to it over and over. Her breath caught and he could feel her muscles tightening.

"I love you, I love you," she panted.

He nipped at her breast playfully and growled softly in satisfaction as he felt her tremble, her orgasm washing over her and feeding his own desire. He lifted his head from her breast and rose up over her. She looked at him, eyes alight as she rolled him over onto his back, surprising him with her strength. She leaned an arm on his chest.

"Can I tell you a secret?"

Lucien's eyebrow rose in a sexy arch, his eyes glittering with desire. "You can tell me anything," he said, a sexy smile curving his lips.

She smiled back as she leaned forward and kissed his nipple, licking it before nipping at it lightly. She felt him shudder beneath her and she trailed her fingers down his gorgeous chest. He really was a stunningly beautiful man.

"Promise you won't tell anyone?" she asked as she watched the muscles on his ridged abdomen dip and ripple at her touch.

"Uh-huh," he nodded, then closed his eyes as she trailed her nails across his navel to grasp his hard length. He was so firm all over. He could be so determined, so focused… She slid her hands along his length, enjoying the feel of his silken strength. She reached for one of his hands, entwining her pinkie finger with his.

"Pinkie swear?" she challenged.

His eyes opened and he curled his finger around hers. "Pinkie swear."

She gently forced the claw out from her index finger and lovingly raked it over his nipple. His eyes widened in surprise, then narrowed in pleasure as she repeated the action.

"Null blood doesn't work on me," she whispered, drawing her claw back in and returning her attention to his lengthening cock.

He frowned, as though it was hard for him to focus. "I don't understand," he said and then hissed as she leaned down to kiss his length. She gripped him as she met his eyes.

"My original transfusion had a little null blood," she reminded him, a knowing smile curving her lips. "Full-strength null blood is like a virus for me. My body fights it off like an infection."

She took him into her mouth, enjoying the sound of his moan. "You…you knew?" he gasped finally.

She nodded. "Mmm-hmm." His hands twisted in the sheets as she played him with her hands and lips.

"I love the way your mind works," he said in a sensual sigh. His stomach muscles clenched and then he reared up, grasping her and pulling her over his body, rolling with her and entering her in one smooth, slick motion.

Her eyes widened at the sensation, the feel of him

stretching her. He moved his hips against hers, his eyes on hers as he touched the deepest places within her.

"Forever starts now," he whispered.

She nodded, unable to speak with all the sensations bombarding her. If this was forever, she'd take it, thank you very much. Her eyes closed as he rocked his hips, thrusting against her with increasing force. Tension coiled inside her and she writhed beneath him, meeting him thrust for thrust. Panting, she opened her eyes, enjoying the sight of his washboard abs rippling as he moved, the bulge of his biceps. She slid her hands up his arms, her nails raking his back as she climbed higher and higher to that summit she knew was waiting for them.

She reached the peak and tipped over, muscles clenching at the tide of bliss that swept over her, and she cried out at the sheer ecstasy in Lucien's arms. He cried out, head thrown back, as he reached his own pinnacle, and she had a few mini explosions as he gradually slowed.

He lowered himself to the bed, sweeping her into his arms so that she was nestled against his body. She traced her hands over his chest, sighing in pleasure. Right here, right now, for the first time in her life, she felt truly, wholly connected to someone. With that sense of intimacy came a confidence and security she could only associate with family. She stretched up to kiss Lucien on the lips tenderly, then met his intent gaze.

"I love you," she said softly.

"I love you," he said right back, leaning down to kiss her just as tenderly. He slid his hand along her back and cupped her butt. She lay her cheek against his chest and smiled. True and utter contentment.

Lucien's hand continued to stroke her hip and butt, and she snuggled up against him, surprised to feel some movement between them.

"Natalie?" His voice was husky and laced with humor.

"Yes, Lucien?"

"Can we start forever all over again?"

She chuckled as he rolled her over, kissing her as his hands stroked her body.

"I can see forever could be a very, very long time," she said, smiling as he kissed her neck.

"Uh-huh. That's what I'm hoping," he said, and then there was no more talking as they made love in the light of the setting sun.

* * * * *

Get 2 Free Books,
Plus 2 Free Gifts—
just for trying the Reader Service!

READERSERVICE.COM

Manage your account online!

- Review your order history
- Manage your payments
- Update your address

> ### We've designed the Reader Service website just for you.

Enjoy all the features!

- Discover new series available to you, and read excerpts from any series.
- Respond to mailings and special monthly offers.
- Browse the Bonus Bucks catalog and online-only exculsives.
- Share your feedback.

Visit us at:

ReaderService.com